Only Six Years

Jenn Lynn Adams

ISBN: 979-8-9869860-9-8 (paperback)

ISBN: 979-8-9869860-8-1 (ebook)

First edition, September 2025

Edited by Cruel Ink Author Services

© Cover design: Ya'll That Graphic

www.jennlynnadams.com

Also by Jenn Lynn Adams

Daughter of the Underworld

Daughter of War & Witchcraft

Just Two Weeks

Just like autumn leaves,
I fell for you.
One by one,
then all at once.

-Unknown

Six Years Ago

CHAPTER ONE

Delia

"What do you mean you bought a house?" I screech into the FaceTime video at my best friend. Two weeks ago, Savannah Smith was gearing up to run her father's senate campaign throughout our home state of Michigan, and now she's suddenly buying a beach cottage on the Emerald Coast in Florida.

What had gotten into her?

"I stopped by the beach—*my* beach—before we left, and there it was: a *For Sale* sign, stuck right in the sand... I couldn't let that opportunity slip away, Del."

I purse my lips and hum into the phone, knowing damn well none of this would've happened if it weren't for her new bodyguard-turned-boyfriend, Jack.

I flush the toilet and lower the lid as my gaze travels around the dingy bathroom of the apartment I share with two other girls. I knock over a bottle of concealer as I flip on the tap to wash my hands.

"Did you just pee while we were talking? Gross!" I dry my hands and I retrieve the phone from the counter. Savannah's dark brows furl, and her lip turns down. Judging *me* for multitasking? Please. Sav is the queen of it.

"It's nothing you haven't seen before," I remind her, hinting at our four years rooming together in college. "Gotta use it when I can. Besides, Jemima and Claire are getting ready to go out and need to get in here, so it was now or never."

"You're not going out on the town with your roomies, too? It's Friday night in the Windy City!"

"Nope. I'm hoping for an early night in. I need to get some extra work done tomorrow morning." Sav's question shouldn't rub me the wrong way, but it does. I've been in Chicago for a little over a month and haven't really connected with my roommates. I found them through a want ad, and while we all work together at the same finance company, Jem and Claire are definitely on the prowl for husbands. Me? I'm just working toward a promotion. Anything to get away from the coffee runs and secretarial duties I've been assigned.

"So, do you miss me yet?"

I suck in my bottom lip and glance at the bathroom ceiling, pretending to ponder. "Hm... well, neither Jemima nor Claire snore loud enough to shake the walls."

"Psh," Savannah practically spits. "Jack doesn't tell me that I snore."

"That's because he's getting laid on the regular. No man wants to mess that up by being honest this early in the relationship, Sav."

She huffs and then goes quiet. "You're probably right. He also lets me choose the music when we're driving."

"Again, he gives you control over the radio. You give him sex. Seems like a smart man." Savannah goes on to tell me something obnoxiously adorable that Jack recently did, but I tune her out as I check my watch.

Two more minutes.

I eye the test, the sleek white plastic tube and blue cap seeming to stare at me from the counter.

My eyes slide down to the solid pink line already forming in the center of the results window. My breath hitches as I glance at the visual aid printed next to the test strip.

Not pregnant.

I breathe a heavy sigh of relief, my eyes closing as my knees nearly buckle. I lean against the wall and rub along my hairline.

Not pregnant.

Thank God.

"Are you even listening? Do you have a headache?" My eyes snap open, and I catch Savannah eyeing me suspiciously through the phone.

"Oh, yeah, it's just the humidity here. It's stifling in the city." I pull away from the wall and start to tidy up the restroom.

"Why don't you head north for the weekend? Go visit Nana and your parents? Get out of that dirty city."

I wipe down the counter and toss the test box in the trash. "Yeah. Maybe," I respond as I glance at my reflection in the mirror. My face is pale, despite it being nearly the end of the summer. The deep purple shadows under my eyes make me look older than twenty-three.

"You've been working too hard. You need a few days to relax."

Easier said than done. My boss, Marshall, runs me ragged sixty hours a week, and even now—on a Friday night—I'm sure I've got an unreasonable number of messages waiting on my computer, all demanding attention first thing tomorrow morning.

"Oh, I know! You should come to Florida and see my house!" Savannah's squeal startles me away from my reflection and back to the scene before me. The timer on my cell phone shows that I still technically have another thirty-nine seconds before the test should be read.

"Hm-mm," I mumble as my gaze drops.

To the sparkling clean counter.

And the plastic test with a giant pink plus sign now darkening in the middle.

Blindly, I reach for the instruction packet from the trash. My throat constricts as I blink to focus. The phone slips from my hand, clattering into the sink.

"Del? Del? What happened?"

I don't answer as my vision focuses and then swims.

Pregnant.

CHAPTER TWO

Dane

"Crystal, you have to show up on time. And on your assigned days!" The woman on the phone rattles off yet another excuse for why she can't come in for her shift, leaving me with my second fourteen-hour day in a row.

I'd replace her if I could, but finding someone willing to work for tips in this economy is nearly impossible.

"I'm going to have to put you on probation," I threaten idly. She cackles loudly in my ear. Crystal may be a lousy worker, but she's smart, and she calls my bluff. "Yes, it is something that exists!"

Honestly my only recourse is to suck it up, and that's what I do after we hang up. I suck it up and go back to the kitchen, where I've got four delivery orders piled up and waiting to be bagged.

I pull the thick slices of garlic bread from the oven and allow them to cool while I carefully place each of the meals in Styrofoam containers. Then I stack the containers and load them into plastic bags with *Thank You!* emblazoned in bright red lettering.

The bell over the restaurant door dings. "Find a seat anywhere! I'll be right out!" I holler over the exhaust fan. It's been running for well over an hour, but it still smells like burned garlic. Antonio, the teenage delivery driver, stepped in earlier to help with an order for spaghetti and meatballs. Judging by the charred meat still clinging to the oiled pan, his cooking skills could use some honing.

I wrap several slices of fresh garlic bread in parchment paper and add the order to the last plastic bag, tying everything with a knot. I wonder who's stopped by the diner this late. The dinner rush is long over, and with the cold snap we've had, most of the town is already tucked in for the night.

"What can I get you to drink?" I ask as I round the corner to the counter. There sits a woman I've never seen before. Her round cheeks are pink from the autumn chill, and there are white snow flurries dotted in her copper tresses.

My hands are clammy—hot—and I instinctively reach for the wet rag I keep to wipe up spills. Just for something to hold onto. "We have Pepsi products." I dip my head to the soda fountain on my right.

Her nose scrunches just so, as though I've offered her a slurry of mud and leaves. "I'll just take a water, please."

Her eyes shift, and I wonder if she's meeting someone. "I've also got a small drink menu. Some local craft beers..."

"Oh, no. Thank you, but I'm—" Her hand dips to rest on her belly that peeks just above the counter. The rounded bump had been so unnoticeable—until she'd drawn my attention to it.

"Right. Water, then." I press my lips together and turn. As I dig the plastic cup into the ice bin, my ears listen for the chime of the bell.

Is she meeting her husband? Boyfriend?

I return with her drink and place it in front of her, making note of her bare ring finger. So, not a husband.

Unless her wedding ring doesn't fit anymore. That's a thing, right? I swallow the lump in my throat and breathe deeply through my nose.

"Do you need a minute to decide?" She hasn't even opened the menu.

She turns her gaze to me. Pale blue eyes latch onto mine beneath full brown lashes. "Oh, no..." She reaches for the menu tucked behind the salt and pepper and quickly scans the contents. "The chicken parmesan, please."

I nod and turn toward the kitchen. Even with it being so late, I've got enough batter and ingredients available, and it's not long before the chicken is frying in a pan of bubbling oil. I head back to the front and see that her stool is empty.

Just then, she saunters around the corner from the restroom, her hand resting protectively over the bump. She's farther along than I thought. And tall, too. I avert my gaze—I'd hate to be the creepy man ogling a pregnant lady—and notice that her glass is empty.

I grab the cup and refill it quickly, setting it down just as she takes her seat. "Chicken parm will be up shortly," I say as I drum my fingers on the counter.

Where'd that rag go?

"Do you know who owns this building?" she asks, digging into her purse. She pulls her phone out and sets it facedown next to her drink.

"Uh, I do, actually. Own the building."

Her eyes widen slightly. "Oh. A-and you own the restaurant, too?"

"Yep, Dane's Italiano. I'm Dane."

"Delia," she responds with a small smile.

I awkwardly stick out my hand to shake hers, but instead swipe the side of the water glass, knocking it over. "Shit!" I look around for the rag but still can't find it, so I race to the kitchen and grab a handful of clean linens. Back in front of the mess, I start wiping up the spill, and my face heats.

She slides down a seat, away from said spill, and drags her purse and phone along with her. Swiping it to life, she taps away before turning back to me. The timer dings in the back. "Let me grab your food, and then I'll refill your water." Taking the stack of wet rags with me, I trudge to the kitchen and mentally berate myself.

I've been working in the restaurant industry for almost fifteen years, yet here I am—tipping over water glasses and misplacing rags. As I plate the crispy chicken and slather a ladleful of marinara on top, I silently pray I haven't messed up the recipe in my idiot-induced stupor. I sprinkle a healthy dose of cheese over the meal and return to the woman at the counter.

Setting down the plate in front of her, I notice her phone—and the apartment listing pulled up.

My apartment listing.

"So you're really here for the apartment, not the food?" I ask, quirking my eyebrow toward the device.

She cracks a sheepish smile. "Yes, but it smelled so delicious, and it's been a while—"

"Since you've eaten?" My face falls as my eyes widen. Who isn't feeding this beautiful woman?

"No, no. I've eaten." She chuffs quietly and rolls her eyes. "Mostly fusion and hipster food from Chicago, though I had a few snacks on the road. It's just been a while since I had my favorite meal. Chicken parm." She eyes the dish in front of her.

I can take a hint.

"I'll let you enjoy it." My throat tightens. I hope my recipe lives up to her expectations. "When you're done, just holler and we'll discuss the apartment."

She nods and grabs the fork and knife before digging in.

"This is the main bedroom." I push the door open and immediately regret not showing Delia the apartment in the light of day. Even with the lamps, the rooms appear dark, almost dingy. The basic beige paint I'd chosen makes the living area look dirty and lived-in.

"And it comes furnished?" she asks, stepping around me and into the small room. Her eyes scan the single window in the corner, then the dusty baseboards I should've cleaned, before finally settling on the simple full-sized bed.

"Yes, and the mattress is new," I add.

Delia approaches the plastic-wrapped mattress and, thanks to her height, easily settles onto the edge before scooting farther toward the middle. Then she swings her long legs up and over and lies back, wriggling her body. The protective covering crinkles loudly in the silence. A small sigh escapes her lips as she closes her eyes, and her hands find her belly.

"I-I'll give you a minute," I say as my mouth turns dry.

"No." She sits up. "I'll take it." She climbs off the bed and follows me down the hallway, past the bathroom and smaller bedroom.

"Let me take down your information, and I'll be in touch tomorrow morning. We can sign the lease, and that will give me time to run a credit check and do my due diligence."

Two identical pink spots darken her cheeks, and she fidgets with her purse. "S-sure, although is there any way I could write you a check now, and"—she shrugs and turns, staring wistfully at the bedroom—"we could wrap this up tonight?"

I press my lips together. Does she not have anywhere else to go?

"Listen, there's a small bed and breakfast just outside of town. I'm sure they have—"

"They don't. I stopped on my way here." She clasps her hands in front of her, wringing them together as she fidgets. "You see, I don't have anywhere else to go tonight." Those pink spots turn darker, reddening as her eyes drop.

My brow crinkles. There's no way the Kingfisher Inn is all booked up. Not at this time of year. "Let me call Mr. Roisin. I'm certain he'll have something available. Even for a single night..." I pull my phone from my back pocket and start scrolling for the owner's personal number.

"No, that won't be necessary." She reaches out and grips my wrist. She smiles, even as her eyes turn watery, shining in the kitchen lighting. "I'll drive over and check myself. Again." Her chin trembles as she turns back once more to the bedroom.

Something isn't right. There's a niggling in my gut that's sending warning signals to my brain. I don't know this woman from Eve. I know absolutely *nothing* about her. She could easily be a con artist. Hell, that bump could be a fake.

And yet...

"It's getting late, and the roads aren't great at this time of night. Lots of deer... I'd hate for you to hit one or get lost. How about I get the bed set up, and you can sleep here?"

She blinks and turns toward the couch—a hand-me-down that belonged to a long forgotten neighbor. "I-I would be fine just taking the couch. And I'd love a blanket, if you have one." Her hand slides over her belly.

I nod and swallow the lump in my throat, because even if I want to protect my interest— my apartment— there's no way I can send a pregnant woman out into the cold.

And so I head across the hall to my own place. While my apartment isn't any bigger than the one for lease, I've made significant upgrades throughout the years. Tile decorates the backsplash behind the kitchen appliances, while a brick accent wall adds coziness to the living space. I grab the afghan from the back of the couch and, as my fingers slide through the crocheted holes, I examine it closely. It's worn and threadbare—handmade by my mother ages ago. Hardly warm enough. I toss it back onto the sofa and head into my guest bedroom. I yank the duvet from the bed, snatch one of the good pillows that's never been used, and—with a sigh—pray I won't regret this come morning.

Present Day

CHAPTER THREE

Delia

The ice-cold water slices through the chilly October morning. It pelts my bare back like razor-sharp daggers, and I yelp as I jump away from the showerhead's assault.

"*Fucking fuck*!" My profanities echo off the crisp white tile.

"Mom, no swearing!" Kayce hollers from his place in front of the toilet.

I peek around the shower curtain at the mop-headed kindergartner. "Aim straight or you're cleaning up the mess this time, kiddo." As he turns to catch my eye with a sleepy smile, he loses focus on the task at hand, and the yellow stream sprays across the porcelain and wall.

"*Kayce*!"

"Sorry..." His gaze returns to the toilet, and the mess that's now dripping down to the floor. When he finishes, he grabs a towel—my *hot-out-of-the-dryer* towel— before smearing the pee all over in an attempt to clean up.

I grind my teeth and flick the shower curtain closed. Nothing like drying off with a piss-covered towel after taking the coldest shower known to man.

I manage a quick rinse and then hop out. I grab a toothpaste-crusted hand towel and dab myself dry before tossing on my robe and diving under the sink to fetch the all-purpose cleaner.

Shaking the bottle, I realize it's almost out, but send up a prayer of thanks as there's just enough left to cover the mess. Then I use the still-warm towel to wipe up the urine.

"You've got ten minutes, buddy! Put the iPad away and eat your breakfast!" I don't even have to look into the tiny living space to know that Kayce's face is glued to some ridiculous cartoon while his waffles go cold.

Instead, I stalk down the hallway, deposit the dirty towel in the basket on top of the stacked washer and dryer, and head into the room I've occupied for the last six years.

Discarding the robe in a pile on the floor, I step into a matching blush pink panty and bra set that I'd selected a few weeks ago from the Target clearance section. Looking at the black skirt I'd laid out the night before, I frown. I'm still shivering from the shower, and there's no way I'll ever feel warm, even with tights, if I stick with the skirt. So instead I don a pair of sleek navy pants and a soft, creamy white sweater.

"Five minutes, kiddo!" I call out again as I catch my reflection in the mirror. Surprisingly, the icy shower has lent a rosy glow to my cheeks. Or maybe it's a bit of frostbite. Either way, I forego the blush and simply apply a quick coat of mascara before throwing my unwashed—and slightly greasy—hair into a high ponytail. On my way out, I kick the discarded robe toward the hamper and raise my fist in victory as it lands true.

As a single mom of a five year old, I'll take my wins as they come.

And today, I need a win.

As Kayce and I tumble from our apartment and nearly roll down the steep stairs to the sidewalk, a bright yellow bus pulls to a stop in front of the building.

"Wait!" I call as I grab him by the book bag, yanking him back against me. I press a quick kiss on his soft blond curls and then release him to the wild. "Have a great day, buddy!" I'm not even sure why I bother to wave; he's already charging down the aisle of the bus and not paying a lick of attention to his affectionate mother.

"Did he even comb his hair today?" As the bus pulls away from the curb, my focus snaps to the man standing next to me, his own hair a mess of tousled waves—only his hair is light brown.

"Did you?" I ask, cocking an eyebrow in his direction as I slide past him and into the Italian restaurant in front of our building.

Dane chuffs as he follows me. "Of course I did." I grab a seat at the counter as he runs his fingers through his hair, pulling it back from his face. But as he leans over and flicks on the coffee pot behind the counter, the strands fall forward once more.

"When's the last time you had a haircut?" The diner isn't technically open for breakfast, but that's never stopped me before.

He pulls two mugs from beneath the till and sets them between us. "It's been a while. Why? You offering?"

"I mean, I'm no stylist, but I can trim and shape pretty well. Would you be willing to take a look at the water heater while you're over?" My chest tightens as I toss the question into the empty restaurant. As though my half-assed hair styling would come close to an even trade.

Dane's jaw tenses as he grips the counter. "Delia, is the water heater out again?"

"If the icy shower I had this morning was any indication, then yes." I eye the brewing coffee behind him as my stomach gurgles.

"Fuck, why didn't you come over and take a shower at my place?" he asks, and I shrug, my cheeks heating at the thought of being *naked* in Dane's apartment. "I'll stop by tonight and see what needs to be done to get it up and running."

My teeth dig into my bottom lip, the thought of accepting charity giving my heart a run for its money. "I can pay. For whatever parts. Or repairs." The lie slips out so easily now.

"I'm the landlord, Delia. This is part of the rental agreement." He says it slowly, like I haven't heard it enough in the last six years.

"But, see, you don't actually charge me the full rent, so it's not—"

He turns away and yanks the coffee pot from the machine. "I told you when you moved in. Pay what you can. I'm not worried about it."

My mind flashes back to that night; it was so long ago. Standing in a completely furnished apartment and praying that I wouldn't be turned away. My bank account had a whole whopping $312 in it. Not nearly enough for a night at the bespoke Kingfisher Inn on top of the security deposit *and* first month's rent for an apartment.

My eyes trail over Dane's features. Not much has changed in the years since he brought me a warm duvet and allowed me to sleep on the apartment's couch. His hair's a little longer, and he could use a shave. The lines around his eyes have deepened slightly. And that duvet now adorns *my* bed. After I'd complimented the softness the next day, he'd insisted I keep it—along with the matching sheet set.

Dane passes the steaming mug of coffee to me before replacing the pot. He pulls two sugars from a box under the counter and then heads to the back. I tear open a sugar packet and add the contents to his mug before repeating the process with my own. He returns with a carton of half-and-half, adding a hefty amount to my cup and then his own.

We each use our spoons to stir in silence, the only sound the cutlery clinking against the ceramic mugs. "So, tonight then?" he asks as he brings his mug to his lips and blows softly.

"Oh, um..." I look down at the swirling caramel-colored liquid before me and purse my lips. "Well, I actually have a...a date tonight. But tomorrow would work. And I could give you that trim, too." I shrug and raise my eyes to meet his.

Except his brows are pulled together, and he's holding the mug away from him as he eyes it with a pinched expression. "I think the half-and-half is bad."

I frown, but, with my stomach still rumbling and reminding me to feed it something— *anything*— I bring the mug to my lips and take a slow sip. "Seems fine to me."

Dane ignores me and heads to the back again. Through the food window, I'm able to see him toss the coffee down the drain and then wash the mug, his lips pressed together as he shakes his head. I eye my own cup and take another delicate sip. I hold the liquid in my mouth, testing it for something off. Anything strange.

Nothing. It tastes like coffee.

"I really think it's fine!" I call to him over the din of the running water. I grab the carton still sitting on the counter and check the expiration date. "You've still got another week left. Maybe it's you?"

Dane cuts off the water and sets the mug on the rack to dry. He towels off his hands and then stalks back around to the counter. "Don't you have work today?" He checks his wrist for a watch that isn't there. "Wouldn't want you to be late when you've got rent to pay."

I flatten my lips and roll my eyes before taking a final, hefty swig of the coffee. "Just because you have awful taste doesn't mean you have to be a jerk about it," I mutter as I dig in my purse. I slap a few dollars down on the shiny counter and hoist my bag onto my shoulder.

I drape my coat over my arm and head for the exit.

"I'll come by tomorrow after work to fix the water heater. And for that trim," Dane adds just as my palm connects with the door handle. "And the offer's still open to use my shower in the meantime, too."

"That's very generous of you," I reply as I swing the door open. "But I'll take the cold shower over your grumpy ass any morning."

CHAPTER FOUR

Dane

"So did you figure out what's wrong with it?" Delia's voice surrounds me in the small utility closet. From my knees, I glance up at her face peering around the door frame. Her pale blue eyes darken in the shadows.

I return to the ancient machine in front of me. "Seeing as I've only just gotten settled? No." I crane my neck and poke around for a second. "But if I had to guess, I'd bet the dip tube detached." I find the cold inlet pipe valve and crank it with a wrench to turn off the water source. My gaze strays back to Delia, now leaning back against the frame with her arms crossed over her chest. "Are you going to stand there and watch the entire time?"

"Yup," she responds as she rises to her tiptoes. "Nobody ever taught me about this stuff. Clearly I need to learn in case it happens again."

I snort, the noise matching the pressure from the relief valve. "If this happens again? You don't think I'm going to fix it correctly or something?"

"That isn't what I said. If there *is* a next time, I can fix it myself instead of bothering you." Her eyes scan over the bucket catching the drain out from the valve and then move to the green tubing in my hands. "What's the hose for?"

"I'm going to drain the system." I pass her the open end. "Take this to your tub, but be careful—the water might be hot."

She grabs the hose and heads farther into the apartment and toward the bathroom. "Can I use this water to shower? It's been two days since I've had hot water!"

"Not if you want to keep that pretty skin of yours," I call back. I wait a few moments until I'm certain she's got the hose situated. "Ready?"

"Ready."

I crank the valve, and the hose flexes. It only takes a few minutes for the tank to drain entirely, and then Delia is right back at her spot in the doorway. "What's next?" She bites her bottom lip as she looks down at my open toolbox.

"Why don't you go have a glass of wine or read a book? I've got this. It's nothing you need to worry about." I stand and locate the connector for the tube before working my pinky into the inlet and pulling the mechanism out. "Besides, it's not a bother for me to fix something for you."

She blows a quick puff of air out of her nose just as I spot a crack in the tubing. "Yeah, but eventually Kayce and I are going to—" She snaps her lips closed as my eyes flick to hers.

"Going to what?"

"Move," she says with a shrug. She's so nonchalant, and I realize she must've been thinking about this plan for quite some time.

"Where are you moving to?" My jaw tightens as I set down the cracked dip tube and pick up the new one I'd brought just in case—and it's a good thing I did.

"We're not moving *now*. But eventually..."

"Ah." I nod, turning my back to her as I insert the replacement. "Well, this should fix the problem long enough for you to find a new place." I try to keep the edge from my voice, but it seeps in regardless.

"Dane, Kayce and I appreciate everything you've done—everything you *do*—for us. But this... it was never meant to be permanent."

"Right. Six years isn't anything permanent. What about your job at the bank, Delia? Do they know you're thinking of moving?" I stand up and meet her gaze.

Her reddish-brown brows squish together, two vertical lines forming between them. "Well, no."

"Ah, I get it. Keep the job but get away from me. Maybe Marigold Fraser has an open room for you and Kayce in her boardinghouse. We all know how much she loves unwed single mothers. I'm sure she'd be a pleasant landlord to have. She even has an entire pew at church for you, for crying out loud!"

"You know what?" Delia says, glaring at me from the doorway, her blue eyes flashing with fire. A flush spreads from her chest, up her neck, and tints her cheeks.

"What?" I counter, stepping toward her. But she doesn't shrink away from me. At five-eleven, I'm not much taller than her five-nine, and we're nearly eye level as we glare at each other.

Just then, the fire alarm beeps, startling both of us from our staring contest. "Fire! Fire!" it repeats between screeches.

"*Shit*! The chicken!" She turns and sprints down the hallway toward the smoke billowing from the kitchen.

And I go back to working on the water heater.

"Thank you for fixing the water heater," Delia says quietly as she leans over me. She pulls my hair gently, and it feels amazing after a long day of standing over the stove at the restaurant.

"You're welcome," I whisper softly, careful not to disturb her concentration as she tests the different lengths throughout my hair. "Thank you for touching up my hair. It's been a minute since I had it trimmed."

"I can tell," she responds lightly with a giggle.

"And thank you for dinner... or whatever that was," I add as my stomach attempts to digest the half-burnt meal.

"It was supposed to be baked chicken, but it just had a little extra... flavoring." She tugs on a piece of hair, and I grimace. "Kayce ate it."

"He's five. His palate is used to sugary cereal and pizza rolls."

"True," she responds, combing through the tresses with her fingers. It's a fleeting massage that sends a tickle down my spine. Too quick to truly enjoy. "So what's *your* favorite meal to make?"

"At the restaurant?"

"Sure. Or wherever. Just something you really like to cook." She leans down close to my ear, the scissors grazing along the skin there as her breath warms the lobe.

"Hm," I say, acting like I'm thinking when I'm really enjoying the feeling of a woman so close. It's been too long. "I think I enjoy making breakfast the most. Bacon, eggs, homemade waffles. Hashbrowns just crispy enough and covered with onions and cheese."

"Mm." Her purr vibrates something deep in my gut. "That sounds amazing. You should start serving breakfast. I'd eat there every day for sure."

"I thought about it. Even tried it for a few days. But the hours were too long. I was up at four just to get the grill going, and I stayed open until ten. It didn't give me time to live."

"You could've hired more staff."

"I've got Crystal. That's enough."

"Yeah, except she calls off every other day, and then you end up working too much."

Delia slides around to my other side, her fingers dragging through the strands as she goes. My entire body is tense as she works. Careful not to move a muscle so she doesn't mess up. I swallow. "I've got nothing better to do."

"You just said you worked too much and didn't have time to live. Yet you're still in that same situation. When was the last time you went on a date?" She pulls away and looks at me, her hand on her cocked hip.

I roll my eyes. "Speaking of dates... how was yours? Anyone I know?" The town of Oselka Harbor, Michigan is small. With the exception of Delia and a few other transplants, most people have lived here their entire lives. With it being the middle of fall and the tourist season winding down, the pickings are even slimmer.

"Oh, no. Just a client from the bank. Some businessman down from Canada who rolls through every few weeks."

"Did it... Did it go well? Do you think you'll see him again?" I try to keep the eagerness from my voice, but even I can hear the way the pitch rises. I clear my throat and swallow.

"Nah. He's not my type." She leans down, her face close to the back of my neck, and goosebumps break out along the skin there. Then a stream of cool air tickles along my spine as she blows off the cuttings. "All done."

I rub the back of my neck and stand as she grabs the broom from the hall closet. "I can get that," I say, reaching for the handle.

"No way, go check out my work. I think I killed it," she responds with a twinkle in her eyes as her gaze dances over my hair.

I pad down the hall to the bathroom, careful not to wake Kayce. His dinosaur nightlight shines through the crack in the door, and I chuckle inwardly at the memory of his face when he took a bite of the burned chicken.

"Mom, this tastes like the time you burned the popcorn. And not in a good way."

I step into the bathroom and check out my hair. It's perfect, the waves are out of my face but still tousled enough to look rugged.

"Looks great," I say when I get back to the kitchen. Everything's cleaned up. The chair's put away and Delia's standing at the sink washing her hands. "Thanks. For dinner and the hair." I point to my head awkwardly.

"It's the least I can do for you replacing the tube thingy from the water heater. I'm excited for that hot shower now." She runs a towel over her hands and folds it neatly on the counter, patting it twice. But I'm caught up with the image of her naked body behind the shower curtain, all curves and soft, soapy skin.

"I, uh, guess I'll see you tomorrow. For coffee?" I grab my toolbox from the floor and head toward the door.

"Throw in some of those eggs, waffles, and hashbrowns why don't you?" Her smile lifts her face as she walks toward me.

"Oh, I only make that meal for the girls I date," I joke as I open the door and cross the narrow hallway to my own apartment.

"Oh, right. Yeah, I mean... right." Her smile falters as she stands in the doorway.

I open my door and glance over my shoulder, her eyes blinking quickly at my back. "Goodnight, Delia."

"Night, Dane."

And then we both close our doors at the same time.

CHAPTER FIVE

Delia

"Del?" My secretary pokes his head through the door just as I look up from the spreadsheet on my computer. "Call for you on line three."

"Thanks, Pete," I say, blinking away the headache I feel coming on. I dig through my desk until I locate the glasses I'm supposed to wear when using the computer and then slide them on. As my vision adjusts, the data sheet in front of me becomes clearer. Crisper.

I don't want to need the glasses, but now that I'm nearing thirty, I suppose this is only the beginning. I make a mental note to pick up some neck firming cream from the drugstore.

The phone beeps, reminding me of the waiting call. I push the button and pick up the receiver. "Delia Evans."

"Ms. Evans, Phil Patrick here." My gut churns as my "date" from the other night's voice curls into my ear. "How are ya now?"

I nearly snort at the way his Canadian accent cuts through the vowels. "I'm fine, Mr. Patrick. How are you doing?" I cradle the phone between my ear and shoulder and return to the spreadsheet on my computer.

"Oh, I'm doing well. I'm calling to see if you're free this weekend."

My heart flutters, but for all the wrong reasons. "Was there something wrong with the contracts?"

"Not at all, Ms. Evans. I had my lawyer look them over this morning and everything's just great." The line goes silent for a brief moment and my stomach drops. "I'm in town for another day or two and thought I'd drop off the contracts in person. Over dinner."

I gulp. "D-dinner? Like a-a date?" Truth was, the meeting with Phil Patrick hadn't *exactly* been a romantic date like I'd led Dane to believe.

"Well, yes, if you'd like to think of it as a date..."

I think back to the other night and rack my brain for any indication I'd given this man that I was interested. I'd brought loan agreements to sign, for crying out loud. There were fancy pens and addendums.

"I just had the best time the other evening. Didn't you?"

My mind flashes back to the ninety-seven minute catered meal in our conference room spent poring over the financial paperwork of Phil's company, a small Canadian supermarket specializing in locally-sourced goods. "Of course I enjoyed our *business* meeting, Mr. Patrick. But, you see, I actually..." I stall, realizing I'm nothing but a coward. There is absolutely nothing wrong with Phil Patrick, other than his two first names. He's kind. Smart. And about as exciting as the Hallmark channel.

Phil Patrick is exactly the opposite of what I want—*need*—in a man.

"Ms. Evans, I don't want to put you in an uncomfortable situation. I'll send the paperwork over tonight. But I will be back to Oselka in a few short weeks. Think about my offer. Until then." The line drops out, and I slowly replace the receiver, still confused as to what actually happened.

I swallow the knot in my throat and return my focus to the data in front of me. It's the accounts for my best friend's non-profit. Savannah Smith, daughter of Senator Paul Smith, started her music venture five years ago on the Emerald Coast of Florida. She works with artists and record labels to bring music education to underprivileged children in the inner city school systems. Now she's thinking of expanding, with the hopes of opening a sister facility in Chicago.

As for me, I'm content at my job running numbers and creating spreadsheets of data as an accountant. Many would find this kind of work boring. Soul-crushing, perhaps. But not me. I find comfort in the cells and formulas. The columns of expenses paired perfectly with rows of itemizations. Everything adds up. Nothing is missing. Nothing unaccounted for. The data can't provide false hope. Data can't let a person down. It's right there in front of someone. Black and white and honest.

It's not until many hours later that I reach into my desk, pull out my cell phone, and notice the time. I've a missed call from Sav. I press *send* on the FaceTime app notification and am instantly connected to her. Horns and other brass instruments blare in the background. "Hey! I'm at the foundation. Let me just step out." It takes a moment for Savannah to locate a quiet space. "What's up? I was just calling to see how your date went the other night."

I roll my eyes. "It wasn't a *date*, Sav. It was a business meeting."

"But you said you told Dane that—"

"I told him it was a date because I wanted to make him jealous, okay?" The truth spills out of my mouth before I can stop it. Ugh, why doesn't my bestie understand the game I'm trying to play?

"Ah, tricky tricky, my friend. So how was this *business meeting*?"

"It was exactly the way you'd expect a financial portfolio evaluation to go with a Canadian."

"So, nice?"

"Precisely." I swivel around in my chair and face the window that looks out to the town square. There's a glimmer of frost leftover on the grass, but everything else is gray and wet. Just like my mood.

"You know, there's nothing wrong with a nice guy, Del."

I chuff. "Maybe for you. But nice has never been my thing."

It's true. Kayce's father, Marshall, was the exact opposite of nice. He was a ruthless financial shark who hunted for companies that were struggling and then bought them out on the verge of bankruptcy. Besides a massive portfolio and holdings throughout the Midwest, his rise up the corporate ladder was spoken about in awe. His only real fault was the trail of heartbroken women left in his path.

Myself included.

"Think about the type of man you want Kayce to be when he grows up. Don't you want him to be... nice?"

I gulp as my throat wobbles. Because yes, I do want to raise a son who is honorable, smart, and kind. But if Kayce never sees those types of men, never learns those types of behaviors, then how is he supposed to grow up to be one of them?

Savannah continues. "And what about Dane? Isn't he nice? It seems like you're interested... especially if you're lying to him about imaginary dates."

"Dane is nice. To Kayce. But to me he's..." I trail off. Because while Dane treats Kayce nearly like his own, there's something different about the way he treats me. Flirty but careful to never cross some imaginary line we both toe. And just when I think he's going to make a move, his attitude pokes through, and I'm back to questioning if he can even stand me. "To me he's just Dane, I guess." I shrug.

"Well, if you're willing to lie and make him jealous, maybe you need to shoot your shot. What have you got to lose?"

I think of the way that Dane cares for my son. The way he rushes to the rescue for us, whether from a cold shower or, like when Kayce was an infant, a sobbing and inconsolable baby with a sleep-deprived mother.

Or, even more recently, this past Christmas Eve...

As I sat on the apartment floor surrounded by what felt like a million tiny pieces of racetrack, I knew that Dane would lend me his toolbox. In my Grinch pajamas and Rudolph slippers, I'd crept quietly across the hall and knocked on his door.

He'd answered in his own pajamas—minus a shirt. My face heated as I took in the defined obliques and deep V, forcing my gaze lower.

"Del? What's wrong?" His hair was askew, as though he'd ran his hands through it a handful of times.

My eyes jetted up to his as my face heated. "Uh, d-do you have a few tools I could borrow? I'm in the middle of building Kayce's present, and it's not going so well." I shrugged and forced my gaze to remain glued to his.

He mumbled something before disappearing. I peered around the open door and into his apartment, noticing that not a single holiday decoration adorned the living room or kitchen. Meanwhile, mine was outfitted with enough décor to stock an entire craft store.

"What exactly do you need?" he asked, reappearing and holding his red metal toolbox. And wearing a shirt.

I shrugged again and held out my hand. "Can't I just borrow the whole thing?"

He harrumphed and stepped toward me. "Let me see what you're trying to build."

"That's really not necessary. I can build a simple racetrack." Lie. I was a Christmas Eve liar. I'd been attempting to build said present for over an hour.

"Did you get him the one I recommended?" Dane walked around me and headed into my apartment.

"Of course. What do I know about the best race track for a child?" I nearly crashed into his back as he came to a halt. He looked around at the mess before his lips pressed into a firm line. Sections of metal track, screws, and a controller littered the floor.

He set down the box and plopped to the ground. "Well," he sighed, "let's get to it then. Santa's not gonna build this himself..."

I held in a smile as I found a spot next to him and reached for the instruction manual. With Dane's help, the track was built within thirty minutes, and the look on Kayce's face the next morning was priceless.

So, to answer Savannah's question... what do I have to lose by telling Dane that I might want more?

Everything.

I stalk through the door to the restaurant and find a tower of pizza boxes and the phone ringing off the hook. "What's going on?" Dane peers through the food window, a sheen of sweat glistening across his brow.

"Been busy. Crystal called off!" he shouts as he grabs the giant spatula and slides an uncooked pizza into the brick oven.

"Again?" She's called off at least three times this month, leaving Dane to fend for himself. He's normally wrapping up for the evening by the time I get home from the bank. "And what about Antonio?" The pizza box tower grows as Dane adds another two to the stack. He wipes his hands down the front of his flour-covered shirt.

"Flat tire, but AAA was on the way when I talked to him a while ago." He glances at the clock over the door. "If he doesn't get back soon, I'll have to deliver these myself."

I press my lips together as the phone continues to ring. "Let me go up and get changed. I'll bring Kayce down— he can play on his iPad— and I'll help."

Something in Dane's expression softens, but he shakes his head nonetheless. "You've had a long day yourself. Don't worry about it. I can handle things." He grabs the phone and lifts it to his ear. "Dane's Italiano. Yes, Mr. Kemper, your order is ready. We ran into an issue, but it'll be to your place shortly."

Dane replaces the receiver, but it rings again and he's immediately re-peating the same spiel once more. "Listen, I'm helping whether you want it or not," I interrupt, striding toward the back stairwell. I take the steps two at a time and key open the apartment door to find Kayce finishing a snack at the table while his babysitter, Maria, plays on her phone on the couch.

"Hey, buddy." I ruffle his hair on my way to drop my purse and lunch-box on the counter. "How was school?"

"Connor taught me a bad word!" He flashes me a toothy grin.

"Oh yeah, which one?" I dig through my purse and pull out a ten dollar bill, passing it to Maria, who hardly glances up from her text messages. Not that I can complain. At five dollars an hour, I'm grateful she even picks Kayce up from school and walks him home. Luckily, I keep her favorite after-school snacks, too, as well as a variety of streaming services for her to use.

"*Shit!*" Kayce shouts from his seat as he bounces up and down with glee. Maria's eyes widen.

"Well Connor's parents may allow him to use that type of word, but I do not. Don't say it again, mister." I frown at him, and his face falls.

"Yes, ma'am."

"Go grab your iPad and your cars. We're going to help Dane out tonight." The smile returns as his face lights up, and before I know it, he's fleeing to his room to collect his things.

"How'd that geometry test go?" I ask Maria as she shoulders her bag.

"I got a B-plus! Thanks so much for helping me study, Ms. Evans. You really helped me understand the difference between sine and cosine."

"Anytime, Maria." I offer her a smile and a shrug. Little does she know that I'm a total math nerd. Explaining geometry terms to her was the highlight of my week.

God, I need to get out more...

"I'll see you tomorrow!" She yanks open the door and bounds down the stairs, her heavy Doc Martens echoing through the apartment.

I heave a sigh and look around, enjoying the quiet, if only for a moment. That headache from earlier pinches behind my ears. "Mom! Can you help me find the red truck?"

"Sure, buddy, but then we've got to get downstairs to help Dane!"

CHAPTER SIX

Delia

"Phew, what a night!" I lock the door to the restaurant and turn to Dane, who's carrying an enormous bag of flour from the pantry.

I pull the wad of tips from my pocket and set them on the counter near the till. "Nuh-uh! You earned those," Dane says as he eyes me through the food window.

I smile sweetly at him, which is hard through the sweat and grease that seems to coat my face. After running back and forth all night between the phone orders and the in-person diners, I definitely need a shower. "Consider my tab cleared, then."

He chuffs. "That doesn't even begin to cover your tab, Delia."

My smile falters, and I swallow the embarrassment that flares in my chest. I don't like taking handouts, and it seems like that's all I've done since I met Dane. I blink. "You know, I never asked—"

"Why don't you help me prep the dough for tomorrow morning, and we'll call it even?" The smile that lifts his lips is genuine, even if slightly goofy. My chest flutters.

At around eight, I'd led Kayce upstairs, tucked him in, and let him know I'd just be downstairs if he needed anything. Now, I glance at the clock, which reads just a few minutes past nine. He's likely fast asleep. I stare at the iPad left on the counter. "Okay, but I've never done that before."

Dane glances down at the stainless steel table between us. "I'll teach you," he says gruffly. He digs his hands into the large bag and grabs a handful of flour. Sprinkling it over the shiny surface, he then smoothes it around with his palm. "Can you grab the eggs from the walk-in?"

I nod and head to the refrigerator. The door snaps open as I yank the handle and step inside. The temperature sends a chill down my spine as I search through heads of lettuce, sliced tomatoes, and cheese until I find the giant pack of eggs. I hurry out, letting the remaining heat from the pizza oven warm me as I close in on Dane.

His back muscles ripple and flex under his basic white tee as he leans over the table, ensuring that the entire top is coated with flour.

"E-eggs," I mumble stupidly, holding them out as he turns to me. His gray-blue eyes darken as our hands touch.

My heart stutters slightly as I take a tentative step forward. Then another. He turns back around, and my gaze peruses the way his tricep muscles contract. The way his jeans fit around his waist. I wonder—

"I need you to crack all twelve eggs into this flour well."

I inch closer and watch as Dane dumps a massive pile of flour onto the center of the table, then circles the mound, hollowing out the middle with his index and middle fingers.

I gulp.

"Del?"

My gaze flashes to his. "Yeah?"

"You okay?" His eyebrow quirks as he looks me up and down.

I blink and shake my head. "I-I'm—"

He sighs. "You're exhausted. And you've got to get up early to get Kayce moving, too. I can handle this. Thanks for your help tonight…" He pulls an egg from the container and cracks it loudly on the side of the table, then dumps the contents into the middle of the flour.

"No. No, Dane. I'm fine. I can help. I *want* to help." Because that's the truth. Right now there's nowhere else I'd rather be. Before he can rebuff me, I grab an egg and follow suit, cracking and dumping one after another until the entire container is empty. "Now what?"

Dane tosses the empty case into the trash. "Now we whisk the eggs." He grabs a fork from a drawer hidden beneath the table and stabs each yolk. Then he passes me the utensil, and I proceed to mix the contents.

"You know, I never asked why you decided to open an Italian restaurant." I want to ask him about his family's heritage, but I'm unsure of the proper way without sounding ignorant.

"My father grew up in New York, and he always raved about the pizza there. Nothing in Michigan even came close, and of course, the signature deep dish style in Chicago 'wasn't real pizza,' as he claimed. It was always his dream to open a pizza place once he retired from the auto plant, but…" He pauses, and my whisking slows.

"I'm sorry." I look down at the dull yellow sludge between us. "I didn't mean to pry or bring up painful memories."

He ignores me and inhales deeply. "When he died, I took the money I had saved and invested in this place. It was originally a diner that served a little bit of everything, but I remodeled. Narrowed down the menu with a focus on Italian, mainly pizza. And that's that."

I nod and hold the fork aloft. "D-do I mix in the flour now?"

Dane grabs the fork— my fingers heating under his touch— and tosses it into the sink filled with soapy water. "It's best to use your hands now."

My throat tightens as he slides his palms under the flour and then rotates his wrists, dumping the white substance into the egg mixture. He repeats the process until the two ingredients are combined, albeit still lumpy. "Grab the salt, please." He nods to the canister across the way.

"How much do I add?" I ask, popping open the dispenser.

"I'll tell you when."

I turn the container over quickly as white flakes sprinkle the mixture.

"More," Dane instructs, the corner of his mouth quirking slightly.

I repeat the process, this time holding the canister upside down for a fraction of a second longer.

"More," he repeats, his eyebrows shooting up.

"Really? That seems like a lot of salt." I eye him skeptically.

"I've never heard you complain about the taste, Delia. *More*," he says, his voice deepening, and I oblige.

Our eyes meet and hold as I flip over the container, the salt falling like lake effect snow into the concoction. Just when I think it's too much, Dane's lips part. "When," he says gruffly.

I push the metal dispenser back into the canister and put the salt away. Only now, my heart is pounding, and my mouth waters. Is it from the excess salt or from Dane? Do I even want to know?

"Help me knead it all together." His hands sink into the wet mixture, forearms flexing and shoulders rolling as he manipulates the ingredients.

I hesitate and bite my lower lip. I'm ready to call it a night as my eyes drink their fill of this man working the dough between capable and expert hands. But before I can bail, Dane reaches out, grabs me by the wrists, and thrusts my hands into the squishy white mass. "Wh-what are you doing?" I ask, my voice rising an octave as the flour and egg mixture squishes between my fingers.

"Come on, Del, you weren't going to go for it unless I gave you a little push." That cocksure smile reaches his eyes, and I feel heat creeping into my cheeks.

We work in tandem, side by side, our fingers and arms brushing against one another's every so often as we fold and knead the dough into smaller sections. My breath hitches each time we touch, and I try—*so* very hard—to keep my composure. Keep my breathing and blinking natural. Only after we've worked through the last chunk does Dane finally pull away and traipse to the sink, submerging his hands in the soapy water.

My body feels suddenly cold without him next to me. "Come wash up," he urges as he scrubs himself clean.

"I'll just wait until you're finished," I respond awkwardly.

"There's plenty of room, Delia. Get over here." Something about the way he commands me has my core warming. I oblige and step toward him. That dominant and aggressive manner is what I like. If only...

I dunk my hands into the warm water, and the flour and eggs instantly dissolve. I rinse and cleanse, my arm pressed against Dane's as he does the same. "I can't wait to get into a nice hot shower." The words are out before I can stop them, and I clamp my mouth closed, embarrassment heating my scalp.

"Me too," he says, drying his hands on a fresh towel as he turns to me. I catch his gaze and hold it, my mouth parting slightly as the thought of Dane in a steaming shower flashes into my mind. "That water heater holding up after the fix?"

"Y-Yeah," I stammer as he passes me the towel. I run it over my hands.

"If it goes out again, you'll come shower at my place." It's not a question. It's a command. And based on the way my heart pumps harder, nearly pounding through my shirt, I clearly love it.

"O-okay." I nod and bite my lip. Blink up at him and hold his stare.

He exhales through his lips. His breath covers me like a blanket on this cold night. "Listen, Del, I—"

A pounding breaks the trance, and we both snap our eyes to the front of the restaurant...

Where my mother and father are staring at us through the locked door.

"What are you both doing here at 9:45 on a Tuesday night?" I stand in my living-cum-dining room with my hands on my hips, eyebrows nearly touching my hairline, as I assess my parents.

"We were invited for Kayce's birthday." My father, an Episcopalian reverend born and raised in Lansing, Michigan, matches my stance.

"Well the party's not tonight," I add dumbly. My parents had never once accepted the birthday invitations I sent. And yet this year they've decided to show up? I watch both of them through narrowed eyes.

My father's gaze is trailing around my apartment, from the threadbare couch to the thrifted kitchen table. The faded red spaghetti sauce stain that is still visible in the carpet between the kitchen and dining room. The crack in the paint between the wall and the ceiling. With his perusal complete, his matching pale blue eyes finally land on me. His lip curls. "You don't answer our calls, Delia, so what else are we supposed to do?"

"We tried the apartment first, but nobody answered," my mother adds.

I push a breath through flattened lips and allow my eyes to close for the briefest of moments. "So who's watching the congregation while you're here?" It's a low blow, and I know it, but I still push past him and my mother and go to the refrigerator. Pulling a longneck out, I twist off the top and hold it out to my parents.

Their expressions look as though I've offered them cocaine.

I lift the brown bottle to my lips and take a satisfying pull.

"Father Joseph is handling the flock this week," my father says stoically. I don't miss the way his jaw tenses as I take another swig of the beer.

"We've booked a hotel just outside of town," my mother adds, her voice barely above a whisper.

"Why now?" I haven't seen my parents in six years. They may have taken me in when I fled Chicago and, unemployed, landed on their doorstep with a duffel bag and a belly protruding from beneath my college sweatshirt. But that kindness hadn't lasted long once the church congregation began asking questions about the reverend's unwed pregnant daughter.

"It's high time we got to know our grandson." My eyebrow quirks as my mother's hand finds my father's arm. She tightens her grip ever-so-slightly.

I exhale a strangled giggle. "Now you want to get to know your grandson? *Now?*" I left the day they suggested I either marry Kayce's father or pair off with an elder from the church who had been more than willing to raise my bastard son as his own.

My father swallows and straightens his shoulders. "Your mother's right, Delia. It's time we put your... *indiscretions* behind us and heal this family."

I slam the half-empty bottle on the counter with such a force that it startles my soft-spoken mother. "M-my indiscretions? Is that what you've come all this way to discuss? After six years?" The backs of my eyes prick, and my nose tingles. I will not cry in front of them. *Not again.*

My father pulls my mother toward the door, his strides long and measured compared to hers. "I can tell this is a lot for you to take in. We'll head back to the hotel now so you have time to compose yourself."

And before I can utter another word, they're gone.

CHAPTER SEVEN

Dane

Coffee brews as my foot taps impatiently on the tiled floor. My gaze strays to the front door and the stairway just beyond. My heart pounds, waiting for Delia and Kayce to fly out to the sidewalk.

Last night...

Last night had been intense. Delia helping me out had been a God send, but once we closed? My chest flutters at the memory.

Delia wrist-deep in dough, a dab of flour on her cheek.

Her smile—how it spread across her face and lit up her eyes as she squished the mixture between her fingers for the first time.

Our hands brushing in the soapy water, and the way I'd almost—

The phone trills from its cradle under the clock. I yank the receiver to my ear. "Hello?" We're not open for another few hours, so I don't have to act like a professional just yet.

"Dane, it's Marigold Fraser with the Rotary Club. How are you doing this morning?"

"I'm fine, Mrs. Fraser. What can I do for you?" My eyes stay trained on the stairwell, my foot continuing to relentlessly tap.

"Well, dear, we're holding a leadership meeting in early December and wondered if you'd be interested in catering the event for us. If you're available, it's scheduled for December 5th."

I swallow and ponder for only a moment. Dane's Italiano doesn't usually cater, nor do I need the additional stress and hassle of this side job. "I don't exactly think I'm outfitted to handle such a job, Mrs. Fraser. I don't even have a full-time waitress on staff most nights."

"That's a shame, Dane. The leadership committee was really hoping to work with you, especially as we know you've discussed expanding your business in the past. Weren't you the one wanting to purchase the abandoned lot on Miller's Run Avenue?"

Damn. I *have* been thinking about building a free-standing restaurant, and there's no way the permits or sale would go through without the support of the busybodies in the Rotary.

"Stepping out of your comfort zone is the best way to grow, Dane."

The bright yellow school bus creaks to a stop outside the building. The door springs open, and I wait.

Where are they?

The stalled engine rattles loudly, vibrating the window panes of the restaurant.

Just then, I catch Kayce's tousled blond hair as he stumbles from the stairwell, takes a bounding leap, and hops onto the bus's black steps. The door closes with a *whoosh*, and the bus pulls away from the curb.

Delia, her red hair pulled into a high ponytail, swings open the door to the diner. A breath of fresh air amidst the fumes of the bus's exhaust, she's wearing a tight pencil skirt and a soft blue sweater that brings out her eyes. Those same eyes that I watched crinkle with amusement last night as we worked so well together.

"You know, Mrs. Fraser, maybe it's time I stepped out of my comfort zone. I'll certainly be willing to cater for your meeting, and I look forward to speaking more about the lot while I'm there."

I replace the phone and meet Delia's wide and inquisitive gaze. "Catering, eh?" She hoists herself onto the stool across from me.

I swipe at an imaginary spot on the counter and shrug. "Yeah, I guess the Rotary wants to test out my skills." I feel my cheeks heat. "Would you—" I pause and worry my bottom lip between my teeth. "Would you be interested in helping out? As a waitress for the event? I'll obviously pay you for your time."

Her peach-hued lips part as she offers me a smile. "Of course I'll help. Which day?" She pulls out her phone and swipes to the calendar app.

"The 5th of December." I grab two mugs from beneath the counter and set them between us. Then I lift the coffee pot from the warming plate and pour, the steam licking around my wrist. "You know, if something comes up and you can't get a sitter for Kayce—"

"Nothing will come up, Dane. I'll be there." She slides her mug closer and, grabbing two sugar packets, rips them open and dumps the crystals into the brown liquid.

"A two-packet kinda day, huh?"

She swirls the mixture with her spoon. "You don't know the half of it."

And then she proceeds to tell me about her parents.

"Dane!" Kayce barrels through the restaurant door and launches his fifty-three pound self at my legs.

"Hey, buddy! How was school? What'd you get on your space project?"

"A check-plus! And I got a sticker!" He holds out his hand and shows me the bright yellow star affixed to his skin.

"Awesome!" I hold out *my* hand for a high five, and Kayce winds up before obliging. I shake my hand, imitating being injured from the sheer force of the smack. "Man, tone it down a little on the protein."

We both turn as the door opens again, and Delia saunters through. She's wearing a pair of dark flared jeans and a tight pink sweater that accentuates... *everything*.

"My mom asked me if she looks pretty," Kayce adds before tumbling over to a booth and climbing in.

My gaze strays from Delia's *assets* up to her eyes just as her cheeks flush a shade of red. "I hope you said *yes*," I say without breaking eye contact. Her lips part, and she inhales just as the door opens again and her parents enter, shaking the rain from their coats.

When Delia told me she was having dinner with her parents tonight, she conveniently forgot to mention they'd be eating *here*.

"They *insisted*," the beautiful woman in front of me says as she slides into the booth next to Kayce.

I plaster a smile on my face, although it probably looks clownish with the way I simultaneously grind my back teeth together. After everything that Delia told me this morning about her parents, I'm not sure I'm capable of being cordial to them.

"Then they sold our house when I was ten and converted a portion of the church into living quarters," she said before taking a swig of her coffee. "I no longer had a room with toys. I had a glorified supply closet with a small hard cot and a few stuffed animals. Nana wasn't happy, so I spent a lot of time at her house. She kept all of my old things and set up a room just for me." Her

smile turned wistful as her eyes dropped. "It was hard cleaning out that room when she moved into the assisted living facility. It was even harder knowing I never came first in my parents' eyes. They always chose the church and their rigid beliefs over me. And now Kayce."

As Delia's father became more radicalized in his beliefs, he often took mission trips and would be gone for months. Building a school in South America. Preaching his beliefs overseas. Delia's mother did all the bookkeeping for the church, but without a steady income, their family was often left without basic necessities.

I stare at the man who slides into the booth. His worn shoes gleam from being polished, and though his coat has seen better days, his appearance is well kept.

"Welcome, Mr. and Mrs. Evans," I say, mustering respect I don't feel for the man and woman in front of me. "What can I get you started to drink?" Kayce passes everyone menus, not that he and Delia need them.

Delia's father glances at me, his pale blue eyes the same color as Delia's. But that's where the similarities end. Where Delia is warm and soft, her father is all hard edges and steely. His gaunt appearance proves he's not one for comforts.

Delia told me her father always made his family forego delicacies and desserts. Anything he considered a treat was banned in their home. Whether it was nail polish or candy—it didn't matter. Delia didn't taste steak or have her first sip of Coke until she went to Florida with her best friend, Savannah.

When I found out that Del despised Pepsi, I quickly switched vendors to sell exclusively Coca-Cola products. And yet her own father wouldn't allow her that one simple treat.

I race back to the soda fountain and seriously consider spiking Delia's Coke with a healthy splash of rum, because judging by the grimace she's wearing as she sits across from her parents, she could use it. I return with two waters, Delia's Coke, and a lemonade for Kayce just as Delia's father pins me with his stare.

"What do you recommend for someone who can't tolerate red sauce?"

I set the plastic cups on the table and pass out straws. "The garlic shrimp linguine is a safe bet, sir." I try my best to avoid Delia's smirk.

"And how fresh is your shrimp? I don't recall Lake Michigan being chockfull of them."

"No, sir. They're frozen." I clasp my hands behind my back to avoid clenching my fists together.

"Hm," he chuffs before returning to the menu. "Someone else go." He waves his hand at the table.

"Pepperoni pizza!" Kayce shouts excitedly. I offer him a fist bump and a nod.

"Chicken parm for me." Delia doesn't even have to look at the menu. She orders the same thing every time.

"Pounded thin and fried extra crispy?" I ask with a wink.

"You know it." She pats Kayce's knee, encouraging him to settle down—he's smashing two Matchbox cars together repeatedly, and loudly. I don't care in the slightest—Kayce can do no wrong in my book—but I think she's trying to calm him for her parents' sake.

I turn to Delia's mother, her eyes downcast on the menu. Her russet hair, with strands of gray along the forehead, is pulled back in a tight bun at her nape. "Just a Caesar salad for me, please." She smiles kindly, if a little sadly, up at me. With lips pressed together, I nod and turn my attention back to the gruff man sitting at her side.

"The marsala, no mushrooms or garlic," he orders, snapping the menu closed and replacing it alongside the condiments. He looks across the table at his daughter and grandson. "When was the last time you spoke to Marshall?" Then I'm dismissed from his presence.

Luckily, Crystal waltzes into the restaurant just as I get the meals going. "Sorry I'm late, boss." She unzips her winter coat and hangs it on the hook in the back.

I hardly register her apology. My ears are cocked to the food window as I try, but fail, to pick up on the conversation in the booth across the diner. "Watch the food." I stalk out of the kitchen.

I pull a box of napkins from beneath the counter and start checking the dispensers. "I don't understand why you won't take his calls, Delia. He's the boy's father."

I attempt to cram a stack of napkins into an already-full dispenser. "Marshall had the chance to be Kayce's father six years ago. Why now? And how did he even get your information?"

Mr. Evans shrugs as he fidgets with a straw wrapper. "It doesn't matter why now," he says. "All that matters is he's interested in being a father. Kayce needs a *father*, Delia." He slides his gaze to the child across from him who's still ramming his toy cars together and making crashing noises with his mouth.

Delia purses her lips together and glances down at her lap. A part of me wants to strut over there and lift her chin. Tell her that she doesn't need anyone but me. *Us*.

Except there is no *us* because I've never told her how I felt.

"You need to do the right thing. As Matthew said, 'For if you forgive others their trespasses, your Heavenly Father will also forgive you.' Let him see his son."

"Hey, boss! Order's up!" Crystal's hollering pulls me from the conversation, and I lift my eyes just in time to catch Delia's. Her face instantly turns a deep shade of red as she puts two and two together and realizes I've been eavesdropping.

I scurry into the kitchen, the tightness in my chest compressing more and more. I hoist the plates along the underside of my forearm and carry them to the table.

Setting them down gently, one-by-one, I avoid Delia's gaze. If I looked at her, she'd surely see all of my emotions written across my face.

Pain.

Confusion.

Cowardice.

And maybe even a little desire.

The desire to pull her against my chest and wrap her in my arms. Let her know she's safe. Taken care of. Show her that I'll be the father Kayce needs.

"Thank y—" Delia's mother starts, just as Mr. Evans interrupts loudly.

"Delia, you'll lead us in the prayer." He holds his hands out, and uncertainty flashes in Delia's eyes. She folds her bottom lip under her top teeth and presses until the flesh turns white. I stand awkwardly next to the booth, waiting with bated breath.

She slowly lifts her hand and places it in her father's. "Actually, Dad, you go right ahead. I'm afraid I'm a bit rusty."

CHAPTER EIGHT

Delia

"Damn!" I rage as the car turns over, the mechanics under the hood groaning but never coming to life. I turn the key in the ignition, trying again. But only the muffled sound of the engine reaches my ears. "Son of a bitch."

"What's wrong?" Dane asks as I exit the car, careful not to slip on the patch of ice right along my driver's side door. He's tossing salt along the sidewalk from a giant yellow bag.

"I'm supposed to visit Nana today, but the fucking car won't start." I search for the latch and lift the hood. Jabbing my hands against my hips, I press my lips together and assess the machine in front of me.

As though I have any idea what I'm looking for.

He saunters over, tossing handfuls of salt around the tires. "With the cold snap, the roads are terrible, Delia. There's no reason for you to be out."

I peek at him beneath the fuzzy beanie that covers my hair. The chill is enough that I can see our breaths mixing between us. "I promised Nana I'd visit."

Two vertical lines form between his brows. "I'm sure she'd understand." He peers under the hood and a rumble percolates from his chest. "Besides, your spark plug is bad. That's why the car won't start."

"Shit," I murmur under my breath as I look in what I hope is the vicinity of the spark plug. "No chance you've got one just lying around?"

He chuffs. "I'm a chef, not a mechanic." He turns to leave, but I grab his coat sleeve with my mittened hand.

"I promised Nana I'd visit. Could I... Could I borrow your truck?" My eyes stray to the silver pickup parked in the alley between the buildings.

He turns, chest puffed and eyebrows raised. "Delia, your grandmother will understand why you can't come today. The roads.... They're awful." He gestures toward the sheet of ice leading out of town.

I press my lips firmly together, not ready to give up on my bi-monthly visit with Nana. "No, you don't understand. She's the most crotchety old woman you'll ever come in contact with. And she *begged* me to bring her medicine, Dane. *Today*!" I point to the small brown bag in the front seat of the car. "So could I *please* borrow your truck?"

He stares at me for a brief moment, his eyes giving nothing away as they peruse my face. But before I can beg again, he's twisting the bag of salt closed and stomping over the sidewalk to the door of the diner.

"So, that's a yes?" I ask, bouncing on the balls of my feet to keep from freezing my ass off.

He sets the bag of salt next to the door and pulls a set of keys from his pocket. Then he sticks the key into the lock and turns, the deadbolt sliding into place with a solid *click*.

"What are you—?"

"There's no way I'm letting you drive *my* truck on these icy roads. Get your stuff." He stalks over to the pickup and slides in before the engine roars to life.

I traipse around to the passenger side of the car and grab my purse and the bag of Nana's medicine.

Then, as graceful as a ballerina, I wipe out and land flat on my back. The ice seeps through my jeans as I lie on the pavement, staring at the gray sky.

Eff my life.

"Jesus, Del, are you okay?" I catch a brief glimpse of Dane's concerned gaze before he's hoisting me up, steadying me as he brushes the muck and salt from my back.

Readjusting my beanie, I pull my mittens from my hands in order to retrieve the brown bag containing Nana's medicine. Only—

"*This*? *This* is your grandmother's *medicine*?" He holds up a handful of miniature plastic liquor bottles and the torn paper bag.

I grab the bag and the bottles, holding them against my coat. "I never specified what *type* of medicine." I tuck the miniatures back into the ruined bag, roll it closed, and shove it all in my purse.

Dane only glares at me, his jaw ticking as his gray-blue eyes darken. "Get in the truck, Delia, before I change my mind."

"So this is the Dane you're always—"

"Nana, look what I brought. Your *medicine*!" I shove the damp paper bag into my grandmother's lap, cutting her off before she can embarrass me with the knowledge she has about Dane.

Because of course I've told her everything. From the way he rented me his furnished apartment for next to nothing when I was eight months pregnant, to the way he's kept Kayce and I fed with his delicious Italian cuisine.

Besides Savannah, my Nana is my best friend.

She cracks the cap of one of the tiny liquor bottles and takes a tiny taste. "Woo, that's strong!" she exclaims with a pinched expression.

"Those have to last you until next month," I remind her. It's our little secret. If my parents knew I was bringing my grandmother spirits, I'd be barred from the facility faster than they could recite the Lord's prayer.

"You know I only like to mix the brown one with my Coca-Cola. The clear ones are for euchre."

Dane sends me a confused look as he hangs back. Close to the door. "Her group of friends have a game of euchre each week where they bet contraband," I add. He offers a tight smile. I'd told him he could wait in the truck, but he'd wanted to come in. Now, as he stands in the entryway, rocking back and forth on his heels, I wonder if he's regretting his decision.

"Don't lurk in the doorway like the grim reaper! Come in. Let me take a look at you," my grandmother demands as she replaces the cap to the tiny liquor bottle and tucks the package into the cushion of her chair.

A flush creeps along Dane's cheeks as he clears his throat. He steps farther into the unit and leans against the wall next to the kitchenette. Nana was originally settled in a bungalow on the facility's property. But, over the years, she's moved to the smaller assisted living quarters. I know she misses the independence of being on her own, but the whole family feels more at peace with the on-site nursing staff close by.

"My, Delia, he is a looker. You didn't tell me he was so... *rugged*." My grandmother's eyes shine mischievously as she takes in all of Dane. From his baseball cap down to his boots, Dane does have a nice physique. He's slightly taller than me, and he's lean. I've never seen him workout, but I know that the muscles beneath his clothes are honed from hours spent doing manual labor. From hauling in boxes for the restaurant to maintaining the building—

"Delia, where's Kayce?" Nana's question thankfully pulls me from daydreaming about the hidden wonders under Dane's clothes.

"Mom and Dad came to town. They offered to watch him, and since the roads weren't the best..."

I'd made both of my parents promise to stay in the apartment and keep the television turned to the Disney channel. My father was happy to settle into the couch and work on next week's sermon while my mother played cars with Kayce.

"Why didn't you tell me the roads were bad? There's absolutely no reason for you to drive all the way to Lansing!" She offers an innocent smile at Dane, who cocks an eyebrow at me. I shake my head, knowing the game Nana's playing.

The innocent granny.

"Luckily I didn't drive. Dane did. And besides, it was only two hours. We were just fine." I take a seat and let her continue this charade.

But, surprisingly, she turns her attention back to me. "Your parents stopped on their way to visit you." Her eyes dart to Dane and then back to me before she leans in. Then, she mock-whispers just loud enough for *everyone* in the room to hear. "They're going to persuade you to get back with that bum."

I sit back and cross my arms, embarrassment heating the top of my scalp. "They already mentioned it last night at dinner, Nana." I shake my head. I can feel Dane's eyes on me, burning my skin, but I can't bear to look at him. To acknowledge that he's got a front row seat to my family's betrayal. "I don't know what to do to get them off my case. I'm not interested in Marshall, or having him in our lives, when he's so clearly not interested in knowing his son." My face heats even more as Dane clears his throat and adjusts himself. I probably should have pushed a little harder for him to stay in the truck.

"Hm..." Nana hums aloud, sitting back in her favorite green velour chair. It's the same chair I used to curl up in at her house as we watched her evening programs together. Before she moved into the facility. Her gaze strays to Dane, and she lets out an exaggerated gasp. "I have an idea!"

There's that charade.

I narrow my eyes. "Go ahead, Nana." I can only imagine what type of cockamamie plan she's cooked up. Although nothing could beat the Great Escape of 2022, where she and her euchre friends talked the poor nursing home bus driver into taking them to the casino nearly an hour away.

"Your father, bless his deluded heart, believes that Kayce needs a father in his life. That married parents are the only way to properly raise the boy, correct?"

Anger leeches from my pores. "Yes, I suppose that's what he's suggesting."

Nana leans forward in her chair. "And you want him to stay out of your love life, right?"

I roll my eyes. "Of course, Nana. You remember that old man he tried to set me up with when I was pregnant." The church elder in question had been older than my grandmother.

"So, you two pretend to get married!" Her slender finger points first to me and then floats through the air to Dane.

The sharp inhale from the kitchenette area is enough of an answer. "Nana! That's ridiculous!" I chance a glance behind me at Dane and already find his eyes on me. "Right?" My neck swivels between the two of them.

"You tell me, granddaughter. When they visited me, they mentioned giving Marshall your *address*."

"What?" I leap to standing and find Dane already beside me, his fists clenched. "Why would they do that?"

"They think your son needs a father in his life," Nana responds, sitting back and setting her hands daintily in her lap. She seems unfazed, even as I hyperventilate and anger radiates from Dane.

"But—" Suddenly everything I've worked for begins to flash before my eyes. The safety and security I've provided for Kayce the last six years. Our cozy apartment. My job.

"I think she's right," Dane mutters as he dips his head toward Nana.

"*What?*" I snap my gaze to him. "Y-you think that pretending to be married is a *good* idea?"

"I do," he responds with a smirk.

My shoulders sag at his pun and I cover my face with my hands. "This isn't a *joke*, Dane! This is my life. *Kayce's* life!"

The man at my side gently pulls my wrists away from my face and then cups my hands in his. I turn to face him, my features surely full of anguish and despair. "No, this isn't a joke. But if it's going to get your parents off your back—and keep you *and Kayce* in Oselka Harbor—then I'll do it."

My eyes drop to my Nana, her face a mask of detachment. I narrow my gaze at her. "Did they really threaten to give Marshall my information?"

"Ask them yourself," she says, pulling her flip phone from her cardigan pocket and holding it out to me. "I'm sure they'd love to fill you in on all the Bible verses about marriage and families."

I swallow the lump in my throat and turn back to Dane, his eyes studying my face as he continues holding my hands.

"Nothing ventured, nothing gained," I recite, the old proverb surfacing from some repressed part of my mind.

"YOLO," Nana adds, her eyes glimmering and a smile stretching her lips.

CHAPTER NINE

Dane

"A-are you sure you want to do this?" The red-haired woman sitting in the passenger seat asks for the umpteenth time as she worries her bottom lip.

I keep my eyes peeled to the road, even as we are only minutes away from the restaurant. The pavement's cleared in most spots, but there's still plenty of black ice and puddles hiding tire-eating potholes. "For the last time, Del, *yes*. I've always been here for you—and Kayce. I'll do whatever you two need."

Her gaze strays to the passenger window as the town limits come into view. She continues to gnaw on that lip of hers as we pass the church and then a row of Victorian houses. We approach Miller's Run Avenue, and my jaw ticks as I spy the *For Sale* sign on the vacant lot. "I just," Delia cuts in, her voice shaky, and my gaze deserts the property and lands on the road ahead. "I just don't want this to get out of hand, especially with the way I feel—" She clamps her mouth closed.

I practically slam my foot on the break. The way she feels? About me?

About her parents?

My senses cut in. *It's likely the way she feels about her ex, Kayce's father.*

My hands grip the steering wheel as I pull into the alleyway next to the diner and cut the engine. Opening the driver's side door, I attempt to race around to the passenger side but slide on a patch of leftover ice and barely catch myself on the front bumper. "Are you okay?" She's there, offering her hand. I take it, my fingers grazing her naked ring finger.

"I have to show you something," I say, hoisting myself to my feet. I keep hold of her hand and nearly drag her up the front stairs to the breezeway between our two doors—hers, still decorated with a leftover Fourth of July wreath; mine, bare except for the numbers of our shared address.

I unlock the door and pull her inside, closing the door behind us. The warmth of the apartment heats my cold cheeks, and I discard my coat and boots before traipsing farther into the unit.

"Should I—?" Delia's finger points to the interior as I turn around the corner toward the bedroom.

"No, it's fine. Stay right there." On socked feet, I pad into my bedroom and over to the bureau where a small wooden box sits, its gold-plated latch turning green with age. I lift the lid and dig through the items within. An old pocket watch owned by my father. Cuff links that belonged to my uncle. At the very bottom, buried beneath a stiff leather wristwatch, sits a tiny diamond ring.

I pinch the treasure between my thumb and forefinger, holding it aloft to assess the stone and its gold band for any imperfections.

There are plenty.

After all, it belonged to my mother. She wore it every day—for decades—until her fingers became so withered that the dainty ring would no longer fit over her arthritic knuckles. Only then did she pass the piece down to me.

"For someone special. Someday," she said, tucking the ring into my shirt pocket.

That was ten years ago. She never got to meet Delia or Kayce, but I'm sure she'd understand.

Before I can change my mind, consider the implications of what I'm doing, I return to the foyer, which is actually just a small tiled area with a rug for my shoes.

"Here." I hold the jewel out to Delia.

Her face instantly transforms. The crinkled brows raise to her hairline as her eyes widen and her mouth gapes. "No, no, no, Dane. I can't take that!" She waves her hands back and forth as though the ring's on fire. "I can easily pick up a cheap piece of costume jewelry at the drug store. This— this isn't necessary."

But it is.

If it keeps her and Kayce here—in my life, in Oselka Harbor—then it's necessary.

"Take it," I insist, but she continues to shake her head. Should I grab her hand and force it onto her finger? How does she not realize how serious I am about this?

So I do the only thing I can think of. Simply so she'll stop refusing.

I drop to one knee. Right there in the muck left behind by my slush-covered boots. My knee digs into the thin wet rug, and I hold the ring up. "Will you marry me, Delia?"

If possible, her mouth drops open even farther as her eyes take in my kneeling form. Those hands halt in mid-air and then slowly raise to cover her cheeks as she stares at me. Unblinking.

"What are you doing? It's... it's too much, Dane! W-we can't—"

"I've already agreed to everything, Del. All that's left is to make it official." I hold the ring higher. "If this isn't your style, I'll gladly go down to Jacobson's Jewelry Store, and you can pick out something you *do* like."

At that, her brow furrows and she finally snaps out of the trance, her hands falling to her hips. "No, that's ridiculous—to spend money on something that's a farce!"

"So you'll wear this ring? Solidify this 'farce,' as you call it?"

In answer, she holds her right hand out, palm up to accept the ring. "Nuh-uh," I admonish, rising to my feet. I reach for her left hand and slide the ring on her finger.

It fits perfectly.

"Now all that's left is to—" I glance behind her. Beyond my closed door. "Tell my parents," she finishes.

"What do you mean you're engaged to be married?" Mr. Evans's nostrils flare as his eyes nearly bulge from his skull. "And why are you just now making us aware of this?"

My gaze strays down the hallway to Kayce's eyes peering out from his room. I subtly shake my head, and he disappears.

I furrow my brow and turn to Delia. "Sir, we wanted to wait until we spoke with Kayce, but felt it was important for you both to know before returning to Lansing." I pull Delia to my side, her body rigid and shaking.

Her father ignores me. "And you think this—this *diner* owner—can provide for you and my grandson?"

"Tom!" Mrs. Evans's admonishment goes unnoticed from her seated position on the couch.

"What will I tell the congregation, Delia? What will the church elders think when they hear of this?"

If possible, Delia's body goes from simply rigid to granite. Stone cold. She pulls away from me slightly and stares through her father. "I don't give a damn what you tell them. I left your church when I left your house. I want nothing to do with any of that anymore! And if you're not accepting of *my* life choices, I'll have nothing to do with you, either."

The threat lingers in the air of the apartment. An enormously large elephant stuffed between the four of us.

It's Delia's mother who finally pushes past the proverbial pachyderm. "That's enough, Tom." She grabs hold of her husband's arm and tugs him toward the door. "Delia, Dane, we'd like to take you both to dinner after Kayce's party tomorrow. A true and *proper* dinner to celebrate," she adds as an aside.

The door slams behind them before we can confirm, and Delia immediately slumps against me. Her hands cover her face as I pull her in for a hug.

But it's Kayce's voice that has us leaping apart from one another.

"Mom? Can I come out now?"

Shit.

I follow Delia to Kayce's room, where we find him sitting cross-legged on his bed with a pillow tucked in his lap. Those big doe eyes, the same pale blue as his mother's, flick between the two of us. But it's Delia who strides toward him, takes a seat on the navy duvet-covered bed, and pulls him onto her lap. Her long fingers slide through his messy waves as she meets my eyes.

"I'm sorry you had to hear that, buddy," she says. Her jaw clenches, and her shoulders sag. This is all taking a toll on her, and I don't like it one bit.

"Are you and Dane going to get married?" He pulls away and glances up at her before turning to face me. I gulp.

Delia and I hadn't discussed how to deal with Kayce. What to tell him. And now, as my mother's ring winks in the soft light of a five year old's room, I wonder how to resolve this. How to fix this before it blows up in our faces.

"What's this?" I ask, pulling a bright yellow flyer from a stack of papers on Kayce's dresser. It's crumpled around the edges.

Kayce sits up. "Baseball team. But there's no one to coach," he says, a touch of sadness seeping into his voice.

I skim over the paper. "You ever played before?"

Kayce shakes his head back and forth as a frown pulls at his lips. "All the other kids asked their dads, but I don't have a dad to ask, so..." His voice trails off.

I don't have a dad...

My throat tightens, and my nose tingles. I think back to all the times my own father stood out on the diamond, the shadow of his baseball cap covering his eyes as his tongue stuck out the side of his mouth. He always tried to throw the ball *just so*, so that I and the other kids on the team had the chance to whack it out of the park and make our parents leap to their feet with applause.

"I'll do it," I say, tucking the paper away in my back pocket. Kayce deserves as much.

Delia's gaze flashes to mine. "Dane, you don't have to—"

"Yes," I interrupt. "I do. I'm going to be Kayce's step-d-dad now." Even as I stumble over the word, my heart in my throat, I can't deny the way I feel when Kayce flashes that thousand-watt smile at me. His face practically glows.

"Really? You'll coach?" He leaps from the bed.

"Of course, buddy. I'd do anything for you." And I mean it. With all of my heart and soul, I mean it. "But first we need to get you a glove. C'mon, I think I have my old one tucked away somewhere."

His tiny hand finds mine as I lead him out into the hallway, and I don't know if it's his grasp or the way Delia looks as I glance back at her. Her eyes shimmer with unshed tears as she mouths, "Thank you."

But I've never felt happier.

CHAPTER TEN

Delia

"Connor! No, that's not a toy!" I shout over the congregation of boys shooting Nerf darts at one another in the church gymnasium. I frantically glance around for the demon child's mother, but she's nowhere to be found.

Before I can swoop in, Dane approaches the offending child and hoists him over his shoulder like a sack of flour. "Nope, this area is roped off for a reason. Stay over here." He plunks the kid back into the fray of foam bullets. "Aggghh!" The boys turn their weapons on him, and he playfully cowers.

I watch all of this from behind the dessert table, which is laden with blue and green cupcakes. A smile pulls at my cheeks as I watch my fake fiancé interact with the youngsters. "Uncle! Uncle!" he finally cries, waving his arms in the air. But the boys refuse to give in and simply grab more darts from the ground, reloading with glee.

Glancing around at the other parents, I work up the courage to approach and offer refreshments. Most lean against the sidelines, separated by gender. The moms hold their trendy water containers while the men, their button down shirts tucked into slacks, discuss whatever football team is doing the best in the season. I can't help but compare their outfits to Dane's. While they look like they've just come from the office, he's wearing black joggers and a tee; his hoodie long ago discarded as he worked up a sweat playing with the boys. The same backwards baseball cap covers his wavy hair.

"There are drinks in the cooler. Help yourself," I offer as I move between the two groups. The moms smile and hold up their giant water receptacles while most of the men simply ignore me. I press my lips together and fight the awkwardness coursing through my gut. I wish Savannah were here, but, understandably, flying in for a six year old's birthday party hadn't exactly been in her and Jack's budget right now. And while I'm cordial with the parents in Kayce's class, I'm not exactly Miss Congeniality. Joining the PTO and knowing the juiciest town gossip has never been my thing.

I saunter over to my parents, standing on the outskirts. They've found the only other person in the room over fifty— Marigold Fraser. As the church party planner, she was only here to lock up and ensure that I'd properly cleaned up and wiped down the rented area— the only space in town big enough for fifteen boys to run amok while also being within my budget.

"My dear, I didn't know you and Dane had finally made it official!" She reaches toward me, and it takes a solid fifteen seconds before I realize that she wants to see the ring.

I hold out my hand.

"I recognize this ring. You know, I always thought you and Dane were perfect for each other. I'm glad I was right about that." I swallow the lump forming in my throat and keep my eyes down, lest my father know that I'm a liar and con-artist. "And his mother, Cora Lynn, would've loved you, dear. She was my best friend, you know."

I force a smile and withdraw my hand, shoving it into the pocket of my sweater. "And you never told me that your parents were of the faith." She turns to my mother and father, beaming with bright eyes.

"I'm surprised Delia hasn't sought you out, Mrs. Fraser," my father admonishes, his steely eyes landing on me. I shrink into myself and feel like a scolded child who forgot her Bible verses all over again.

"Yes, well, there's—"

Kayce's shrill holler interrupts our conversation, and I've never been more grateful in my life. "Mom! I'm thirsty!" Suddenly all the other boys decide they're also dying of thirst, and it's a mad dash for the refreshments.

"Excuse me." I nod politely and hurry away. After all, dealing with a herd of sweaty kindergartners demanding sustenance is much more appetizing than speaking about religion with my family.

Dane meets us in front of the building. Gone is his backwards baseball cap and joggers. Instead he stands before me in pressed khaki slacks, a crisp white tee, and a dark green utility jacket. His hair's neatly combed back from his face, but a few stray waves curl around his forehead.

"W-wow...," I mutter as I take in how good he looks. His gray blue eyes seem to darken as he looks me up and down, too.

He sucks his bottom lip between his teeth and presses, the deep pink hue turning to a dusky rose. I imagine those lips pressed against my—

"Mom! My shoe came untied!" I immediately shift my gaze to Kayce and the wet shoelace dragging on the leaf-covered concrete. I hesitate, wondering how I'm going to demurely bend down to tie the offending lace without my pencil skirt riding up or ripping.

It's been six years and I still haven't lost all the baby weight, no matter how hard I've tried. My brow furrows.

"I've got it, bud," Dane insists as he crouches and laces up the sneaker. The task is over within seconds, but Dane stays low on the ground, his gaze trailing up my exposed legs. The tip of his tongue flicks out and those winter storm eyes flash. I feel his eyes on me, the heat searing my ankles up to my core, despite the frigid temperature in the air.

"It's cold!" Kayce hollers before racing toward our car.

"Actually, I'll drive." Dane's hand falls to my lower back as he leads me around the icy puddles and cracks in the sidewalk. With wedge ankle boots on, I'm nearly eye level with him, but his wide shoulders make me feel petite as he guides me toward the passenger side and opens the door.

Kayce tumbles into the backseat like a blizzard.

Dane offers his hand as I climb from the sidewalk into the truck, and I take it. An electric shock, akin to touching a doorknob on a dry winter's day, jolts through my body at our contact, and I snap my eyes to his.

Did he feel it too?

"Got it?" He asks, pulling away far too soon as I situate myself into the seat.

I nod and pull the door closed as he strides around the front.

When he finally slides into the driver's side, I'm hit with a wave of his scent. It's a heady mix of herbs and dough from the diner as well as mint and bergamot. My saliva glands flood at the mixture of savory and clean. Like a man who just cooked dinner and then cleaned up after.

My elbow rests on the console between us, my hand dangling precariously close to his, which grips the gear shift as he maneuvers into drive. It's like there's a string from my palm to his, pulling us closer.

Until finally he grasps my hand in his and gives it a tight squeeze. "Everything will be okay," he says with a small smile, his eyes flicking to me briefly before returning to the road. "It's only dinner with your parents."

"Yes, please," I respond to the waiter when he asks if I'd like a third glass of white wine. Because, at this point, dinner is already a nightmare, and it appears that alcohol is the only way to soften the hardness in my father's eyes as his gaze once again flicks to the diamond ring on my finger.

"And when will the date be, Delia?"

Dane grabs my hand, his thumb circling the joint at the base of my thumb. My heart rate slows as I meet my father's eyes.

"We haven't discussed it, but I'd love a winter wedding," Dane interjects before I can answer.

Heat pulses in my core. Whether from the wine or the way his touch sends shivers up my forearm, I can't say. But as he glances at me and offers a slow smile, the image of snowflakes dancing around us as we stand before our meager guests flits through my mind.

My breath hitches.

"You'll have the ceremony at the church. In Lansing. I'll preside over the nuptials." It's not a question, and my shoulders sag as I deflate in my seat.

"Actually, there's a lovely park just around the corner from our building. It's where Kayce—"

"Took his first steps," I finish as the smile pulls at my cheeks.

"I always imagined that's where we'd get married..." Something flashes in Dane's eyes, and his jaw twitches as he turns back to his plate and releases my hand.

Either Dane is the best actor in the world or just perfectly prepared.

I face my father. "Thank you for the offer, but Dane and I will handle the arrangements." I set my elbows on the table and clasp my hands together, as though they can protect me.

"You *will* marry in a church, Delia. Else you'll not be wed in the eyes of the Lord. You know this. I raised you better!"

"You can have the reception outside in the... *park*," my mother adds, the word falling from curled lip. "In a tent."

I breathe deeply in order to relax my shoulders, which are nearly buried behind my ears. "*Where* we marry isn't important. What's important is the people who celebrate with us."

"Then you'll have no problem marrying in a church. Marigold Fraser was only yesterday telling us all about the lovely weddings she plans."

Dane's fork clatters to his plate and he sits back, arms crossing over his broad chest. "Delia has said—"

"It's fine," I interrupt, my hand finding his elbow and squeezing in warning. "It's fine," I repeat as I look across the table at my father. "We will *look* at the church."

"And the bridal suite is just here," Marigold Fraser says as she opens the door to the Sunday school room the next day.

My eyes scan the nursery, from the miniature chairs fit for someone of Kayce's size to the bins full of supplies. "No vanity?"

"There's a connecting restroom just through there." Mrs. Fraser points to the water closet, complete with a child-sized toilet and a basic sink-mirror combo.

"Hardly enough room for a makeup artist and hair stylist." I'm thinking of every possibility to postpone this wedding, and getting rid of a potential venue is priority one. As I take in the lack of counter space and tiny toilet, it's as though Dane has read my mind.

"Charm is deceitful, and beauty is vain, but a woman who fears the Lord is to be praised," my father recites from memory.

"I just love that Proverb," Marigold smiles winsomely at my father before turning to me. "It's a shame that you haven't sought us out on Sundays, dear."

"Yes, well, we all worship in our own ways." My gaze flicks to Dane, and I silently plead for him to intervene in some way. *Tell her we'll think about it, and get us out of here*!

"Marigold, is there any way we could utilize the Reverend's office for Delia's bridal suite?"

"Dane, that's not—"

I'm interrupted as my father exclaims, "That is ridiculous! A minister's office is sacred. It's not to be used for hairspray and beauty products."

"It would be highly irregular, Dane, for the Reverend to allow an *outsider* to utilize his private chambers, but I suppose..." she trails off just as a single eyebrow quirks up.

Dane crosses his arms over his chest. "I'm sure there are numerous odd jobs and repairs the Reverend needs done around here."

Embarrassment heats my cheeks, but I'm equally enthralled by Dane's persistence. Marigold's face cracks into a smile. "Now that you mention it, the toilets in the men's restroom need to be snaked, and the Sunday school teacher has been begging for a set of cabinets to house all of the arts and crafts supplies."

Dane sticks his hand out and Marigold Fraser meets it with a shake. "Deal," he says before turning to me and pulling me into his side. "Anything for my future wife."

Chapter Eleven

Dane

"My God, that was a long weekend," Delia muses as she takes a sip from the coffee. "I'm so glad it's over." The purple crescent moons under her eyes, along with her glasses and hollow cheeks, lead me to believe she didn't sleep well last night. "I think you bought me some time by mentioning a winter wedding. I mean, my parents can't expect it to happen in just a few weeks! So we've got at least a year to come up with *something* that caused us to break it off..."

"Hm," I mutter noncommittally as I roll the mug between my hands. The weather's turned, and the sun shines through the front windows, basking the diner in an eerie morning glow.

"Oh! I almost forgot!" Delia straightens up and pulls at her ring finger, sliding my mother's jewel off. "Thank you so much for all you did. If my parents ask, I can pretend we're in no hurry to get married." Her throat works as she places the gold band on the counter between us. "I think you'll want this back for when..."

I don't move. I simply eye the ring as my gut bubbles with anger. "Right," I murmur. "For when I find someone."

The truth is I've *already* found someone.

And she's sitting in front of me.

Delia takes one last swig from the mug and places it loudly next to the ring. "Oh, Kayce wanted me to remind you—"

A burst of air leaves my lips. "I know, I know. Practice at 5:15 at the park." I pick up the discarded ring and tuck it into my shirt pocket. I don't miss how Delia's eyes track my movements. How she swallows and her eyes shutter slightly.

"Thank you again, Dane," she responds as she grabs her bag and hoists it over her shoulder. "For everything."

"Dane!" Kayce runs at me full tilt, his baseball mitt bigger than his head.

I grab him and swing him around. "Hey, buddy!"

"I thought you weren't going to make it. Mom was pacing. She looked worried." He points his mitt in the direction of Delia. Her hands are on her hips, and her lips are thinned.

I stalk over, ready for a lecture on punctuality. But before either of us can say anything, Elijah Jorgenson's mother approaches.

"Dane! It's so nice of you to volunteer to help out the boys. I know my Elijah just adores you!" Her hand finds my bicep, and she squeezes slightly. "Now, if I recall, you played ball in high school, didn't you?"

"Yes, ma'am, I did." My gaze strays to Delia's. Her eyes are wide, and a smile is breaking out across her face as she watches the interaction with a mixture of glee and curiosity.

"I can tell you've been keeping up with your athletic regimen." She squeezes my arm again before stepping back and scanning me from head to toe. "My, my, my."

"Mrs. Jorgenson, would your husband be interested in assisting with practice today? It's always easier with additional adults helping out."

"Oh, no, dear. My husband is in Chicago on business. Besides, he wouldn't know a thing about baseball." She leans in. "He was in the *math club*," she whispers like it's a deep, dark secret.

"Right." I nod amicably. "Well, if you'll excuse me. I need to get practice started." I stalk over to the dugout and drop the large duffel on the bench.

But before I can unzip it and rifle through the contents, I catch Delia's legging-clad legs in my periphery.

"You're late." I turn to her just as she leans against the dugout post and crosses her arms over her chest. Her pale blue eyes, even lighter in the sunlight, burn a hole through me.

"Crystal didn't show, so I had to close the diner." I return my focus to the bag, unzipping it with more frustration than I mean to.

"Shit, Dane. Again?" She shakes her head and bites her lip as her gaze trails to the boys running around the bases. "I'll head over to the diner. Get everything going. I'd hate for you to lose out on business because of me."

"No." I pull my mitt from the duffel and jam it onto my hand before giving it a squeeze.

"What do you mean *no*? I won't have you missing out because of us."

I inch closer to her, my hand punching into the glove again and again as I warm up the leather. "I'm tired of you insinuating that I'm missing out, or losing out, or in any way inconvenienced because of you or Kayce. I *chose* to be here. I *want* to be here." I push forward as my body and brain sync up. I crowd against her as a flame sparks in my gut.

She nods slowly as her eyes scan from my broad shoulders to my face, the words sinking in. "All right." A slow smile stretches her cheeks. "Can I at least help with practice?"

I eye the way her black workout leggings hug each and every inch of her calves and thighs. "I thought you'd never ask."

Delia's athleticism is impressive. Not only can she lob the ball from home plate to the outfield, she can also tip the ball off the bat with perfect precision.

"This one's coming to you, Cooper!" she shouts as she tosses the ball in the air and sends it his way with the swing of the bat. Cooper cowers behind his outstretched mitt.

"Coop! Man, that was totally yours!" I say by way of encouragement. I jog over and gently take his arm, hoisting it into the air. "Send us another one, Del!"

She nods and obliges, hitting the ball directly our way with a *clink* of the metal bat. It soars through the air, and as Cooper turns into me, I keep his mitt aloft. "Watch, Cooper, we've got it!"

The ball lands softly in his glove. "I caught it! I caught it!" he squeals as he jumps up and down.

I can see Delia's grin from home plate as she sets the bat down and cheers for Cooper. "Great job, Coop!" His teammates rally around him, patting him on the back and ruffling his hair.

"All right, kiddos! Huddle up!" I head toward the dug out as the boys circle around me. Taking a knee, I give them all an encouraging smile. "That was a great first practice! Can anyone share something they learned about baseball?"

Several hands go up, but I call on Cooper first. "I learned not to be afraid of the ball!"

I chuckle. "Yes, great! And you caught a pop fly, too!" I turn to the others in the circle. "Jordan, what'd you learn today?"

"I learned that the Detroit Tigers are the best baseball team and the Cubs suck!"

My face reddens as several mothers on the periphery tsk over the word, but I nod nonetheless. "Yes, although let's say the Cubs stink instead, okay?"

Kayce's hand waves in the air. "Kayce, what'd you learn today, buddy?"

"I learned that Coach Dane is the best, and we're going to beat the other teams!" A resounding cheer goes up from the boys, accompanied by a few whoops and fist bumps. I love the energy and let myself get caught up in their fun.

"That's right! But most importantly we're going to have fun, yes?"

"Yeah! We're gonna have fun beating their butts!" The boys are clearly obsessed with the word and giggle over and over as they repeat it to one another.

I turn my attention to the parents. "Who can bring a snack this week?"

"My mom makes the best chocolate chip cookies! She can make some for the whole team!" Kayce yells.

That sets the boys off again.

"I want chocolate chip cookies!"

"Chocolate chip cookies are my *favorite*!"

"*Gimme all the cookies!*"

"All right, all right. Calm down everyone." I make eye contact with Delia. "Coach Del, can you make the team cookies for after the game?" I send her puppy dog eyes and encourage the kids to do the same. At once, all eyes turn to her, and they follow my lead.

"Please, Coach Del?"

"Will you make us the cookies, Kayce's mom?"

"*Gimme all the cookies, Coach!*"

She playfully narrows her eyes at me, but nods along with the fun. "Yes, I'll make all of you cookies. But only if Coach Dane agrees to help!"

The boys cheer as though they've won the World Series. My gaze catches on Delia's again, and she shrugs. The funny thing is, she didn't even have to ask. I was going to help either way, just to spend more time with her.

Chapter Twelve

Delia

"**M**a'am, you can't just go in there without—"

"She's expecting me."

Marigold Fraser stalks through my doorway and immediately closes the door behind herself as I stare from behind my computer, speechless. "Mrs. Fraser, what can I do for you today? Have you come to see about a loan? Have some interest in playing the stocks?" I can't say I enjoy the way her eyes pinch at me, but I don't *not* enjoy it either.

"Delia, you should know why I'm here, dear." She takes a seat without being offered and scoots the hefty office chair closer to my desk before digging into her bag and pulling out magazines, binders, and finally a pen with a giant cross on the top.

I gulp.

"I-I'm afraid I don't. But I do have an appointment in the next fifteen minutes, so if you'd like to set up a meeting with my secretary, he can tell you my availability." My gaze lands on the title of the binder. *Celebrating*

Matrimony. "What is *that*, Marigold?" All manners have gone out the window.

She tuts at me like I'm a crazy person. "There are only a few short weeks until your wedding. And you haven't stopped by the church, so Reverend Frank sent me to find you."

"Wait, what are you talking about? We never set a date."

She fingers a tab in the binder and flips open the hefty book. "Your father called me just this morning, didn't you know? Luckily the date he selected was available! December 10th."

My stomach bottoms out and I hold back a dry heave as I look at the date on my computer. November 18th.

"Now, let's discuss your answers to the matrimony match quiz, and then I'll compare with Dane. I'm certain he'll be easier to get ahold of than you, what with his long hours at the diner." She clicks her pen and pushes her glasses higher on her nose. "Number one. How often do you and your partner talk about the future?"

I glance at the clock over the door and realize my next appointment should be here any moment. I tidy up the area before us, stacking the wedding magazines and notepads and pushing them toward the well-meaning woman in front of me. "Whatever option is never. That's the one to circle."

A disgruntled noise escapes from the back of her throat, and she eyes me over the rim of her glasses. "Delia, this is no way to start a marriage!"

I stand and pace, wondering how I can usher her out without being rude.

"Number two. Do you both agree on the subject of kids?" She presses her lips together, thinning them until they're nearly invisible. "I mean, Dane certainly must enjoy children considering..."

My molars grind together as I take in the hypercritical woman in front of me. Except she meets me, glare-for-glare. The judgement seeps from her pores. "You know, how about I just take the quiz with Dane and then drop off the form to you in the morning?" I swipe the papers and move to the doorway, crossing my arms.

Even though she may be pushy, Marigold Fraser isn't stupid. She eyes me under furrowed brows and packs away her things. "It's highly irregular, but as long as you promise to bring the papers back tomorrow morning, I'll allow it." She adjusts the bag on her shoulder and heads out the door before turning back. "You know, I always thought you and Dane were perfect for each other. I'm glad I was right about that." My anger dissipates slightly, and my belly gurgles with guilt.

"Thanks, Mrs. Fraser." My head drops, and I feel like absolute shit. I almost think things can't get any worse until I turn and find Phil Patrick seated just outside my doorway.

Of course Phil would take it upon himself to show up early to our meeting. "I'm sorry to keep you waiting, Mr. Patrick." I hold out my hand for him to take a seat while I circle behind the desk and jiggle my mouse, pulling up the latest financials for Canada's culinary market.

"It's not a problem at all, Ms. Evans. And apparently congratulations are in order?" There's not a single shred of sarcasm or snark in his voice. His eyebrows lift, as does his smile. Gosh, the Canadians really are lovely people.

"Yes, well, it was certainly unexpected..." I settle down and turn to my computer, clicking away on the keys to log into the system. "So, about the budgetary constraints for the store—"

"So when is it? The big day, I mean." He pulls his phone from his suit jacket and swipes up before turning expectant eyes on me.

Heat sears from the top of my head down to my neck. I'm a horrible human being. First, I lied to my son. My sweet six year old who idolizes Dane. And now I'm lying to a client who entrusts me with his company's financial holdings.

"December 10th," I manage behind my clenched jaw.

He taps on the device. "Excellent. Your fiancé must be pretty amazing to sweep you off the market, eh?" There's that expectant look. The innocent look of a Canadian who has zero ulterior motives and is nothing short of a gentleman.

"Yeah." My gaze lands on my left hand. It feels suddenly empty without Dane's ring. Naked. "He's pretty amazing."

"Please, allow me to take the two of you out for dinner while I'm in town. It's the least I can do, seeing as I've been remiss in getting you an engagement gift."

"Oh, that's not necessary, Mr. Patrick."

"Well, at least tell me where you're registered, Ms. Evans." His earnest gaze has me smiling—even though I'm panicking inside. Like an out-of-body experience. What is it about our neighbors in the north that makes them so damned likable?

And will Dane feel the same way when he realizes that we have a stack of paperwork to complete as well as an entire bridal registry to fake?

"Where do you keep your vanilla extract?" Dane asks as I crack another egg into the mixing bowl.

"Top shelf of the far left cabinet. In the back."

Dane takes a single stride across the expanse of the apartment's kitchen and flicks open the cabinet door before reaching his arm overhead. My gaze instantly tracks the hem of his shirt. It rides up, exposing obliques and the sensual deep V that cuts down into his low-slung jeans.

"Delia?" I don't even notice when he hands me the brown liquid; my mind has short-circuited with arousal. "You good?" He waves a hand in front of my face.

"Oh, yeah. Yeah, sorry," I mumble. My hands hold either side of the broken egg shell, unsure of what to do.

"Let me get those from you." His touch sends an electrical shock of desire straight to my gut as he slides his hands along mine, and I relinquish the shell. "You're clearly exhausted, Del. Go sit down; I'll take care of the cookies."

I start to protest, but think better of it. Not because I'm actually tired. No, it's simply so I can sit at the table and look my fill at Dane. But as I settle into a chair around the small kitchen table, my gaze falls to my open bag and the stack of papers inside, including the compatibility quiz.

"Your parents make it home safely?" he asks as he adds a splash of vanilla to the cookie dough.

"Y-yeah. I think so," I murmur as my eyes track the way his palm wraps around the wooden spoon before he scrapes the side of the bowl. His pectorals flex under his shirt, and he deftly spins the container with his thumb and forefinger.

My mind flashes back to the last time we cooked together. In his restaurant. Our hands slick and soapy as the heat of the industrial kitchen wrapped around us. Was it only a week ago? Between my parents showing up and the fake engagement, it seems like so much longer.

"So what was the verdict?" Dane asks. He sets the spatula in the sink and grabs the spoon.

"Verdict?" I watch as, forearms flexing, he scoops out the dough and then drops it onto the baking sheet.

"Yeah. Their verdict about me. Did I pass the future husband test?"

I know he's joking, but there's no way I can regale him with the truth.

"What are you doing, Delia?" my father questioned. "Not only have you allowed your faith to lapse, but now you're marrying a non-believer?"

"We raised you better," my mother added from the couch as she worried her hands in her lap. "I knew we never should've allowed her to attend a public university, Tom."

"This has nothing to do with ECU! And Dane and I haven't exactly spoken about our particular religious affiliations."

"What?" My father's eyes nearly bulged out of his head as he digested the information. "You've accepted a marriage proposal from this man, and you haven't discussed this simple thing?"

As though religion, and all its many facets, were just a simple thing. That's what my father didn't understand. My belief system was hardly simple, especially given how I was raised.

"We cannot approve of this marriage." My mother frowned and squared her shoulders with a harumph.

"I don't need you to approve of this marriage," I responded with my hands on my hips. "I'm almost thirty years old and raising a child of my own! When will you two realize that this is my life?"

"If you won't consider yourself, at least consider Kayce. He should be raised the right way, Delia." Despite knowing he was fast asleep, my gaze still strayed to the hallway and Kayce's open door.

"And what is the right way, exactly? Being raised in a household of bigotry and unwavering adherence to a book that was written thousands of years ago?"

"That is enough! We will not stand here and tolerate your hatred of our Lord and savior." My parents had quickly fled, as though I was a madman—a devil. And maybe I was. Maybe I was purposefully fleeing from a religion and a set of rules that hung over me throughout my childhood and adolescence. But that didn't make what they did any better.

They scheduled my wedding day in a church—in a location they knew I didn't want.

I turn my attention back to the man scooping the last spoonful of dough onto the cookie tray. "They hardly like me, Dane. In case you didn't notice, they aren't the most welcoming people."

He drops the utensils into the empty mixing bowl before sliding the sheet into the preheated oven. "Eh, they weren't so bad," he says as he turns the dial on the timer. The contraption ticks loudly. "I've met worse."

A flare of jealousy boils up in my gut. How many parents has he met? I push the question down just as my phone rings. The name on the screen is one I've been avoiding answering for months. Nay, years.

Marshall Hampton.

I frown and click the side button, silencing the ring and sending it to voicemail.

"So the worst parents you met, they were—" My phone interrupts me. Again.

Marshall.

My eyebrows pinch together, and I repeat the same process as before as I send the call to voicemail. Then I turn my focus back to Dane. "They were your, um, girlfr—" The phone trills once more. "Shit, sorry," I say as I finally swipe and answer the call. "What, Marshall?" I try to keep the contempt and anger from my voice, but it leeches into my throat as I watch Dane turn away in order to give me privacy.

"You're getting *married*, Delia? Since *when*?" Apparently the contempt and anger goes both ways. I stand and move into the living room. Suddenly I'm twenty-three again and standing in front of the man who impregnated me. I vividly see the disgust curl his lip into a frown. The way his eyes turned lifeless and shuttered as he appraised my physique.

I swallow and push down memories of the past. "Marshall, seeing as you're not in my life, I'm certain you can understand why I wouldn't tell you that *private* information." Damn my parents. I should've known this would happen.

"This isn't just *your* life. It's Kayce's, too. *My* son. Has he even *met* the guy?"

I grind my molars to dust as the urge to throw the phone across the room surges through me. But I refrain, if only because I can't afford to replace the device. "Of course Kayce's *met* the guy. He's the guy who stepped up, Marshall. But you'd know that if you spent even one *ounce* of time with Kayce."

The line goes silent, and for a brief moment, I wonder if he's hung up on me. But then I hear him sigh. "You're right, Dee. I fucked up. Big time. But that was years ago. And it's time I made it right. For our son."

My heart pounds wildly in my chest. "What does that mean? And why should I give you a second—no, a *third*—chance?" Uncertainty bubbles in my gut.

"I've changed, Dee. You'll see. Can I come to Oselka Harbor for a visit? This weekend? To see Kayce."

My heart stops. How does he know where we live? And then it hits me—*my parents*. They've shared everything with the man who refused to be a father to his son.

I close my eyes and take a moment to process what's happening. It's been nearly six years since I've seen Marshall. He met Kayce once, in the hospital when he was born. Since then it's been birthday cards sent via my parents' address and the occasional phone call.

I take a deep breath and try to think logically. I know I can't deny him the right to see his son. And I certainly don't want to get the court system involved. Even if it's not my preference, I have to be the bigger person. For *my* son.

I eye Dane's back.

"All right. You can come visit him. But I swear to God, if I tell him and then you don't show up—"

"I'll be there, Dee. I promise. You'll see I'm a changed man."

I end the call on that promise and with very little reassurance. Because, not so many years ago, Marshall Hampton promised me a lot of things. He promised if I worked hard, I'd go far in the company. He promised if I went on a date with him, he'd keep me in mind for the next opening in the accounting department. And then, when he invited me back to his penthouse for a night cap, he promised he was a good guy and had "never done anything like this before." I was young and naive then, but I've learned that Marshall's promises mean absolutely nothing.

CHAPTER THIRTEEN

Delia

"Nana?" I swing the door to her suite open and toe off my boots. The kitchenette and sitting area are both dark. I glance at the clock on the microwave. 1:30. "Nana?" My voice rises an octave as the concern leeches into my pipes, but it's not like her to *not* be up and moving around.

I tiptoe through the home as the fear takes over. My breathing becomes labored and, as much as I knew this day may one day come, I'm still unprepared. Turning the corner, I find her bedroom door ajar.

She's lying on her bed in her nightgown. Hands overlapping on her sternum. I swallow over the stabbing pain in my throat as my eyes prickle. "N-nana?" She doesn't move.

I inch closer as my hand reaches out and covers her shoulder. I give her a decent shake. "Nana?"

My gran's eyes pop open, and she sits straight up like one of those Halloween decorations. I scream and stumble back, hitting the wall. A hanging photo crashes against my shoulder and falls to the carpeted floor.

"Jesus, Nana!" My heart pounds out of my chest, and I'm certain I've just taken years off my own life.

"Why didn't you knock?" Her brows crinkle, and she swings her feet to the floor. I crouch down and help her into her slippers. They're worn around the toes, and I make a mental note to pick her up a new pair on my next shopping trip.

"I did knock! I thought you were dead!" I stand and hold out my hand to help her from the bed. She's frail, and if I'm not careful, I'll yank too hard and hurt her.

"Psh," she says as she shuffles past me and into the bathroom across the hall. "That bitch Linda would love that. Then she'd never have to pay after I beat her at euchre last week."

I step toward the doorway. "D-do you need any help?"

"No, Delia. Pick up the mess you've made!" She gives me a stern look before slamming the door in my face.

I crouch to pick up the picture frame and frown at the giant crack across the glass. "It's broken," I holler.

"What?"

I raise my voice. "It's broken!"

The water runs as I hold the memento in my hands. It's a photograph of the two of us at a resort in the Upper Peninsula. The lake is behind us with the sun setting just over our shoulders.

Nana appears beside me. "Oh, I do love that picture." She reaches for the broken frame, and I pass it over. Her soft fingers trace my photographed face and a smile blooms across hers. "I loved our girls' trips."

Tears fill my eyes, and I try to blink them back before she notices. Nana was never one for tears. "What do you say we plan another one for the summer?"

"Oh, you don't want to take a trip with your old grandmother. You and Sav go. Have fun." She pats my arm and sets the frame back on the nail hooked into the wall. She shuffles from the room, and I allow myself one last glimpse of the photo before I follow. I wish I'd known how precious those trips were when I was that age.

Nana takes a seat in her favorite armchair while I perch on the couch. "So you don't bring Kayce to visit me anymore?"

"He stayed at his friend's last night, but he has a baseball game this evening. I'll text you pictures, and you can FaceTime this evening."

She narrows her eyes. "I don't want to see *pictures*. I want to see Kayce."

I know what she's hinting at. "Nana, it's simply too cold this time of year for you to be outside at a baseball game. I promise I'll bring him up next weekend, and you can have lunch and play Bingo together." I reach for her, but she harrumphs at me.

"I suppose you're right." She pulls a blanket from the back of the chair and covers her lower body. "How's that fiancé of yours doing? My, he's quite the looker, isn't he?"

My cheeks flame as I try to hold in the smile that blooms across my face. "Dane is fine. We're... fine, I suppose."

"You better not run him off, Delia. A man like that won't wait around forever."

"What do you mean?" I furrow my brow as my smile drops.

"It's clear that he's completely head over heels for you. I figured it out within just a few minutes of meeting him. The way he looks at you?" She pauses and stares at me. "Did you really not know?"

I chuckle and shake my head. "Dane's just a-a friend. He's doing me a *favor*." Nana's having a rough day.

She sits back and crosses her arms over her chest before raising a thin eyebrow at me. "Hm-mm... and I'm the queen of France."

I swallow the lump that suddenly flares in my throat and think back to my time with Dane. The years he's been by my side. Helping me with Kayce, the apartment, and everything in between. But there's never been anything like that between us. I mean, lately I've been noticing him differently and feeling... things... about him, but he surely doesn't feel the same. "No, Nana," I finally decide, "you're mistaken. Dane's just a friend." I repeat myself once again, if only to be certain.

But what if she's right?

"Goddamnit," I curse as I break a nail pulling the cooler of drinks from the back of the car. I assess the damage and shake it off. I've got bigger things on my mind this morning—mainly telling Kayce that his father will be in town in a mere two days.

"Need some help?" I turn to find Dane watching me from his truck's bumper. The way he leans against the shiny fender with his hat turned backward and his long-sleeved tee stretched across his chest has me nearly salivating.

"Oh, sure. Thanks," I mutter as he comes closer and easily hoists the cooler bag over his shoulder. I lean back into the trunk and pull out a second bag. This one has tiny cellophane-wrapped cookies tied with baseball-printed ribbons and adorned with a matching baseball keychain.

"Wow," Dane mutters as he eyes the bag. "You went all out." We saunter toward the ball field together.

"You're not the only one who can jazz up a meal, Chef."

He chuckles, but I don't miss the way his cheeks redden slightly at the nickname. Does he like it? "Chocolate chip cookies constitutes a meal?"

"Paired with a box of Blue Berry Blast fruit drinks, yes." I shoot him a smile as we near the dugout. "Listen, about the other night. That call was unexpected. *Unwanted*," I add.

"Delia, you don't owe me any explanation."

I stop and turn to him, my eyes searching for any chance that he actually cares. The way that I do. "I know I don't owe you one, but—"

"Mommy!" Kayce's weight hits me from behind like a ton of bricks as he barrels into my legs. I fly forward and nearly sprawl headfirst into the infield dirt when Dane's arms wrap me up and pull me against his chest.

"Kayce!" I proclaim from my position nuzzled against Dane's neck. But I can't be too mad as I inhale the fresh scent of his soap and wonder what he'd do if I simply pressed my lips—

"I had so much fun at Hunter's house! He has an Xbox!" Kayce throws his overnight bag at me before he's off again, this time headed for the dugout and his friends.

"Hunter has an Xbox," Dane jokes as I right myself and slowly pull away. Regrettably.

I roll my eyes. "Well I've got cookies." I adjust the bag over my shoulder.

"I'd choose your cookies any day."

I can't believe I ran all the way to second base!" Kayce yanks open the door to the car and tumbles onto the sidewalk. "I'm fine!" He reaches back into the vehicle and pulls out his mitt, the game ball tucked reverently between the worn leather. "I did good today, right Mom?"

"You did great, buddy!" I unload the trunk as Kayce races up the stairwell. "Be careful with your cleats!" I admonish, turning my attention back to the vehicle. The cookies and juice had been a hit with the team, and as I pull the empty cooler out, something warm glides along my lower back. Dane's palm.

"We should've driven together," he says, his hot breath tickling against my exposed nape. Before I can protest, he reaches beyond me and pulls everything from the trunk. My gaze follows his muscles rippling under the tight baseball tee with Coach emblazoned across the chest. "I'll dump the ice out and then be right up." His timbre sends shivers along my spine.

My nipples tighten, and I swallow. All this cat and mouse between the two of us... it's starting to get to me. My body hums with desire, and even the chill of the cool November day can't tamp down the heat warming my core. I think back to what Savannah had said when I'd told her about the whole fake engagement.

"Is it really fake if you actually want the guy?"

I'd snorted into the phone and blown off the question.

Now, my breath stuttering as I watch Dane walk away, I clench my fists and decide that enough is enough. It's time for me to be open with him about how I feel. It's time for me to tell him that, for as long as I can remember, I've wanted more...

The man who's been by my side through thick and thin over the last six years? Yeah, I want him. I want to spend the rest of my life knowing that he'll continue to be my rock. My safety net. He'll be there for both Kayce and me. And I want to be all that and more for Dane, too. I want to be the person he comes home to. The person sharing his bed. The person who trims his hair when it gets slightly long and the person who grocery shops for him when he's busy at the diner.

I want it all.

"Mom!"

"I'm coming!" I traipse up the stairs, my thighs burning as I hit the last landing.

"Mom!" I meet my son's eyes and then quickly register the stranger next to him. Leaning against our door.

No, not a stranger.

Marshall. Kayce's biological father.

"What are you—?"

"Delia, who's this?" Dane's gruff voice echoes behind me.

I take the final step up to the landing and— eye to eye with my son's father— watch as he reaches his hand out to introduce himself.

"Hi, you must be Dee's fiancé. I'm Marshall. Kayce's father."

"Can I get you anything to drink?" I ask from the corner of the kitchen where I've retreated to collect my thoughts. I don't know what I thought would happen when I agreed to letting Marshall visit for the weekend, but it certainly wasn't an unannounced arrival on our doorstep a day early. Kayce tumbles from his room, his baseball gear discarded in exchange for a pair of off-brand sweats and an Oselka Elementary sweatshirt.

"Come see my room!" Kayce's tiny hands yank Marshall to standing. I should be proud that my son never met a stranger, but at the same time, something about his comfortability with his father doesn't sit well with me.

"Just a water, if you have it," Marshall responds as he traipses after our son. *My* son.

I open the fridge and retrieve the pitcher from the shelf. The filter's never been replaced, but it's either this or tap water. I pull a glass from the cabinet and scrunch my nose at the water spots leftover from the ancient dishwasher. Using the sweatshirt tied around my waist, I polish the glass clean and then pour.

I mentally prepare myself for what I'll see when I take the drink to Kayce's room. A father and son affectionately embraced? Kayce's face alight with joy as he shares his treasures with the man he doesn't know?

"Everything okay?" From the entryway, Dane's question pulls me back to the kitchen. I'm holding the glass aloft with feet planted firmly in the same spot. I haven't moved.

"Oh," I clear my throat, "of course." I turn my attention back to Kayce's doorway. And yet I don't move a muscle.

"Allow me." Dane reaches for the glass, but I snatch it back, sloshing liquid all over myself.

"Shit," I mutter, setting the glass on the counter and searching for a dish towel. But Dane is already there, dabbing the wet spot on my shoulder with the cotton cloth. His gaze lowers, following the trail of water down the front of my chest to where the thin white baseball shirt has turned see-through. He presses the towel lower, to the crease between my arm and my chest. My tailbone finds the countertop as my hands grip the rounded edge tightly.

The cloth pats its way lower. Lower. Until he's pressing it against my—

"Ahhh!" Kayce's high-pitched squeal has both of us jumping apart and then racing toward his bedroom.

"What's going on in—?" My eyes track Marshall as he swings Kayce around the room, a giant smile plastered to my son's face as he giggles.

Oh.

Seeing Marshall wrapped around my son—*our* son—unfurls something in my gut. Something I didn't know was there twisted into a million knots. Their smiles are infectious. Their laughter fills the apartment.

Marshall's eyes find mine, and his face falls. "Sorry about that. I suppose we got a little rowdy, didn't we, big guy?" He gently places Kayce onto the bed and ruffles his hair. Seeing them next to one another... they share so many features.

Same hair color.

Same lip shape.

Same eyebrows.

I swallow and nod curtly. "Well, I'm glad everyone is getting along." As I turn back toward the hallway, I catch Dane's eyes as he lurks behind me. Those knots in my belly tighten once again. "We should talk."

CHAPTER FOURTEEN

Dane

Delia pulls me into her bedroom and quietly closes the door behind us. I can't remember the last time I was in here, but as I glance around at the essence of her, I never want to leave.

My gaze lands on the comforter. The same one that used to adorn my guest bedroom. Upon closer inspection, the edges have frayed slightly through the multiple washings and years of wear and tear.

Delia's never been one to spend money on herself, but the urge to spoil her— to buy her every single thing she desires courses through my veins. I want her wrapped in a thousand thread count Egyptian cotton sheets.

Wearing absolutely nothing, my brain adds as an afterthought.

"Dane, I don't think I can keep up this charade." Her soft voice pulls me back to the here and now. The two of us standing mere feet apart while she worries her bottom lip between her teeth.

"What are you talking about?" I press forward, closing the space between us to inches. Centimeters. A breath.

"I just—" She plays with her ring finger. Her *naked* ring finger.

Ah, it suddenly dawns on me. She's regretting giving back the ring so quickly. And now that Marshall's here, she's worried that he'll notice the lack of an engagement diamond. "Here." I reach into my pocket and withdraw the jewel. "You don't even have to ask, Del." I hold it out to her.

She releases an audible intake of breath. Her eyes dip to the ring. "Y-you still...? Why do you just have that on you?" Her hand floats toward the diamond like Sleeping Beauty reaching for the spindle or Snow White the apple.

I reach out and grab her extended hand, my large digits finding her ring finger. Her eyes snap up to mine, and I pull her into me.

Kiss her, my brain implores as my cock presses painfully against the zipper of my jeans.

But I can't. Not yet. Not with her ex in the other room. Not with her son on the other side of the wall, his squeals of laughter echoing beyond the closed door.

Soon.

I look into those pale blue eyes, wide and waiting. "I, uh, I need a favor from you."

She blinks once. Twice. Stands up slightly straighter and pulls away from me just so. "Sure, whatever you need. You know I'd do anything..." she trails off and leaves the rest unsaid.

For you. My throat narrows, and I force an inhale. *I'd do anything for you, too*, I want to say.

"I've got a boat. A small fishing boat." She nods knowingly. "And I need help cleaning it up. Winterizing it."

Her brow crinkles and a slow smile breaks across her cheeks. "You want me to help you do manual labor?" She cocks her hip.

"Well, it's kind of a two-person job. And I thought if you weren't doing anything, you wouldn't mind offering me a hand."

She tucks her bottom lip under her teeth and nods. "Just tell me when."

"Tomorrow" tumbles from my lips before I can stop myself. The truth is that I just want to spend as much time as possible with her. "If you're free," I add.

"Let me text Maria and see if she can come by for a few hours." She looks at me awkwardly because I'm still holding her finger.

We both look down as I slide the ring over her knuckle. It fits like a glove. She knows I'm not asking permission this time. Not that she'd have the power to deny me.

I've wanted Delia Evans for a long time. And it's high time I got what I wanted.

"I thought you said we need to winterize your boat?" Delia glances at the small fishing vessel bobbing against the dock. There's a cooler and fishing gear nestled between the seats.

"We do. But first I thought we'd take her out for one last spin before I put her away." I step gingerly into the boat and hold out my hand for Delia to follow.

Our palms connect, and I try to ignore the electricity that thrums through my veins. "Her? Your boat has pronouns?" She steps around me and settles into the passenger seat.

I work my way around the boat, untying knots and pushing away from the dock. "Of course my boat has pronouns. *She* was my first big purchase after I finally paid off the business loan for the restaurant."

Delia watches quietly as I finally sit down in the captain's chair and crank the engine. "Does *she* have an official name?" I slowly pull away from the dock.

"It's nothing official, but I like to think of her as The Cora Lynn, after my mother."

Delia's quiet as we sail away from the marina and toward a secluded inlet. There aren't many others out today, even with the sun and more temperate weather. Most have already pulled their vessels out of the water. The trees dip yellow-and-orange leafed branches into the chilly water, and with the sun hitting them just right, they appear to be on fire. "How often do you come out?" Delia rolls up the sleeves of her flannel and then leans back, allowing the sunshine to paint her face.

"Not as often as I'd like." I motor toward the shore of a secluded beach and cut the engine. "I'm thinking of selling her." I pat the steering wheel. "You hungry?"

She nods as her eyes track my movements to the front of the boat. I toss the anchor onto the sandy shore and then return to her side to grab the cooler.

"You want to eat on the boat or the beach?" Delia looks around at the cramped quarters and motions toward the shore.

In just a few moments, our feet are back on land and I'm spreading out a blanket as Delia digs out the fare. I'd carefully packed cold fried chicken, homemade potato chips, hummus, and carrot sticks—and of course a few beers. She lays everything out before taking a bite of a carrot. "Why are you thinking of selling her?"

I take a swig of the beer and lean back on my forearms. While it's not quite warm enough to discard my shoes and socks in favor of the sand between my toes, I hike up the sleeves of my hoodie and turn my baseball cap forward to shield the sun from my eyes. "Lots of reasons. But mostly because I don't have anyone to share this with." I nod to the sunlight dancing on the water. The lazy lap of the waves as they kiss the shore.

Delia curls her legs up to her chest and rests her arms on her knees. "You have me. And Kayce. We would love to come out here with you. And you could teach us to fish, too." She smiles as she bumps my shoulder with hers.

"You don't know how to fish?"

"Nu-uh."

"Well then, I think it's about time you learned." I push up to my feet and return to the boat, grabbing a single pole. It's already set up with a hook and bait— some sparkly worm I'd picked up at the sporting goods store on my last trip.

"C'mere." I hold my hand out, and she takes it. Again, that electric shock shoots straight to my veins. I fight the urge to run my palm over her ass and down the length of her jeans and instead focus my attention on unfurling the fishing line.

"All right," I instruct as I hold the pole toward the water. I maneuver behind her and then inch in closer so our bodies are flush. "Hold here..." I guide her hand to the rod and wrap my own over hers. "Now you'll want to fling the hook into the water, but make sure you release the line without letting go of the pole entirely." I mime the movement, our hips sliding together as my chest presses to her back. "Got it?"

She turns her head back and I catch a glimpse of her profile, the sunlight behind it giving her an angelic aura. "Y-yeah. I think so..." I step back to give her some space and watch as she mimics my movement, releasing the line farther than I'd expected.

"That was great!"

"So now I just wait for a fish to bite?" She glances out at the water, her bottom lip trapped under her top teeth.

"Yup. But you can reel it in slowly if you want. We can try to bait the hook with a piece of chicken."

She slowly turns the crank until the sparkly fake worm jumps from the water. Then she watches me wordlessly as I slide a piece of chicken onto the hook. I step back and watch as she effortlessly flings it into the water beyond the boat.

"You're a natural, Del." I settle down into the sand at her feet. It's an odd position, but still comes natural to me. Worshipping this woman for six long years has always felt a bit like this.

She joins me, the fishing rod situated between her knees. "Don't sell the boat, Dane." Her eyes track the way the vessel bobs over the shallow waves.

My brow furrows. "Why not?"

"Because..." She glances down at the fishing rod, passes it from one hand to the other.

"I told you... I don't have anyone to share this with." I lean in closer, my eyes tracking the way the skin under her jaw pulses in time with her heartbeat.

She swallows and turns to me. Those clear blue eyes catching mine. "And I told you"—she meets my lean with her own—"you have me."

Demolishing those last centimeters, I dip my head and find her mouth.

I expect Delia's lips to be lush. Pillowy, even. But the reality is even better. Her mouth is satiny-soft, and as those lips part, warm and willing, I press my tongue into the depths. Slowly. Expertly.

It's been a while since I kissed anyone. But the wait, the dry spell, it was all worth it for this moment in time.

The velvet warmth of her tongue collides with mine as we explore each other. I'm consumed by her. By the fact that *her tongue is in my mouth.* It takes everything within me, all my self-control and restraint, not to hoist her onto my lap and have my way with her right here on this beach. To give in after *so long*. Instead, my hand finds the side of her jaw. I glide my fingers slowly over her skin as I attempt to pace myself.

Until she releases a soft moan.

My dick stiffens, and I surge onward. The beast within me that's been caged for *six long years* yearning to be released. I devour her, my tongue sweeping behind her teeth and around the tender interior of her mouth as my hand falls down her back to a rounded ass cheek lifted away from the sand.

We both come up for air at the same time. Chests heaving. Her freshly-suckled lips glisten wetly in the sunlight as rosy circles dot her cheeks.

And then the fishing rod flies into the lake.

Monday morning dawns dark and gloomy, an anomaly compared to my mood. For the last day I've thought of nothing but Delia. Her succulent lips. The taste of her mouth. Her tight ass in my palm.

I'd decided to give her and Kayce space on Sunday evening and waited impatiently for a text or a knock on my apartment door. But when neither arrived, I wrote it off as the dilemma she was facing with her ex.

So, I go about my duties. I prep the restaurant for the inevitable lunch rush, and when Delia still hasn't appeared by her usual time, I organize the walk-in freezer. Anything to get me away from watching the door like a hawk.

I'm still digging through the frozen food when I hear the telltale *ding* of the bell over the door. My heart nearly leaps out of my chest, but as I inhale the chilly air, I realize being nearly frozen may have its benefits.

At least on my cock.

I step around the wall separating the kitchen from the dining area and feel as though I've been nuked in a microwave. My body heats at light speed, going from frost-bitten to molten in a matter of seconds.

Our eyes meet, and I offer her a small smile just as she hitches herself up onto the stool at the counter. I clock the diamond ring still on her ring finger and simmer down—slightly. Because then I'm met with an eyeful of her cleavage nearly popping out of an unbuttoned white blouse.

"Kayce have a dentist appointment or something?" I casually ask as I fill a mug with coffee that's no longer fresh. All that time in the freezer and I never thought to refresh the pot.

"No." She watches me as I slide the mug across the gleaming counter. "Marshall dropped him off this morning on his way back to Chicago."

Nodding slightly, I drop my elbows to the counter and come eye-to-eye with the woman I haven't stopped thinking about for the last twenty-four hours. I don't want to scare her away, and I know she's got a lot going on in her life right now, but there's no time like the present. Or so they say.

"Del, I want to talk about—"

She sets her cup down as her eyelids flutter. "I know. I do, too. But this weekend... everything that's happened... I just can't get my mind wrapped around anything but Kayce's father coming back into our lives right now. Can you understand that?"

I straighten. Step back from the counter. From this angle I'm really able to see all of her. The wrinkled shirt. The missed button. The circles under her bloodshot eyes.

Delia's not okay.

And how selfish and stupid am I to make this about me—about my needs—right now?

I mentally berate myself for being so blind to her plight.

"Of course I understand." I retake my place at the counter and pull her hand into mine. It's ice cold. "I'm here for you. You and Kayce. Whatever you need, Del. I'm not going anywhere."

"I was hoping you'd say that," she adds as she pushes away the mug. "Because Marshall wants to come back next weekend."

CHAPTER FIFTEEN

Delia

"Five more minutes, buddy, and then you're getting out!" I holler at Kayce in the tub just as a knock rattles the door. I traipse to the small entry, grabbing toys and discarded socks in my path before glancing through the peephole.

Dane.

I unlock the deadbolt and swing the door open. "H-hi," my voice catches as my gaze travels over him. His hair is still slightly damp, likely from a post-work shower, and the scent of his cologne drifts into the apartment.

"The diner was slow tonight, so I had extra cannolis." He holds out the box and I take it gently. "There's chocolate chip and pistachio, too. I thought you could use a pick-me-up."

Despite what I said earlier this morning, I can't stop the way my body responds to Dane. I can literally feel my nipples tightening. Pressing against the fabric of my bra so uncomfortably that I just want to rip it off right here in the foyer. But I gulp down that base urge and instead stand aside, inviting the kryptonite into the apartment.

"Kayce's just finishing up a bath, and he's already had dessert for the evening." I look around for a place to hide the telltale pink box.

"Wait, don't you want one?" Dane slowly advances and takes the box from my hand, setting it on the counter and flipping the lid open. His heady scent wraps around me while the powdered sugar-dusted pastries taunt me from their nest. My mouth waters.

"I shouldn't..." Usually I'm not one to deny a dessert, but I've also been feeling a bit more comfortable in my own skin and have noticed my dress pants fitting slightly tighter. "I already had dessert," I lie.

"C'mon," Dane practically whispers. Our faces are so close I can nearly taste the toothpaste he uses.

"Mom, I'm done!" Kayce's holler echoes off the bathroom tile, and I snap out of my cock—I mean cannoli-induced thirst.

"Be right back." I hurry to help Kayce from the tub and get him dried. Wrapped up like a burrito, we scurry across the hall. "Say goodnight to Dane!"

"Goodnight, Dane!" He gives a flapping wave and shakes his wet hair like a dog.

I quietly close the door to his room behind us as I wiggle him into his Spiderman pajamas. I run my fingers through his curls, which have always reminded me of Marshall.

Although Marshall's since buzzed his curls, a change I hadn't been expecting. I hadn't been expecting any of this. Marshall. A son at twenty-four. A life outside of the big city.

Dane.

"Mom, is Dane going to spend the night?" I blink at my son, and his innocent expression from under the covers.

"W-why would Dane spend the night, sweetie?" I keep my hands busy as I tuck the blankets and stuffed animals around him.

"Hunter's mommy and daddy spend the night together." He toys with a stuffed bear.

My throat tightens as my brain works to come up with a seemingly appropriate response. How can I explain this mess to a six year old? *Mommy wasn't good enough for your daddy, and grandma and grandpa are religious zealots who believe she's a whore, so now Dane is helping protect Mommy from everything so she doesn't have to face it all alone.*

Yeah.

"Listen, Dane brought cannolis, so if you're good and go right to sleep, I'll pack one in your lunchbox tomorrow, okay?"

Way to dodge the bullet. *Mother of the Year, ladies and gentlemen.*

"Really? Okay, love you. 'Night 'night!" Kayce immediately rolls away from me and snuggles farther into the covers, burying his face into the stuffed bear. I pat him gently on the back and turn the light off on my way out before cracking the door ever so slightly.

The exhale of relief I release is audible. But as I approach the main living space of the apartment, I find Dane sitting on the couch. The box of cannolis is open on the coffee table, and a glass of wine beckons for me to relax.

"I can go, Del. Give you some time to yourself." But his eyes beg to stay.

"No, it's fine." I curl my legs under me as I settle on the two-person couch next to him. The apartment isn't big enough for anything more. Not with Kayce's toy race track in the corner or the dining table that we rarely use. The small couch has always been enough for us...

Until it wasn't.

The marriage compatibility papers taunt me from my work bag by the door. I'd completely forgotten to return them, let alone complete them, in the time Marigold Fraser allotted. "Dane—"

"Try a cannoli," he interrupts as he lifts one of the delicious fried pastries from the box. It's covered in crushed pistachios. My favorite. The anticipated mixture of salty and sweet has my mouth watering, and I hold out my hand. But Dane bypasses my waiting palm and raises the delicacy into the empty space between us.

His eyes darken, and my mouth salivates even more at the implication. *Come and get it.*

Forgetting the matrimony discussion I'd planned on having, I zero in on the cannoli, its shape so suggestive, and lean into the moment. After all, I want this—both Dane and the dessert. So why bother denying myself?

My lips wrap around the flaky confection, and I bite down, savoring the creamy ricotta that fills my mouth. I pull away, but Dane has other plans. He carelessly deposits the cannoli into the box and then presses himself against me. His body covers mine. Large hands wrap around the back of my head and tip my chin upward before he's claiming my mouth with his.

I swallow the bite just as his tongue breaches the barrier. In the next moment, we're all lips and teeth. Tongue and heat. Somehow, my body slides farther down, and my back is pressed against the couch cushions with Dane hovering over me.

I'm needy with desire. One bite of cannoli—one kiss thirty-six hours ago— wasn't enough. I wrap my legs around his hips and allow my hands to explore. Under his shirt. Up and across his chest. Down his back. But it's still not enough.

"You want more?" Dane murmurs against my mouth as though he can hear my innermost thoughts. I nod like I'm starved.

Because I am.

It's been years since I've been held, touched, kissed.

Fucked.

And I want it all.

I reach for the button of his pants just as he thrusts against my core. I feel *all of it.* Every inch of him. I release a moan and grind back as my hands find his hips and pull him against me.

More.

"Del."

I thrash under him. My body needing friction as the heat creeps up my spine.

More.

"Del."

I don't actually hear him until he pulls away. His navy eyes flick between mine as he holds himself aloft.

"Why'd you stop?" Did I do something wrong? Is it something I said?

"Del, let's go to your bedroom. So Kayce—"

Shit. My mind instantly flashes to my son. My sweet innocent six year old asleep in his room. What if he'd come looking for me and found…?

I sit up and push away from Dane. My back finds the armrest of the couch as my eyes see nothing except the image of Kayce. His sleep-tousled hair and wide eyes not comprehending…

"Come on," Dane urges as he stands and reaches for me. But I cringe. Shrink against the couch, away from his touch.

I don't even want to look up into his eyes. Those eyes that are surely full of disappointment. Disappointment in me. What I've done. I've seen a man look at me like that before, and I don't want to ever again.

So instead, I shut everything down. "No. You should go." The person speaking is far away. In a tunnel. It's not me, even as I hear myself say the words.

Dane doesn't immediately respond, but his hand drops, and he sighs. I can practically *feel* his body deflate. It sucks all the energy out of the room, his disappointment in me. "Is…is that what you want, Delia?"

I swallow the shards of glass in my throat and nod as my eyes tingle. Blinking back the sting, I turn away from him.

From *Dane.*

And rather than watch him leave me, I close my eyes and shut out the world.

CHAPTER SIXTEEN

Delia

I've been avoiding Dane all week, but when Marshall calls my phone while I'm at work and reminds me that he's coming to Oselka for the weekend, I know that I've got to swallow my pride and approach the man whose ring I still wear. So at noon sharp, I saunter across the town square to the diner.

Usually on my lunch break I'd be working on Savannah's monthly metrics. I'd research grants and other financial pathways she could utilize as a non-profit. Losing myself in the numbers and finding ways to work the system for the good of my best friend's dream gives me a high unlike any other.

Except sex, of course. Which I haven't had since... well, since Marshall. Six years is a long time to go without, and I can't even recall if the dick was even *good*. It obviously wasn't memorable.

Dane, on the other hand... I hadn't even truly experienced it, and I knew it would likely destroy me.

So why'd you stop? the horny voice inside me rages.

I pull open the door to the restaurant and find Dane with his back turned, giving me the perfect view of his ass in a pair of low-slung khakis. An apron is tied tightly around his waist, accentuating the thickness of his glutes and thighs.

What I wouldn't give for a second chance to wrap my legs around that. I saunter over to the counter and grab a stool. "Hey." My voice comes out no louder than a whisper, and I'm almost certain he hasn't heard me. But then he turns, a plate of chicken parm in his hands. "H-how'd you know I was coming for lunch?"

He looks at the plate. "I didn't. This is for table seven, Delia." I turn and notice an elderly couple in a booth. Their hands joined across the table.

As Dane delivers the food, my eyes catch on the glint of the diamond ring. It twinkles in the bright overhead lights of the diner. And suddenly, the glass shards are back, coating my throat as I try to swallow down the embarrassment. I've made all of this—everything—about me. I've just assumed that Dane would always be there for me. Always save me. How selfish and reckless I've been, taking advantage of this man and his generosity.

"So what can I get you, Del?" There's not an ounce of resentment or coldness in his voice. Has he so easily forgotten the other night? Or is he just putting on a brave face and allowing me to exist without embarrassment?

Probably the latter.

I know I've got thirty-seven dollars in my account until payday, and Kayce has a field trip coming up that costs twenty-two. "I'm not hungry. Just a coffee, please."

He narrows his eyes at me before turning. Like he knows I'm lying. Despite how delicious that chicken parm looked, the cold ham and cheese sandwich in my lunch bag will still be on my desk when I return.

He slides the mug my way. "Anything else you need?" His Adam's apple bobs like he wants to say more. Ask for more.

"About the other night—"

"You told me you weren't ready. And I didn't respect you, Delia." His arms hang at his sides. "I'm—"

"Dane, no." I hold up my palm before he can continue. This man certainly does not need to apologize to me for anything, let alone giving me exactly what I've been wanting for as long as I can remember. "I wanted you. I *want* you," I clarify as my cheeks warm. I glance down at the cup of coffee wrapped in my hands and the diamond ring that scratches against the ceramic mug. "I want you," I repeat.

The tip of his finger finds my chin and tips it up so my eyes meet his. There's understanding and validation in those gray-blue irises. "You've got me, Delia. You always have."

I reach into my bag and pull out the stack of papers that I've been ignoring. But when Marigold Fraser's text came in early this morning, demanding that I drop off the papers or lose the date, I knew it was time to face the music. Despite being surprised that she knew how to text—and had my number—I knew I'd been nothing short of a coward. I slide a blank copy of the quiz across the counter to Dane.

"What's this?" He flips it around and frowns as he inspects it.

"Marigold Fraser dropped it off the other day. I... well, my father set the date for us, Dane. He booked the church. And this is part of the whole..." I wave my hand in the air. This is part of the whole charade? Game? Con?

He flips through the stapled packet and nods, not saying a word about having a date set for our fake marriage. Is he really okay with this happening? "All right. So I fill out my part and then we compare answers?"

"Yes, but if it makes things easier, I can fill out yours to match my answers and then just turn it in to Marigold. I don't want to put you out or add to your plate." I reach for the papers but Dane is faster and pulls them closer to him and out of my reach.

"No, I'll do it, Del. I told you; I'd do anything you need me to do."

My eyes go misty, and I struggle to swallow. I've never been someone's first priority, and while it feels amazing, I still can't get used to it. Not when I know the pain on the other side.

He takes my hand, just like the older couple behind us in the booth. "So, when exactly is the date?"

"Just under a month. On December 10th."

The moon is bright overhead when Kayce flings open the passenger side door and tumbles out of Marshall's BMW X5. "Hi, Mom!"

"Hey budd—" My boot hits the last step, which happens to be covered in a patch of slick frost, and I lose my footing. My feet fly over my head, and I'm certain I'm going to need an entire new spine when Marshall's arms wrap around me.

"Your boyfriend doesn't salt the steps or sidewalk?" His lip curls as he sets me down on the equally-icy pavement.

"He's not my boyfriend." Once the words are out, my scalp prickles. *Oh shit...*

"Boyfriend. Fiancé. *Whatever.* As the landlord, he needs to do his job, Dee." I swallow at the nickname. Nobody had ever called me that until I met him.

Del sounds like a dude's name, he said when I told him how Savannah and my roommates addressed me. *Besides, calling you Dee reminds me that you've got these.* And then he'd buried his face in my chest.

I cringe at the memories. The fact that I was so easily swayed by an overgrown frat bro who kept me on a rotation and needed a nickname to remember I was the girl with big tits.

"Dane's been busy coaching Kayce's baseball team and running his own business. I'm sure he'll get around to it. If not, Kayce and I can help out. After all, we live here." I ruffle my son's hair as he races past me up the steps without a single slip or stumble. "I'm sure Kayce had fun at the arcade. I hope he thanked you for taking him."

Marshall's eyes track Kayce. "He did. You've done a great job raising him, Dee. But I'd like to take a more prominent role in his upbringing."

I narrow my eyes at the man who, up until a few weeks ago, wanted nothing to do with *my* son. "Kayce isn't a company you're trying to manage, Marshall."

The man in front of me has the audacity to roll his eyes. "I know that. And I know you're probably concerned about my motives here. But I promise you, I just want to get to know our son."

The fall chill seeps beneath my sweater, at least that's what I tell myself as I shiver on the sidewalk. It has *nothing* to do with the fact that I still don't trust Marshall. "I'm not so sure..." I manage to get out before I wrap my arms around myself.

"Listen, you have a right to be worried. But I can assure you, I only want to do this on your terms. No courts. No lawyers. I want to take this slowly and make sure it's what's best for Kayce." He blinks at me. "I-I think I'm already starting to love that little guy."

My brow furrows as I appraise the man in front of me. From his bespoke loafers to his expensive haircut, I have a hard time finding the genuine man beneath the facade. And yet, a part of me always wanted this. Maybe I've become jaded and should give my son's father a second chance. "All right," I concede. "What do you have in mind? Another trip to visit next weekend?"

"Actually, I'd like to have Kayce come to Chicago. Stay with me for a weekend."

"Ha!" The exclamation is out before I can stop myself. He cannot be serious. "You've visited *twice*. I hardly think allowing *my* son on an overnight trip out of state with a man he hardly knows is realistic."

"*Our* son, Dee. *Our* son. Kayce is mine, too. And I'm trying here."

I bite back the retort that's begging to be spewed from my mouth and, instead, grind my molars.

"There's no way that's happening." Whether it's the cold seeping through my thin sweatshirt or the anxiety of the situation, my shivers turn into all-out body shakes.

"I knew you'd—" he starts and then suddenly stops. He exhales and places his hands on his hips. "What if... what if you came along with him? There's enough room in my penthouse for both of you."

My shivers dissipate, and suddenly I'm itchy all over. "Are you serious, Marshall? I really don't think that's the best idea."

He nods and bites the inside of his cheek. "I know it's not ideal, but I'd like Kayce to be able to see the room I've made for him. See my home and the place he could have as a part of my life."

I suddenly feel like I need to move, so I push off the brick wall and copy Marshall's stance. Hand on my hips as I rock side to side, my chest feels like it's caving in.

"I'm really trying, Dee," he repeats. "Can't you see that?"

I'm not sure if visiting twice in nearly six years can be construed as really trying, but I want to be the bigger person. I want to prove to Marshall that *he's* the one who should be ashamed of his past—a father who left his child—*not* me. I clear my throat, the tension in my jaw still there. "Fine. But not next weekend. That's Kayce's baseball championship game."

"The weekend after, then. Got it." He pulls out his phone and types something in. "Thank so much, Dee."

The luxury of scheduling in time with a child. I wouldn't know anything about that.

I nearly nod and say, "You're welcome," but instead, I finally stand up for myself. "It's Delia, actually, Marshall. I always hated you calling me Dee."

And then I watch him drive off back to Chicago, where I'll be headed in just two weeks.

CHAPTER SEVENTEEN

Dane

"Let's go, boys!" I holler as the T. Rex T-Ballers race to the field. Tucker and Elijah both argue over who is actually assigned to shortstop while Samson runs straight to his mom, begging for a snack. "Tuck, fall back to left field!"

Luckily, Del is already dealing with Samson and scooting him toward the inside of the fence, so I head to the other team's dugout and greet their coach.

"Dane! I thought for sure it was a typo when I saw your name on the coach's list this year." Joshua Jenkins sticks his grimy palm out, and I cringe inwardly as I grip and shake. Maybe a little too hard. He's one of Crystal's ex-husbands. And while we went to school together, playing ball on the same team for years and years, I never liked the guy. There was always something smarmy about him—still is. From the way he gnaws on the toothpick between his teeth to the way his beer gut hangs over his sweats, not much has changed. "I didn't realize you had a son. Finally give up on the eternal bachelorhood, eh?"

"No, not quite. Just helping out," I murmur, turning to face the field. The boys are kicking at the dirt as their anticipation bottoms out and boredom sets in. According to Delia, a six year old's attention span is only about five minutes long. Because of her advice, I'd introduced more movement and less lecturing during practices.

"Helping out, eh? You talking about that fine piece of ass over there in the leggings?" I turn around just as he eye-fucks Delia. "All the dads at school have been trying to nail her for years. Can't believe you're the one to finally get it done." His double chin wobbles as he chortles.

"What did you just say?" I advance, my sneakers coming toe to toe with his.

He retreats slightly into the dugout. "Hey, I didn't mean anything by it, man. Just didn't expect you to be the one to fuck her first. We all figured Daniel's dad would hit that. Even had a bet going with Reggie from the boatyard."

I see red and squeeze my fists together, ready to make a scene. "That's my fiancée you're talking about, Jenkins." I crowd him against the dugout's bench, my chest burning with the fire of a thousand suns. "You tell Daniel's dad, and Reggie, and whoever else— *all the other dads*— that Delia Evans is mine. You got that?"

Jenkins's hands go up in surrender as he slides onto the bench, eyes wide and mouth agape. "Like I said, man, I didn't mean anything by it."

"Fuck off," I mutter as I turn and head back to the field. As I take my place behind the batter, I find Delia's eyes on me from our team's dugout.

"What's wrong?" she mouths with her eyebrows drawn together.

I shake my head and glance out to the field. The boys are fucking around and already bored with waiting. "Are we gonna do this or what?" I shout as the anger and annoyance seep into my voice. And for the time being, I honestly don't know if I am directing my question at the herd of six-year-olds or the woman still watching me from the dugout.

"Welcome," I say after opening the door and finding Delia standing before me in that soft pink sweater and tight flared jeans. After Kayce begged to stay at his friend Hunter's house, I decided to offer to cook for Delia so we could spend some time going over the matrimonial compatibility quiz.

I wish I could say I'd cooled off from earlier, but seeing her curves on display has my blood heating again. This time for an entirely different reason.

"Wow, something smells delicious." She toes off her shoes and stands aside with her hands clasped in front of her.

"Have a seat." I follow her to the couch, but on second thought, take the recliner. After our last foray seated together on furniture, I'm not so sure I could contain myself again if she asked.

She glances toward the kitchen and then back at me. "It smells good. What are you making?"

I don't break eye contact as I tell her what I've whipped up. "Eggs, waffles, and hash browns. You know, breakfast for dinner..."

Her cheeks heat, and a timid smile lifts her lips. Does she remember that conversation from so long ago? *I only make that meal for the girls I date.* Because if she hasn't realized it yet, Delia and I are doing just that. Dating. And I've waited six achingly long years to date her. This is not a chance I'm squandering, and I'm willing to pull out all the stops, including making her an entire menu's worth of breakfast items to satisfy whatever she wants.

"So, um, the quiz..." She digs in her purse and uncurls her packet while I pull mine from the end table drawer. "I did mine in pencil so we can adjust the answers to match."

I release a chuckle. "Del, do you really think our answers need to be 100% alike for us to be compatible?"

She glances down at the page. "No, I just don't want there to be a reason for anyone to doubt this."

I'm not sure why anyone would doubt the thought of her and I together. It's always made perfect sense. At least to me. And maybe it's taking her longer to see it, but eventually she'll get there.

I turn past the directions and start reading. "Question one. I feel like my fiancée and I are best friends." While I chose *very much so*, I already know that Delia likely chose *sometimes*. Her best friend lives in Florida, although I'm not sure how often they chat. Certainly not as often as we do.

"I chose *very much so*. What did you pick?" She peeks up from her paper with two pink circles on her cheeks.

My mouth pops open. "But what about Savannah?"

She snorts and rolls her eyes. "Sav is my best *girl*friend. You're my best *boy*...friend." Her smile drops, and she looks down at the paper. "Besides, who has best friends in their thirties? This quiz is lame."

"Right. Well, I chose the same." I make a check in the air with my finger. "Next one. I have a strong sense of craving 'oneness' with my fiancée. Such as missing them, desiring sex, etcetera.'"

Delia keeps her eyes trained on her packet. But I don't miss the way she curls her bottom lip under her top teeth. "*Very much so*," she mumbles.

"What was that?" I want to hear her say it again.

"I said 'very much so.'" This time her eyes meet mine, and there's a flash of passion in those baby blues.

I clear my throat and keep my eyes locked on hers. "I said the same thing. Although if there was an option for *all day, every day*, I would've chosen that, Del."

Her chest heaves under the pink sweater, and I so desperately need to bury my face between her breasts that I nearly pop out of my seat and crawl to her. But eventually, her eyes drop back down and she reads the last question on the page. "I am willing to do whatever it takes to make this relationship last a lifetime."

My insides burn in anticipation as I wait for her to say it. Say the words that I need to hear to know that all of this has been worth it. The waiting. The pining. The aching.

"I put *very much so*, Dane." She blinks at me, and I know that, *maybe*, she's finally realizing what this is. It's not a con. It's not a game. I was all in from day one when she showed up at my restaurant looking for a place to live. I've been *hers* for six years.

"Me, too, Del. I put that, too."

We stare at one another as the cord holding us together tightens. Like a guitar string ready to be plucked and make the sweetest sound. And then the oven timer dings.

"And you've got to try this homemade brown sugar butter syrup for your waffles." I pass Delia the dish of warm liquid. My chest flares as she ladles a decent amount on her fluffy waffles.

"I don't even know where to begin," she says, eyeing her full plate.

I sit back and enjoy a piece of crisp bacon and watch, rapt, as Delia spears a few hash browns onto her fork. "Now that baseball is over, how will you and Kayce spend your weekends?" I keep my tone light, when I really want to ask how can I continue to be a part of their lives on a regular basis.

Del swallows her bite and then takes a swig of her mimosa. After all, breakfast for dinner goes wonderfully with champagne and orange juice. She takes another moment. "Actually, Marshall invited Kayce to Chicago next weekend. And I'll be going, too."

I drop the last bite of bacon onto the plate. "Wait, *what*?"

This time she loads a huge bite of waffle onto her fork. Syrup drips from the cutlery. "Yeah. Marshall invited Kayce, but I don't really feel comfortable just letting him go alone. So Marshall suggested I come along, too."

"And where will *you* be staying, Del?"

"With Kayce, of course. Marshall has the extra space." She says this so nonchalantly it's like she hasn't even considered how this might look to me. *Her fiancé.*

Her *fake* fiancé.

But there's something more here...

Still a fake engagement.

The voices in my head war back and forth until I finally shut them up for good. "I'm coming, too."

Her head snaps up and her eyes meet mine from across the small table. "What? Why?"

I narrow my gaze as my shoulders crawl toward my ears. "Do you really not understand, Delia?"

My question lingers unanswered for what feels like forever.

It finally dawns on her. "You think I'd get back with Marshall?" The sneer that lifts her lip is comforting.

"Well, not now, no. But who's to say he doesn't have plans of his own?"

Now she's the one sitting back, her fork dropped to her plate and her arms crossed over her ample chest. "And you assume I can't handle myself, is that right?"

"Well, yeah!" The sentiment is out before I can stop myself, and I instantly know I've said the wrong thing when her eyes widen and her mouth falls open. *Shit.*

"Are you kidding me right now, Dane? We just got on the same page and now you're doubting me?" She pops out of her chair.

"I'm not doubting *you*! I'm doubting *him*!" I stand and move toward her. "Who's to say he won't realize what a colossal mistake he made by letting you go and want you back?"

She inches toward me as her blue eyes narrow. "Who cares if he wants me back?" Her voice is barely above a whisper.

I grab her. One hand circles her waist while the other grabs behind her neck. "Fuck, Delia. Do you really not get it? *I* care!"

Her chin lifts. "Why would you care?"

I can't keep the truth inside anymore. "Because you're *mine*, god-damnit!" I pull her to me, and our lips crash together. It's like a fire's been set as we ignite. Her arms snake around my back and under my shirt. "I've wanted you for so long— so fucking long, Delia."

"How long, Dane?" Her tongue pushes through the seam of my lips.

I break the connection. "Not that long, I promise," and dive back in again. Fuck, I can't even think straight. What'd she ask me again?

"How long is 'not that long?' Tell me." Her nails scratch along my spine, and my body spasms at the sensation.

"Only six years." I pull away and watch as her face transforms. The understanding dawning in her eyes as she finally realizes that I've wanted her since we first met.

"You—?" But before she can ruin the moment with all her overthinking, I reach behind her and swipe all the dishes to the floor. Hash browns. Syrup. Bacon. All of it. It's gotta go. She yelps and looks at me like I've gone mad.

I grab around her hips and hoist her onto the kitchen table. "You're the one thing I've wanted for six *long* years, Delia. And I'm about to take my time tasting every inch of your body if you'll let me."

CHAPTER EIGHTEEN

Delia

My ass connects with Dane's kitchen table, but my eyes trail over the mess on the floor. Plates of food coat the rug. "You didn't have—" Dane grabs my chin and pulls it toward him and those soft lips.

"I'm only hungry for you." He leans in and sucks my bottom lip between his before dragging his mouth along my jaw and down farther to the sensitive skin beneath my ear. Heat shoots through my core, and I arch against him.

His breath tickles along my collarbone as his hands trace my curves to the bottom of my rib cage. I moan and inch closer to the edge of the table. I need friction like I need air.

"Nuh-uh," he murmurs as he pulls away. His palm finds the middle of my chest, and he presses gently. I go willingly, laying back until I'm staring at the ceiling and he's nestled between my thighs.

"We'll break the table."

"Which is why I'm staying right here, Del." He grinds his hips against me before flicking the button of my jeans and then pulls down the zipper.

Thank God I wore cute underwear.

I rise to my forearms, but he *tsks* and pushes me down again. "I'll let you know when you can watch. Until then, eyes on the ceiling."

The gruffness in his command has my nipples turning to glass beneath my sweater, the fabric suddenly feeling too tight.

He wiggles my jeans over my hips and ass and down my legs before tossing them over the back of the couch. "I've waited *six long years* to do this, Delia." His palms run up my shins and under my thighs. "I'm going to savor every bite." My feet connect with the surface of the table, and I'm nearly on full display; only a thin pair of pink cotton separates us.

I wiggle my shoulders to the side and watch as Dane glides two fingers along my fabric-covered slit. "So fucking wet for me, aren't you?"

I nod as our eyes connect. I thrust and writhe against the table, needing him to touch me.

"You want me to keep going, baby?" I nod again and suck my bottom lip in anticipation.

His fingers find the band of my panties, and he yanks them down. The warm air of the apartment hits my sensitive skin as he works the thin material over my knees and ankles before they're discarded with my jeans. "*Fuck*, this soaked pussy looks delicious, Del." He rolls his lips together before seating himself between my legs once more. I thrash against him as the ache grows.

"Touch me. *Please.*" My hands slide over my hips and thighs. My arms aren't long enough to grip him fully, but if they were, I'd pull him on top of me and relish the weight. Damn the table.

"I thought you'd never ask." Those skillful chef fingers glide over my clit and coat themselves in my desire before parting my lips. Then he's entering me, slowly, but with a force that tells me he's fighting against his own restraint.

His fingers edge my perfect spot. I gasp and buck against his hand as our eyes lock.

His thumb finds my clit, and he presses against it *just so* while he finger-fucks my pussy. My breathing increases as he glides in and out, the tempo building and matching the thrum in the base of my spine. My ass grinds against the table as I find the rhythm.

"Dane..." I moan and writhe as the friction builds.

"Nu-uh, baby. Not so fast." He withdraws from me, and I mewl in disappointment. "That was just the beginning. I can't have you finishing before the main course."

He drops to his knees and sends me a wicked smile over the edge of the table. Then he presses his nose straight into me and inhales. "I'm going to enjoy every lick. Every suck. Every inch of your pussy, baby."

I gasp as his tongue flicks out and finds my sopping wet flesh. He drags it through my lips and up to my clit before pressing against the bundle of nerves with the tip. I let out a squeal and buck against his face as my toes curl over the edge of the wooden surface. His fingers find my entrance as he continues to roll his tongue over the button at the apex of my thighs.

"*Fuck*!" My fingers claw at the table.

He chuckles against my flesh before withdrawing his fingers and sliding his tongue down to my opening. Then he's entering me with the wet muscle and using his slick-covered fingers to massage my clit. He switches again—tongue at the top and fingers fucking in and out of my cunt. He continues this back and forth between his fingers and tongue until my legs are shaking.

"I-I—gonna come!" I manage before my body spasms, and I lose all function of my limbs. I'm pulsing against his face while my fingers grip the edge of the table. I'm moaning, squealing, and speaking in gibberish as my soul exits my body and glimpses the pearly gates.

"That's it, baby. I'll lick all of it up. Come all over my face." And I do. I use his face to satiate the dry spell —six long years devoid of a man's touch. A man's *tongue*.

I have no clue when the orgasmic rollercoaster of emotion ends, but eventually, my body slows and my mind returns to the here and now.

A table.

Dane.

My desire all over his face.

My arms fall uselessly to my side as my feet slide off the table. I'm literally wrung out. A meal completely devoured.

And before I can even wonder if my legs are going to work, Dane gently lifts me from the table, cradles me in his arms, and sets me on his couch. A well-loved afghan covers me as he props a pillow behind my head. He kneels next to me as I turn to him.

I brush a stray curl back into his hair. "I'd never get back with Marshall."

His fingertips trace along my jaw. "I know."

I grab his hand before he can pull away. "No, you don't know." He stills. "When I was heavily pregnant with Kayce... before I came to Oselka." I inhale deeply and force out the words I've kept hidden for so long. "I went back to Chicago."

Dane's brow crinkles and he sits back on his heels, eyes darkening.

"I needed to give Marshall one more chance. To change his mind." My hand falls to my belly, long flattened as I recall the rounded bump that once held my son. "My parents were pushing me... trying to set me up with someone from the church." My cheeks burn. "So I went to Marshall's place. Knocked on the door."

The air is sucked from the room, as though Dane's stopped breathing.

"He answered. Shirtless. Another woman was behind him on the couch. He acted like he didn't know me, told me I was lost and had the wrong apartment."

Dane's face is inscrutable, but the anger radiating from him is palpable. I can feel it, as hot as my own as I reminisce about that day.

That was the day I promised myself I'd raise Kayce all on my own because I didn't need a man— or anyone else.

Tears burn in the corner of my eyes as I look up at the ceiling. But then Dane's body is covering mine, his arms wrap around my neck, and his face sinks into the gap between me and the couch.

"You weren't lost, Del. I just hadn't found you yet."

The tears slide down to my temples. Tears of happiness. Tears of safety. And I fall asleep with a drowsy—and satisfied—smile on my face.

"You've got to be kidding me!" Savannah squeals through the FaceTime screen. "Dane done *goooood*!" I bury my face in the dish towel that's flung over my shoulder. "*Hey*! You can't share that Chef Dane went down on you and then hide from me, Del!"

"Shush, Kayce will hear you!" I admonish as I crane my neck and peek around the corner of the kitchen. I can't see into his room, but I can hear him slamming his Matchbox cars into one another.

A devilish smile spreads across Sav's face. She's sitting on her front porch, and I can hear the waves crashing in the distance. "I still can't believe your front yard is the ocean."

"Yeah, it is pretty bad ass. Unless there's a hurricane. Speaking of which, there are a few out in the Gulf we're watching. We were thinking of heading north sometime soon."

My smile widens. "Well, how would a visit on December 10th work for you, Miss Maid of Honor?"

She lets out a squeal, and I have to hold the phone away from my ear lest I lose all sense of hearing. "Wait... that's less than a month away, Del!"

I exhale. "I know. My *parents* booked the venue. A local church."

Savannah makes an awkward noise on the phone that sounds like an upset stomach. "And you're okay with that?"

"I have to be, at least for now." Eager to change the subject, I turn the conversation back to Savannah. "You wouldn't fly to DC to visit your dad?"

"Nah. DC in November and December isn't all that fun, to be honest. Lots of crazies. Besides, Dad will be too busy schmoozing with all the newly elected officials to spend any time with me."

"Well you're always welcome to stay here, of course."

"Would there be enough room for Jack, too?"

I glance around at the apartment and worry my bottom lip. There's hardly enough room for me and Kayce. "Sure. You two can take my bed, and I'll bunk with Kayce."

"Absolutely not, Del. We aren't putting you ou—"

"Wait a sec!" I turn on my heel and head out to the breezeway and across to Dane's apartment. I rap my knuckles on the door.

"What are you doing?" Sav's voice squeaks from the screen.

Before I can respond, Dane opens the door to his place, and I'm immediately sucked back to last night. Laid out on his kitchen table with his face in between my thighs.

Gasping in pleasure as he lapped me up like the last bite of dessert.

"Hey." His voice is scratchy, like he just woke up from a nap.

"Did I wake you?" My eyes trail over the mass of brown waves as he raises his arm, bicep flexing, and runs his fingers through them.

"No, just watching the game. Come in." He reaches for me before opening the door farther.

"Actually, I was just making dinner... and Kayce's home."

"Ah, so that's what smells so good."

"Why don't you join us? I made plenty." Compared to Dane, I know I'm not the best cook, but the way his smile lights up his face has me feeling like a Michelin-star chef.

"Ahem!" The voice from my hip startles me, and I nearly drop the phone.

Dane's eyes zero in on the screen. "Oh, yeah. Say hi to Savannah." I hold her up to him, and he waves awkwardly. "She and Jack are wanting to come visit. December 10th. I asked her to be my maid of honor. But there's not enough space at mine and—"

Dane crosses his arms and leans against the doorframe, his shirt pulling tight over his chest until I can see the outline of his pecs. "Of course they can stay at my place, baby."

I practically melt right there on the concrete breezeway at the way he addresses me, but then Savannah cuts in. "Great! Thanks, Dane. I'll call you later, Del!"

The screen goes blank, and I slide the device into my back pocket.

"So, about that dinner..." His eyes flash as he looks me up and down. Gone is last night's cute outfit. Today I'm in nothing but joggers and an Emerald Coast University sweatshirt. My hair tossed haphazardly into a bun.

"I-I don't think it'll be as good as last night," I hint with a small smirk. My cheeks heat.

"Why don't you let me be the judge of that? After all, my cooking was nothing compared to what I *actually* ate."

I shake my head and chuckle as I turn back to my apartment's opened door. Between his cooking and his oral sex skills, I wonder if there's anything Dane *isn't* amazing at.

Chapter Nineteen

Dane

"Dane's Italiano!" Normally the hours of two to three p.m. are the slowest of the day. I use the time to restock, prepare the marinades, and complete any missed inventory.

"Dane?" The voice on the line is thin and confused. "Dane Lukes?"

"Yes, this is Dane's. Will this be pickup or delivery?" Since Antonio isn't in until four, I'll have to drive the order over myself, but our service area isn't large, and I'll be back with plenty of time to spare.

"This is Nana, uh, Grandma Delia. The original one."

I curl my bottom lip under my teeth. Del never told me she shared a first name with her grandmother. "Oh, yes. Hi, Nana... er... Mrs. Delia." I shake my head at how dumb I sound.

The phone cuts out, and I'm certain I've lost her until she speaks again. "Now, Dane, I need you to understand something about my Delia. Are you listening?"

"Yes ma'am, I'm listening." My lips flatten as I try to hold in a smile. I imagine the diminutive lady sitting in her chair, a tiny glass bottle of rum opened next to her can of Coke. "What can I do for you? Wait, is everything okay?" It never occurred to me that something might be wrong.

"Everything is fine. Well... it's really not. This is about Delia."

Panic shoots straight to my chest. The same feeling I get when I'm driving and see flashing lights in my rearview mirror. "W-what's happened, Nana?"

"Oh, calm down. She's fine." She chuckles to herself while I wait, my stomach in knots. "How much has Delia shared about her parents, Dane?"

I sigh and run my palm across my stubbled jaw. "I know her childhood was pretty rough. They didn't have a lot of money, and what little they had went toward the church. Delia said..." I stop, wondering just how much I should tell.

A loud sigh escapes from the phone. "So she only told you the beginning, then."

I swallow and cradle the phone against my shoulder. "What do you mean?"

"My dear, when Delia found out she was pregnant, Marshall encouraged her to get rid of it. He didn't want anything to do with her or the baby."

My molars thrash against one another. I'd suspected as much, even if Delia had never confirmed.

"She knew her life in Chicago was over. It was too expensive, and she could never work with Marshall again, so she had to quit her job. The likelihood of getting hired anywhere else with a baby bump was slim. So she came back home. To me."

I wait for her to continue.

"*I'm* the one who told her to go to her parents and ask for help. I thought, surely this is their time to shine. Show their daughter the benevolence they'd always preached toward others. After all, she had decided to keep the baby. And at first, they did everything right. They allowed her to stay. Helped heal her broken heart. But there were questions from the congregation about the paternity of the unborn baby. An unwed mother, the daughter of the reverend... so her father encouraged her to reach out to Marshall once more. See if those feelings were still there and if he'd changed."

"He hadn't," I confirm out loud.

"No, he hadn't. And when Del got her heart broken all over again, her father suggested he set her up with a nice man from the church. An older man who didn't mind taking another's child into his home."

I swallow the disgust bubbling up from my gut. "Because Heaven forbid the reverend's family be anything other than perfect."

"Precisely. And that's when she started to plan her escape. She applied and got the job in Oselka."

I inhale loudly through my nose and nod. "So why are you telling me all this, Nana?"

"Because, Dane, it was all my fault. The family being torn apart. Delia being so alone and untrusting. And now it's time for me to fix it." She's quiet for a moment. "And when I saw you, well... I want you to know that I *know*."

Confusion settles over me. "Know what, exactly?"

"Why, I know you love her, of course. I've always suspected, actually. The way she talked about all you do for her and Kayce. But meeting you in person confirmed it. You *love* Delia."

I clear my throat and sniff, unsure what to say. But the images of Delia snuggled up on my couch, her eyes closed and her face completely calm has my heart pounding out of my chest.

"I've told her as much, too. But she's stubborn. Won't consider that she's finally found the one."

"Well I—"

"You don't need to say anything, Dane. Just know this... Delia's going to have a hard time trusting any man in her life, as you can imagine. I just hope you can stick around until she figures out that you're one of the good ones."

My throat goes dry. "Th-thank you, Nana. But I'm not going anywhere. I love...". I can't tell her the truth. Delia should be the first to hear those words. "I loved speaking with you."

She's quiet for a moment, and I'm certain I've lost her. "I'm glad. And I'm glad she'll have someone to take care of her when I'm gone. But don't hold in that sentiment forever... tell her before it's too late."

"Yes, ma'am." I nod and replace the receiver in its cradle. My gaze strays out the front window and across the town square to the bank.

And then the phone rings again.

It's been years since I stepped foot in Oselka Elementary. The hallways have been updated with modern photos of smiling kids and the trophy case no longer hosts the awards from the 80s and 90s that I was familiar with. I don't have time to glance into the gleaming case and determine whose kid was the spelling bee champ or fastest runner at field day, though, as I immediately open the glass doors to the office and stalk inside.

Kayce sits slumped in a chair, an ice pack held to his face.

"Shit," I murmur under my breath as I sit next to him. He allows the pack to fall away, and I can visibly feel my eyes pop from my head. The school nurse told me on the phone he'd taken a kickball to the face during gym class, but I didn't expect it to be so... swollen.

His tiny chin starts to wobble as tears flood his eyes. "Oh, buddy, does it hurt?" I wrap my arm around his shoulders and pull him into me.

He nods and sniffles. "It hurts when I breathe. And blink. And talk."

"All right. Let me get you outta here, and then we'll stop at the Med-Check on the way home." I slowly extricate myself and approach the ancient secretary. The same woman has worked the front desk for years.

"Thanks for getting ahold of me, Mrs. Danvers." I quickly scrawl my name on the sign out sheet.

"Oh, it's no problem, sweetie. I'm just glad we were able to get ahold of someone. We tried Delia at the bank, but they couldn't locate her." She raises a sparsely-drawn eyebrow at me.

I don't have time to worry about where Delia is, or why she's not at work. So I nod quickly before grabbing Kayce's bag and ushering him out of the building.

"Where's mom?" he asks from behind the ice pack as I hoist him into the back of the truck. I don't have a booster seat, so instead, I cinch the seatbelt as tight as it will go and hope for the best. And ignore his question, too.

Luckily the MedCheck is only down the street, but I still keep my hands at ten and two as I white knuckle it under twenty miles per hour the entire way there.

As I slide the truck into park, I pull out my cell and dial Delia's number. It rings several times before going to voicemail. I click *end* and instead send a text asking her to call me as soon as possible.

"Did you get ahold of mom?" I can hear the uncertainty in Kayce's voice.

"No, I didn't, buddy. But I sent her a text so she'll call me soon. Let's get you inside."

By the time I get Kayce checked in, I've looked at my phone no fewer than twenty times. No texts from Delia. I slide my phone into my back pocket just as the nurse calls for us. Kayce's eyes look up at me expectantly, but I take his hand and inhale before plastering a smile on my face.

The tentative knock at my apartment door pulls my focus away from the cartoons on the television.

"Hey," I say slowly as Delia rushes past me. She doesn't bother to drop her coat or bag, nor take off her shoes, as she rushes to Kayce.

"Oh, I'm so glad you're okay, sweetie," she says as she pulls him close. He peers around her hug at the TV.

"I'm fine, Mom. The doctor said it's not a cone... cone...cuss."

"Concussion," I add as I lean against the wall between the living room and kitchen. "He's got to take it easy for a few days, but there are no signs of a concussion. His nose isn't broken, either."

Delia gently trails the pad of her finger over Kayce's bruised skin. She inhales through her teeth. "Does it hurt?"

"Nah." Kayce shakes his head. "Dane got me ice cream!"

Her eyes finally land on mine and they soften as either side of her lips raise slightly. "Get your stuff." She stands and pats Kayce on the knee before approaching me. "Thank you so much for being there." Her hand lands on my forearm and squeezes.

My ribs tighten in my chest as I stand upright. "You know it's no problem. But where were you, Del?"

She blinks. "What do you mean? I-I was in a meeting. I couldn't get away." Her face turns to Kayce, who's hoisting his bag over his shoulder while still glued to the TV.

I grab her chin between my thumb and index finger and turn her back to me. "No, you weren't. Your secretary told me you'd left for the day and went home feeling sick. But you weren't there either." I purse my lips and fight the urge to clench my fists. "So where were you?"

She clears her throat as her eyes dart back to Kayce. Then she leans in. "Dane..." her eyes find mine and then drop. "I-I had a job interview. Okay?"

I exhale silently and my shoulders relax. "Oh. Well that's great. Why didn't you just say so?" While there's only the one bank in town, there are a few bigger branches not too far from Oselka. I can't be upset with her for that.

She wets her lips as two deep lines form between her brows. "I didn't know how to say it exactly."

My eyes narrow and she fidgets with the hem of her blouse. "Say what?"

"The job... it's in Lansing, Dane."

CHAPTER TWENTY

Delia

Dane's been radio silent and standoffish for days, but now that we're stuffed together in his pickup on our way to Chicago, he can't escape my ability to force a conversation that neither of us wants to have.

As we near the suburbs, I lean forward to turn the knob of the radio. If there's one thing I enjoyed about Chicago, it was their plethora of radio music selections. Oselka's lucky to get a smattering of top 40 hits on the four or five stations we manage to pick up within the town limits.

I land on a station blasting some pop star's newest hit and dial up the volume slightly. As I lean back, my gaze lands on Dane's hands. He's white-knuckled as we merge onto the major highway that will take us into the city.

"Do you want me to drive?" It's been a few years since I navigated the Illinois drivers and their pothole-filled roads, but I'm sure I can handle their Nascar-style escapades.

"Nope." His eyes stay trained to the road.

I press my lips together in defeat. Instead, I prop my elbow against the window and watch as the trees and terrain turn to apartment buildings and warehouses. "You okay back there, Kayce?"

When he doesn't answer, I turn in my seat and find him fast asleep. His neck at an odd angle and his mouth gaping wide.

"I'm just gonna…" I murmur aloud as I unbuckle and maneuver to my knees. I shimmy between the driver and passenger seat and reach back, adjusting him so he's leaning against the headrest of his booster seat. My ass presses against Dane's shoulder. "Sorry," I mutter again as I return to the seat. I click the belt back in place.

We ride in silence for another song. My gaze drifts out the window, and I try to recall the last time I was on this road. It must've been just over six years ago as I traveled from Chicago to my parents' house. My hopes and dreams packed in the trunk—along with my meager belongings—as I felt the uncomfortable press of my belly against my too-tight jeans. I'd taken to looping a hair tie around the button for some extra give, but I knew it wouldn't be too much longer before even that wasn't enough.

My hand drifts to my stomach, and I place my palm against the fabric of my shirt.

"Are you feeling okay?" Dane asks as his gaze finally lands on me.

I smile slowly and nod. "Just thinking about the past." My hand falls to my thigh. "I haven't been back to Chicago since I was pregnant with Kayce." I'm hopeful Dane's finally coming back to me.

He sighs heavily and chews on his bottom lip. "You think you'll ever move back?"

I track the sites passing by. Billboards announcing clubs and events. Multi-storied apartment buildings surrounded by parking lots and strip malls. I shake my head. "Chicago was never my home. It was just a temporary stop on my way to Oselka." I rest my hand on his thigh.

His eyes briefly land on mine before returning to the road, as though to gauge if I'm serious. "Then why'd you have a job interview in Lansing, Del?"

"I applied for that job *months* ago. And honestly, I never thought I'd even get an interview. But I figured I'd give it a shot so I'd be closer to Nana. Plus it's like, twice my salary…" I shrug.

"And you didn't think to tell me any of this beforehand?"

"I honestly didn't think it was worth noting. Besides, I don't want to continue burdening you with my problems, Dane. It's not your job to fix my life."

Dane speeds up the car slightly and moves over to the right before exiting on the approaching ramp. "What're you—"

"We need gas," he says gruffly.

I stay silent, wondering if the conversation is at an end, as he turns into the nearest station and cuts the engine. Wordlessly, he exits the car, and I tune out the noises around me. I turn to check on Kayce, who's still fast asleep, when my door is yanked wide open. Dane stands there, his arms situated overhead on the top of the truck as he stares down at me. The hem of his shirt rides up as he flexes his biceps.

"How many times do I have to tell you that you and Kayce *are* my job? I want to be there for you both. I willingly signed up for this, Delia." He leans farther into the cab, crowding me against the worn seat.

"I don't want to be reliant on you all the time." I *can't* be reliant on anyone, I want to say as my eyes bounce between his. My reservations are pointless, though, as the only thought running through my mind is how his lips taste.

"Too bad, baby. I'm not going anywhere, so you better to get used to it." As though he can read my mind, we both lean toward one another at the same time. Our lips touch, and the tension crackles and then splits apart.

All that's left is the desire—to be wrapped in his arms and feel his weight on top of me.

The gas clicks off with a loud *thunk*, and we pull apart at the same time. But he doesn't immediately retrieve the lever or even leave my side. Instead, he rolls his lips together—as though he can taste all of me. I have no idea what's running through his mind, but I can imagine it's full of the same dirty thoughts running through mine.

How are we going to survive sharing a bed at my ex's house?

The ride in the elevator to Marshall's penthouse is fraught with tension. The lift dings as we soar to the top floor, but my stomach drops incrementally as we rise.

If his seeking out my hand to hold is any indication, Kayce's nervous too. We hold tight to one another, but for very different reasons. He's likely nervous to see the place in which his father lives. I, however, am nervous to relive some of the most painful moments of my life. The moment that I showed up at this very same penthouse, my first ultrasound pictures tucked in my purse. I was three months along, not even showing, and looking for answers.

Of course, the answer I found was a man who wanted nothing to do with me or the baby.

"Get rid of it," he demanded, his eyes cold and his jaw set. When I refused, he pulled out his checkbook and offered me any amount just to go away. I was too stunned to refuse the check, but I tore it up the moment I returned to my shared apartment. Shoved it deep into the trash can and poured a lukewarm can of Coke over the top.

I swallow the thick lump in my throat as the elevator opens to a brightly-lit foyer. A slim end table adorned with freshly-cut flowers is nestled against the wall. Kayce's eyes go wide at the opulence. It's something neither of us is used to. And it's only when I feel a comforting hand along the small of my back that I remember Dane. When I turn, I find his other palm covering Kayce's shoulder.

"C'mon, buddy. Let's do this." I offer encouragement and bravery I don't feel as I hoist my son up and approach the door. "Go on." Kayce reaches out and grabs the gold-plated door knocker and slams it a little loudly.

Once. Twice.

I retreat, finding my space next to Dane. Something about his nearness eases my discomfort. My anxiety. I glance over at him just as the door opens and Marshall appears.

My ex is wearing dark fitted denim and a pale blue cashmere sweater. A large-faced silver watch gleams on his wrist. It could not be further from Dane's outfit of slouchy, worn jeans and a black tee. A full-zip hoodie and a leather jacket, along with a backward baseball cap, complete his ensemble. But it's not Dane's duds that have me head over heels. It's the way his eyes don't stray from Kayce.

"Welcome, welcome!" Marshall's smile seems forced and doesn't quite reach his eyes as he tracks Dane's presence. "How was the drive?"

"Long." I adjust Kayce, who seems to snuggle closer against my neck.

"Well, come on in." He moves aside and ushers us in. I attempt to toe off my shoes but the weight of Kayce is too much. "I'll take him," Marshall suggests, reaching across the entry for our son.

Except Kayce reaches for Dane instead. I press my lips into a firm line, careful not to show the smirk I feel coming on, as I pass him over to Dane.

Marshall clears his throat. "Not much has changed." He directs us to follow him into the penthouse.

I keep my hand pressed against Kayce's back as Dane holds him. I pull off the palm-sized trainers and set them next to my own.

Marshall's right, his penthouse hasn't changed much in the years since I was last here. His style favors modernism, with hard lines and minimal clutter. Leather and stone are the two main textures, and everything feels cold and harsh.

"Nice place you've got," Dane murmurs from beside me. I can tell he's not impressed. Something about his tone, something only I would notice. It leaves me with a sense of warmth in my belly. Knowing that I am so acutely aware of his mannerisms.

Marshall hardly acknowledges Dane's compliment. Instead, he turns to Kayce and attempts to draw him from Dane's shoulder. "You ready to see your room, kiddo?" The smile is bright, if a little strained.

Kayce nods solemnly and wriggles free of Dane's grip. Dane gently lowers him to the sleek tile floor, and he takes off. "Careful on the tile with your socks!" I chastise as I quickly chase after him.

Marshall attempts to take Kayce's hand as he leads him around a corner and down a hallway. I follow in their tread as my mind flashes to the first time I stepped foot in this very penthouse.

How enthralled I was by the pseudo-erotic artwork that still lines the hall. Marshall had espoused about his art dealer and how much he loved acquiring paintings from up-and-coming artists who "pushed the limit."

Now, the pieces look gauche. Like a college frat bro playing at being an adult.

"I've been meaning to replace these pieces with something a bit more... kid-friendly," Marshall adds, as though he can read my mind. "My art dealer's working on it."

"You should get a *Paw Patrol* poster! Rubble's my favorite," Kayce adds.

Marshall looks confused. "Is that a TV show?" From behind me, Dane snorts.

"Welp, kiddo, here's your room!" Marshall stops in front of a nondescript door, and as Kayce bounces on the balls of his feet, he throws it open.

And I instantly see red.

Luckily, Marshall's penthouse isn't far from the aquarium and field museum—both which are world-renowned. And, as the day has warmed considerably to feel more like September than late November, we decide to walk.

"I can't believe you installed a television, an Xbox, *and* a PlayStation for a six year old, Marshall!" I glare behind my sunglasses.

"You get to decide what his room looks like at your place, and I get to decide what it looks like at mine." He's unnerved by my outburst and continues to point out various sites to both Dane and Kayce, who trail behind us.

"That is *not* how this works. I get to decide because I'm the parent who's been in Kayce's life, raising him from birth."

"So I should run every decision by you?" An eyebrow cocks beneath his couture sunglasses.

"Exactly." I stomp ahead. I may not have lived in the city for several years, but everyone knows the way to the Museum Campus. Not only is it home to the aquarium and field museum, it's also the location of the Adler Planetarium and Soldier Field. As I traipse along the sidewalk, the sun glinting off Lake Michigan has me missing the city. I forgot how beautiful the autumn days were, and I'd be lying if I said I wasn't a little nostalgic for those days before I was a mom. "Listen," I say, turning to Marshall. "I just want what's best for Kayce. And all the books say that a television in a child's room isn't a good idea. So why don't you turn your guest room into a... boy cave? Like a play room for Kayce?" I want what's best for Kayce, and compromising with Marshall is ultimately going to go a long way in keeping the co-parenting relationship intact.

Marshall slows and comes to a stop. He beckons for Dane and Kayce to continue walking, and I nod as Dane sends me a questioning look. "I know this is hard for you. And I'm glad you want what's best for Kayce, too. Maybe that involves you moving back to the city." He glances around at the pedestrians and bites his lip. "I could pull some strings, you know." He drives his hands into his hips and stares out at the lake.

I chuckle. "Marshall, absolutely not. Just get rid of the television in Kayce's room, okay? Oh, and I'll send you a list of child-rearing books that should help." I add as I pat his arm. Then I jog ahead and catch up to Dane and Kayce, who are wearing dual smiles of glee as the aquarium comes into view.

CHAPTER TWENTY-ONE

Dane

The city is disgusting. There's no other way to put it. Litter dirties the streets, there are crowds of people everywhere, and even the lake has a distinctive rotting fish smell that permeates the air.

Suffice to say, Chicago is a shit hole.

"Dane! They have an octopus!" Kayce grabs my hand and pulls me toward the *Oceans* exhibit, where, lo and behold, an enormous sign announces that Sawyer is a giant Pacific cephalopod.

Kayce's been obsessed with octopuses for weeks. Ever since his kindergarten class completed a unit on sea animals, he's been sharing random facts with Del and I. I trail behind the tot as he leads me to the glass enclosure where the sunset-orange octopus is settled atop a rocky crag.

"Read it to me?" Kayce points to the informational blurb.

"The average arm span of a giant Pacific octopus is fourteen feet—"

"How big is that?"

I look around and spy another visitor. "About from me to that guy."

Kayce's face lights up with excitement. Man, I love this kid. His enjoyment over something so small as the length of an octopus's reach is contagious, and I smile. I return my gaze to the blurb. "It also says that Sawyer the octopus can squeeze through a hole smaller than two inches. And he can camouflage himself, which means blending his color, texture, and shape to catch his prey!"

"Wow..." Kayce presses his nose against the glass, enraptured by the squishy sea creature in front of his face.

"Plus, they're absolutely delicious." Marshall chuckles. He turns and winks at me just as Kayce's face falls.

"You eat them?" I don't miss the way his childlike voice cracks or the tremor in his chin. We're about to have a code red meltdown.

"Ha, n-no, you're dad's just—".

"Of course I eat them," Marshall says, interrupting me. "Octopus is one of my favorite foods. Only it's called *calamari*," he enunciates, blindly ignoring the fact that he's traumatizing his own child.

Kayce's eyes fill as he glances back at the gentle creature behind the glass. "B-b-but I learned that octopuses can feel pain." His small palm presses against the glass, and he sniffles. His shoulders begin to shake.

Fuck.

Anger and annoyance course through my veins. I clench my fists together and attempt to tamp down the urge to throttle Marshall.

"What'd I say?" The dense moron looks around, first at me and then, when he realizes I'm two seconds away from beating his ass, at Delia.

"Kayce's favorite animal right now is the octopus. He's been reading everything about them for months, and he's learned that they are sentient," she replies calmly. But I know there's a mama tiger raging inside of her. I can see it in the set of her jaw and the coldness in her eyes.

"Shit," he says loudly. Several parents give him the side-eye and move their children away from us. Only Marshall doesn't notice. He's crouched down, face-to-face with his son. Kayce's tears have left dual tracks down his cheeks. "Hey, kiddo... I'm so sorry, I didn't know."

Kayce doesn't look at his father. He keeps his gaze trained on Sawyer, who's stretching a tentacle toward the glass, his suction cups pulsating through the water. "It's okay. But now that you know, will you stop eating cal-cal-whatever it's called?" The suction cups stick to the glass, and Kayce's features brighten.

"Of course. No more *calamari* for me." He gives his son an awkward side hug, but Kayce's still too enthralled with his new cephalopod friend to notice.

Dinner is another disastrous affair. Kayce's exhausted after spending all day walking around the aquarium and field museum, and when we enter the upscale restaurant, we're told there's a forty-five-minute wait for a table.

"But I'm hungry," Kayce whispers to Delia. She digs through her bag and comes up with a lint-crusted applesauce pouch. She twists the top and hands it to him.

He scrunches his nose, but before he can complain, I send him a severe stare and a subtle head shake. He sticks the tip of the pouch into his mouth without another word.

"This place has the best deep dish pizza," Marshall adds as we take a seat on the bench near the door.

"I lived here, remember?" Delia rolls her eyes.

"Oh, that's right..." He nods and slides his phone out of his pocket. "I've just got to make a call. Excuse me." He steps outside.

The moment the door closes, Delia groans and tilts her head back, letting it hit the wall. "Can we go home yet?" she whispers as she catches my eye over Kayce's head.

I chuff and want to tell her that I wish. I wish this was all a nightmare. I wish that Chicago was just a city we read about in the news. I wish Kayce was my son, not Marshall's. But unfortunately, none of that would help the situation. So instead, I plaster a fake smile on my face and shrug. "It's not so bad," I lie as my molars fuse together.

Kayce finishes the applesauce pouch and passes it to his mother. "I'm bored." None of us are used to waiting for a table. In Oselka, the restaurant options are slim. And of course neither Kayce nor his mother have ever had to wait for a table at my restaurant.

"Let's play I Spy," I suggest as I hoist him onto my lap. "I spy with my little eye..."

We continue the game for all of six minutes. At that point, his eyes grow heavy, and he leans his head against my shoulder.

Another four minutes later, he's passed out.

Del and I make small talk, mostly about what we miss most in Oselka, before Marshall returns and our table is suddenly called. I carry Kayce to a secluded booth in the back and settle him in his mother's lap.

Which means Marshall and I are crammed next to one another.

Lovely.

I don't purposefully push my elbows as far out as possible, but I don't *not* push them, either.

And when we're told the signature, Chicago-style deep dish pizza will be an additional forty-five-minute wait, I force yet another shrug and fake smile as Delia catches my eye across the table.

While Delia tucks in Kayce, I retreat to the bedroom we're to share. With an en suite bathroom and spacious walk-in closet, it's nearly bigger than her entire apartment. A hefty cupboard hides an enormous television, but the plethora of remote controls has me too nervous to switch it on. So instead, I grab a pillow and settle onto the floor to make my bed for the evening.

"You, too," I hear Delia call from the hallway. Then she's standing in the doorway, her eyes perusing over my place with an inquisitive cock to her eyebrow. "What're you doing?" she whispers as she closes the door behind herself.

"Making up my bed."

She crosses the wide expanse and opens her mouth. But before she can utter a single word, she glances behind her at the closed door and then approaches the cupboard. Grabbing a random remote, she powers on the television and then switches to a rerun of an old sitcom. The volume rises before she tosses the controller onto the bed. "Why are you on the floor?"

I sit up, my sweatpants-clad legs stretched out before me. "Where else would I be, Del?" Does she truly not understand? I glance around once again at the sprawling room before turning my gaze to hers.

Arms cross over her bust, breasts pressing against the cotton tee she wears. Her long auburn hair, which was neatly curled this morning, has fallen free and hangs over her shoulders in waves. Her under eyes are rimmed with purple semicircles.

"It's been a long day. We're both exhausted." I lean back against my pillow and pull the blanket I'd found in the walk-in over myself.

I don't miss the way her throat bobs as she looks at me—or the way her face goes flat. And try as I might, I can't ignore the way she saunters to her overnight bag, which happens to be tucked next to the cupboard in my direct line of vision.

She squats down, her jeans stretching over her ass and thighs. She peeks over her shoulder at me, as though my gaze would be anywhere else in this dull beige bedroom. I swallow over the tightness in my throat. Is she really going to make this so hard?

She unzips the bag and pulls out an oversized T-shirt. *My* oversized T-shirt. "Where'd you get—?"

She shrugs and stands, the worn cotton hanging loosely from her fingers. "I may have found it once upon a time."

And suddenly, I remember. Two years ago, when Kayce was four. I'd been washing my truck in the summer heat. Buckets of soapy suds and a coiled hose lay in the alley. Peeling the wet shirt from my chest, I'd tossed it nonchalantly to the sidewalk just as Del and Kayce approached. "Can I help?" the tot asked, his face beaming with glee. He was enamored with big trucks. Still is.

So, under my tutelage, Kayce helped me wash the truck and gave it a proper vacuum, too, while Delia had gone upstairs to make dinner.

"You had my Lions shirt this whole time..."

She doesn't say anything. Only bites her bottom lip and turns away, her back to me, before lifting her fitted tee over her head. My breathing speeds up as she unhooks her bra and drops it into her bag. Then she quickly slides my shirt on. It hangs loose down to her upper thighs. But she's not done yet. No, still facing away from me, she unbuttons her jeans and, hips wiggling, slides them down her legs.

I swear I catch a glimpse of lacy red underwear before she neatly folds her pants and sets them, along with her tee, beside her bag. Then, without a backward glance, she saunters into the en suite bathroom and closes the door quietly.

I lie back, my eyes trained on the ceiling, as I contemplate my life's choices. Only moments later, she's padding across the plush carpet and sliding under the covers. The television clicks off, and the room goes dark.

"Del?"

"Hm?" She rolls toward me.

"You know why I'm on the floor, right?"

She's silent. Doesn't say a word.

So I continue. "There's no way I can share that bed with you. I wouldn't be able to control myself."

She's still quiet, but I hear her subtle intake of breath. Then, after a few moments, "So I'm safe up here?" The question hangs in the darkness like a taunt.

I shake my head back and forth on the pillow. "I'm not sure, baby, but I'm trying."

CHAPTER TWENTY-TWO

Delia

The pain that wakes me up is unbearable. It feels like my body is being torn apart. A white-hot poker stabbing straight into my guts. I sit up, my pregnant belly as hard as a rock.

Fuck, he's coming! I press a hand to the overlarge bump. It's only then that I realize my bottom half is completely wet. My water's broken and soaked through the brand-new sheets and duvet Dane was kind enough to give me.

I need to get changed and—another contraction hits. I double over as it radiates up my spine and wraps around my body.

Fuck! I grind my teeth and hold in the scream, rolling into my pillow and letting out a wretched wail into the fluffy down.

It dissipates just as quickly as it started, and I tenderly change into fresh pajama bottoms, toss on an ECU sweatshirt, and toe on my clogs. My hospital bag has been packed for weeks and sits near the door. I swing it over my shoulder just as another wave of pain sears within my pelvis. I manage to grab onto the door handle as my legs collapse. This time I'm better prepared and try to breathe through the agony like I've seen in the movies.

I was too frightened to go to any birthing classes alone. Not in a town that I'd just moved to. Not without a friend in the world.

Hee hee hoo. Hee hee hoo. The Hollywood technique does nothing to stop the pressure that radiates around my core. I'm just grateful there's no one here to hear me hissing in pain.

I ride out the contraction and carefully stand when it's passed. I need to hurry if I'm going to make it to the car before the next one hits. Opening and closing the door, I take the steps as quickly as possible and make it to the sidewalk safely.

I toss the hospital bag in the passenger seat, and just as I'm walking around the front of the car, another contraction brings me to my knees.

Only this time it's worse.

So much worse.

I grind my teeth and try to hold in the scream of pain, but I fail and release a keening wail into the night air. It echoes off the empty brick buildings, but I'm in too much pain to care if I've disturbed the sleepy town I now call home.

"Fuuuuuuuck!" I roar as another spasm wracks my body. I decide then and there that I'm just going to curl up and die in the street. It's been nice knowing you, Oselka. I hope someone will identify my dead body.

"AAAARRRGGGGG!" The contraction ebbs, and then, on its heels, another rages again. I think that means the baby's close, but at this point I don't even care as I see stars and flashes of lights behind my eyes. Goodbye, apartment. Goodbye, bank. Goodbye, rough pavement that feels so cool against my cheek.

Suddenly, I'm lifted to my feet. Strong, capable hands wrap around my back and under my knees and tuck me into a truck. I have no clue where I am—who I am—as I writhe against the seat in agony.

Then we're moving—quickly—along the road away from town and toward the hospital.

A bright light flashes, and I'm in a hospital bed. "I don't want to be alone," I say as a nurse holds my hand. The hospital gown is tucked up under my breasts, and a sheet covers my bottom half. A doctor examines between my thighs.

"You're not alone, honey. I'm going to be right here to walk you through this." She squeezes my hand as her eyes catch the doctor's, and they share a nod. "But it is time to push, okay?"

Panic seizes my chest, and I shake my head. "I-I can't do this alone. I need..." A sob escapes my throat because the truth is, I have no one. My parents don't even know where I am. My best friend is a thousand miles away. And the baby's father would rather pretend I don't exist. That we don't exist.

"The man who brought you here?" the nurse asks.

Only I have no recollection of how I got to the hospital. I fall back against the pillows as the pain returns. I squeeze the metal railing at the side of the bed, the nurse and her soft hand gone. Perhaps she's one of the people peering between my legs.

"Push!" The command comes through the haze of agony, and my body takes over. I bear down and scream. It feels like my body's being torn in two. I'm being split apart, broken beyond belief, yet I push again.

A hand takes mine, calloused and coarse compared to the feminine one before. "Push, Delia!" the deep voice commands, and I do as I'm instructed.

I grip the roughened hand and squeeze as a loud growl rattles from my chest.

"C'mon. One more!" the doctor encourages. I sag against the pillows, my energy depleted and my body completely broken.

"I can't... I can't—" Tears stream down my sweat-soaked face. The pain below feels like I'll never be healed. Never survive this.

"Delia... Del... look at me." Strong fingers take my chin and snap it toward dark blue eyes. An errant curl dips to his lashes. "You can do this.

You need to push. Now!" He doesn't break eye contact. Only shakes his head until I'm following suit. Nodding up and down. "Now, Del. Push now!"

I bear down and press as a roar of power thunders from within. There's a moment of searing pain followed by instant relief.

And then a baby's soft cries.

Those calloused hands cover my sticky cheeks. "You did it," he whispers. "You did it, Delia." The voice fades. "I knew you could do it."

My eyes snap open, and as my hand slides down to my flat stomach, I immediately breathe a sigh of relief in the darkness. I'm not pregnant or in labor. The sheets are dry.

Just a dream.

It was all just a dream.

I stare at the darkened ceiling, backlit by the moon's glow from the window. Marshall's penthouse is high enough that we aren't bothered by the lights and sounds of the busy streets below.

And yet I miss the quiet of home. Oselka.

I roll over and find Dane snoring softly on the floor. His arms are thrown wide and the blanket kicked off. I gently press my bare feet to the floor and drop to my knees, the rug not as plush as I'd expected. I can't believe he's slept like this.

I wouldn't be able to control myself.

My fingers find his wavy brown tresses, grown long again over the last several weeks. The ends curl around my thumb as I trace his features. Over his eyebrows, around the eye socket, and down his grizzled jaw. Just as I round his chin, his hand reaches up and grabs my wrist and he pulls me on top of him, those dark blue eyes catching mine in the moonlit room.

"I dreamt of you," he whispers as his palm finds my neck.

"I dreamt of you, too." Dane was there, both in my dream and in actuality, as I brought Kayce into this world. I wasn't alone. Although, without him, there would've been nobody by my side. "You were there. You're always there." I lean in and press a gentle kiss to the side of his mouth.

"And I'll always be there. Whatever you need, baby." His hands slide down my back and under my panties, cupping my buttocks. He squeezes and I grind against him. His length hard against my core.

And while I know I don't need to thank this man who would literally give me the clothes off his back, the sudden urge to show him how appreciative I am is overwhelming. My mouth waters as I slide lower, my legs widening to accommodate his thighs.

He watches, his lids drooping as his stomach tightens. "Del, you don't—" Those large hands find my cheek before sliding down to tilt my chin up.

"I know. I want to." As I maneuver his pajama pants over his hips, his cock springs free. It lands thickly against his stomach as I reach overhead and pull off the oversized tee.

My breasts are heavy, the nipples hardening against the air. Dane reaches for me, the pads of his fingers dancing over the soft flesh, and I lean into his touch. Press myself against his palm as he fondles the tightened bud between his fingers.

"*Fuck*, these tits are magnificent," he whispers. I crawl over him again and, once I'm level with his face, lower my chest toward his mouth. He grabs and suckles at one while his fingers massage the other before switching. His saliva makes the perfect lubricant. "Let me fuck 'em, Del. *Please.*" His hips grind upward with need, and I slide back down once again, this time my face stopping just inches above his navel.

I press my chest against his length, my breasts surrounding him fully. Completely. I use my hands to cup the sides and squeeze the heavy flesh tightly against his velvety cock. He thrusts into me, moaning slightly as he sucks air in through his teeth. "*Fuck*, baby."

I match his movements, my stomach taut as he fucks my tits. "I want you in my mouth, Dane." My eyes catch his, holding his gaze.

He nods slightly, his hand finding my cheek again. I sit up and take his length in hand, running my palms up and down the thickness. My heart pounds as I dip lower and draw him into my mouth. The salty tip glides smoothly over my tongue, and I work my jaw open to take him completely until he's hitting the back of my throat. I bob up and down, my eyes watering as I breathe through my nose. But it's worth it for the look on his face.

His eyes glint under heavy lids as his thighs quake beneath my forearms. His breathing is ragged, and yet I hollow my cheeks and swirl my tongue over the tip. One hand steadies the base while the other reaches under and fondles him gently between my thumb and forefinger. He releases a gasp as his cock pulsates in my mouth. "Stroke me, baby," he begs as his hips rock.

My hand slides up and down his saliva-lubed erection as the other continues to press under the root. His breathing goes erratic, and the quaking thighs are now throbbing. "I-I—"

But he doesn't get out the words as I lean down once more and take him in my mouth. *All of him.* He spills into me, hot and fast, and I open my throat to swallow it all. He continues to throb, slowly and then not at all, as I sit up and wipe at the corner of my mouth.

"C'mere," he says sleepily, beckoning me into his chest. I go willingly as the fringes of sleepiness pull at my brain. He presses a kiss to my mouth, one hand wrapping around the base of my head while the other tangles in my hair, and pulls me against his side. "You're amazing, Del."

We stay like that, breathing each other's air, until we fall asleep.

CHAPTER TWENTY-THREE

Delia

Kayce and I wait in the lobby of Marshall's building while Dane retrieves his truck from the underground garage.

"It'll give you time to say a proper goodbye," he insisted when I pleaded to come with.

Dane's right, though. Marshall has come to Oselka twice now, and after this visit, I realize that perhaps I'm becoming more comfortable with the idea of giving Marshall a third chance to get to know his son. After all, he's been respectful of Kayce's and my schedule and has promised to work with me, sans lawyers and family court, to be a part of his son's life.

But I'm still not ready to admit that to Marshall yet. And I definitely don't have my hopes too high, although as I watch Kayce's excited smile, I pray he doesn't get his heart broken.

"Did you have a nice weekend, kiddo?" Marshall's wearing fitted joggers and an expensive name brand hoodie. Fashionable trainers complete his athleisure ensemble. His entire outfit probably cost more than I pay in rent. I swallow and glance down at my own worn sneakers. I haven't had time to work out, let alone the extra cash to purchase new.

"My favorite part was the octopus!" Kayce hugs the stuffed animal that Marshall had surprised him with this morning.

"Because I know how much they mean to you," he'd said. I smiled, my heart warming at the change happening to the man I once thought I'd never see again.

"Of course it was." Marshall winks at me over Kayce's head.

"But I also liked Sue, too!" Prior to his fascination with octopuses, Kayce, like all little boys, loved dinosaurs. Seeing the largest and most complete T. Rex at the Field Museum had been another highlight for him.

"Maybe the next time we go they'll have discovered even *more* bones," Marshall adds.

Kayce turns to me, his eyes shining. "Mom! When can we come back?" My forced smile falters slightly.

But Marshall saves me. "I'm sure your mom will be busy with the wedding plans the next few weeks. Maybe we can set up a plan for your winter break from school. If that works for your mom, that is."

I nod in gratitude just as Dane returns. His comforting presence as he slides his palm along the small of my back has me recalling the details of last night.

And waking up tucked against his chest.

My smile turns genuine as he grabs our bags and returns to the truck just beyond the lobby doors.

Suddenly Kayce darts past me and flings himself against Marshall's lower half, engulfing his legs in a robust hug. Marshall pats him gently on the back before lifting him up, appearing to muster more fatherly affection than I knew he had as he holds Kayce close. "I love you, Dad!" My heart falters, and I struggle to breathe as Marshall doesn't say it back.

I blink as I sling my purse over my shoulder and plaster on that forced smile once more. Because while my brain knows I should love the fact that my child is finally forming a relationship with his father, my heart is breaking as he attaches himself to someone who, at one time, didn't want him. And maybe, once he realizes how intense raising a child is, may decide to back out again.

"All right, buddy, it's time to head out." Marshall sets Kayce down, and I take his hand, gently pulling him back to my side. "Thank you," I say to Marshall as I nudge Kayce to say the same.

And as we walk away from Marshall and toward Dane, who's standing at the passenger side ready to help load Kayce into his booster seat, I suddenly feel like I can breathe easier than I have in days.

"There it is!" I point to the *Welcome to Michigan* sign as we cross over the state line. Kayce claps from the back seat, his octopus plush still snuggled into his lap.

"I'm just glad to be back in a state where the residents can actually drive," Dane adds, his grip finally loosening from the steering wheel.

I chuckle slightly and glance out the window. I, too, feel the relief. As though my body has been thrown in a washing machine and then tumbled dry, I relax into the worn passenger seat.

Just then, my phone dings. I reach into my purse and pull it out, my brow furrowing as I notice Marshall's name on the notification.

"Did we leave something behind?" I murmur to myself as I open the alert.

Dane's gaze slides my way just as my heart lurches into my throat.

I read the message once.

Twice.

And a third time, just because my brain still can't comprehend what I'm seeing.

> *I'm sorry I wasn't brave enough to speak with you face to face. But you know what they say… "The brave man is not he who does not feel afraid, but he who conquers that fear." So that's what I'm doing. I've spoken with my lawyer, and I'll be filing for joint custody of Kayce. I thought you'd like to know before the papers arrive, and I'm being the bigger person by not blindsiding you. I recommend that you also retain a lawyer, and that we have no further communication until the courts sort everything out.*

"What is it?" Dane asks. Only my entire body begins to shake. "Del?" He repeats, patting my leg. "Whatever you forgot, we can replace. Or he can mail it to us?"

I blink back the angry tears that well and force myself to focus on the road ahead. The road to our home. The road that will take me to safety. "H-he promised. He *promised* he wouldn't do this," I whisper, as a single hot tear rolls down my cheek.

"Do what, baby? What's going on?"

"He's filing for joint custody. He's got a lawyer and everything. When he promised he wouldn't!"

Dane glances behind him at Kayce in the back. Then he leans in and whispers, "Are you sure? What does it say?"

I pass him the phone, and while he reads, I try to control my breathing. Only, it's getting harder now as the severity of the situation settles over me. I'm nearly panting, unable to catch my breath.

"Whoa, Del. Breathe." He slows the truck and signals with his blinker before pulling over to the side of the highway.

"What's happening?" Kayce asks from the backseat.

"Nothing, buddy." Dane tosses his own cell phone at Kayce. "Why don't you watch something on my phone, okay?"

"Cool!"

The second Dane slides into park, I leap out of the truck and double over on the side of the road. My stomach rolls as it empties. The hot tears stream down my face, and I gag, cough, and spew snot and spit all over myself.

"I always knew this could happen. But when Marshall promised we'd keep this just between us, I believed him. I'm so stupid!" I sink to my knees and press my hands against the tall grass. "I'm not ready to share him yet. He's *my* son!"

"It's going to be okay." Dane rubs my back, his body protecting mine from the windy chill of Lake Michigan.

I shake my head as I stand, swiping across my face with the back of my hand. "Y-you don't know that, Dane. He's rich. He'll give Kayce whatever he wants, and eventually Kayce will want to live with him. He'll choose Marshall over me and there's nothing I can do." My chest is pounding like I'm having a heart attack, and I can see nothing except my son through the back window of the vehicle. "I never asked him for *anything*— child support, school fees, new shoes— *nothing*! Th-this is going to cost a fortune and I-I—"

"Del, stop this!" Dane grabs my shoulders and pulls me into his arms. Wraps me up in a hug that squeezes my insides. His palm finds the back of my hair and he strokes, tangling in the tresses at the nape of my neck. "I've got you, baby. Kayce's yours." He pulls away and levels me with an intense stare. "Your son. Nothing will change that." His navy eyes bore into mine. Grounding me. "I've got you. I've always got you."

I nod as the tears continue to fall. But my breathing returns to normal after a few moments, and I'm able to make it back into the truck, albeit shakily. Dane watches me the entire time. His hand finds mine over the shifter, and he squeezes.

"I knew his promises meant absolutely nothing, and I still believed him." A sob escapes from my chest. It's gut-wrenching and breaks my heart. "Take me home," I beg as I lean my head against the window. "I just want to go home."

CHAPTER TWENTY-FOUR

Dane

"That's the last of it," I say as I set Kayce's overnight bag and octopus stuffed animal next to the kitchen table in Delia's apartment.

The woman on the couch doesn't look up, her gaze remaining trained on the empty space to the left of the television.

"Del? You okay?" I move to sit beside her, my arm instinctively wrapping around her shoulder as she sags against my weight.

She nods, but as her throat bobs, I know she's not. She's not okay at all.

When we arrived on the outskirts of Oselka, I'd glanced over to find not only Kayce asleep, his head tilted up and mouth wide open, but also Delia snoring softly in the passenger seat. Her hands were curled under her chin as she leaned against the window. I pulled into the alley next to the building, and upon opening my door, Delia startled awake. Her eyes shone brightly in the truck cabin light. "Will you help me carry him up?" she asked quietly, nodding to Kayce in the back. She followed with both my overnight bag and hers, even after my admonishment that I'd get them.

I carefully laid Kayce in his bed while Del removed his shoes and tucked him in, my mind not comprehending that anyone would wish to separate these two for even a single moment.

Delia stirs next to me, pulling me back into the here and now. "I-I should go," I say.

"Don't..." She tilts her head up, those bright blue eyes boring into mine. Sadness pools in them, and I wish I could tell her that I feel the same way. I don't want another man in Kayce's life either. I want to be the only man, the only father figure, in his life.

But I'm not.

So while she's hurting more, I'm still hurting, too.

"Do you want to talk about it?" My hand finds a russet strand of her hair, and I twist it between my fingers.

"I thought all of this was behind us. My parents *gave* that deadbeat our address. They told him exactly where to find me. And now this?" She shakes her head. "I don't want to think about any of it, Dane. I'm so tired of thinking. Of worrying." I don't want to ask what she worries about and ruin the mood, but if she told me, I'd surely wake up tomorrow ready to fix every problem she has.

I swallow, my nerve endings firing with anticipation as I wait for her to continue. This line is thin, and I don't want to make the wrong move. I've done it before. Scared her away and made her shut down. And dear God, I can't let that happen again. Not now. Not when we're finally making headway.

"Del, I—" But before I can continue, she stands from the couch and links her hand with mine, pulling me up as well.

"Stay with me."

And like a man in love, I follow willingly.

Delia's bedroom door closes with a soft *click*. She flicks the lock before turning to me, her long hair falling gently down her back.

A hum of desire surges through my chest and settles in the base of my spine. I itch to reach out, take her in my arms, and undress her slowly, but I'm like a predator stalking his prey. I don't want to scare her.

She approaches me quickly, and I immediately realize that perhaps the roles are reversed. Perhaps she's the hunter, and I'm the defenseless deer. She's ready to take what she wants, what she needs, and God help me, but I'm willing to give her all of it.

Her arms wrap around my neck as she pulls me down and captures my lips with hers. My palms find her hips, her curves pressing against me and edging me back against the bed. I settle onto the mattress and try to pull her on my lap, but she hesitates.

"Are you sure?" I ask, although I needn't bother as she lifts her sweater over her head and tosses it to the floor.

Then her thighs are bracketing mine as she climbs onto my lap, searing me with the feel of her soft skin against my palms. Her perfectly round tits are at eye level, and I bury my face between the flesh before sliding my tongue along the curve of each globe. Her skin smells like vanilla and some kind of flower. I could live here in the crevice between her breasts. Happy and satisfied by the warm flesh. I drag the pad of my forefinger up the curve of her spine. She arches into me and releases a gasp.

"Del, I'm not going to be able to stop…" I exhale against her bra as my tongue traces the lace.

"I don't want you to stop." She leans down and presses soft kisses against my neck. Plush lips flutter against taut flesh that throbs as my heart races. Then she reaches down and raises the hem of my tee over my head, discarding it on the floor with her own.

Bare-chested, I grip her ass and roll us onto the bed. With myself on top, I press her into the mattress with my weight, desperately resisting the urge to grind my hard cock against her softness.

Our mouths find each other, and we're tongue and teeth, exploring and delving into one another as our hands caress and touch. I push her bra up, exposing her tits before leaning down and sucking the plump flesh between my lips. She writhes against me, her breath coming in quick gasps as I flick my tongue over the budded nipple.

"Th-the other one," she begs as her hips grind up into mine.

"Beg for it." My mouth continues to assault her flesh while her fingers dive into my hair, pulling against the strands and guiding me to the left.

"Please. *Please*…" Her skin glimmers with my saliva in the moonlight that trickles through the window, and I eagerly pull the neglected nipple into my mouth to match its sister. She pulls air through her teeth as I suckle the tightened flesh until the nipple is as hard as glass.

She unbuttons her jeans, and I watch with fascination as she wiggles the denim down over her hips. A black lacy pair of panties greets me, and my mouth waters as I eye the damp spot at the top of her cleft.

"Already so wet for me, baby?" I run my finger through her slit as my cock presses painfully against my boxers.

She nods, all doe-eyed with her bottom lip tucked under her top teeth. "I-I've wanted this for so long…"

"Me too," I mumble as my hands drag along her curves. Under her breasts, across her stomach, and around her thighs to her ass. I've dreamt of this for years and years. And even now, I know that nothing will ever be as good as this. For the rest of my life I'll think back on this day as the peak of my existence. The day I finally got to be with the woman I've loved for six years.

She leans forward and unhooks her bra, disentangling her arms from the straps, but all I can focus on is how badly I want to lick along her hip bone and use my teeth to rip the thin fabric from her body.

So that's exactly what I do.

Chapter Twenty-Five

Delia

"Oh my god," I exclaim as Dane's teeth nip against my hip bone. His breath tickles along the sensitive skin, and my nipples tighten to the point I'm certain they could cut glass. Then the sound of fabric tearing, mixed with the feel of his warm breath on my clit, has me glancing down to see my panties in shreds. "Did you—"

"Fuck, Del, I couldn't stop myself." I kick off the torn underwear as he stands and dips his hand into his joggers, his forearm flexing as he eyes my wet center. "Lemme have a taste. *Please.*"

My chest tightens, and I nod. "But first, lose it all. I want to watch." That tightness instantly dissipates as he lowers everything, and I'm left staring at him. I knew he was big. I knew in Chicago. But seeing him now—standing over me and so close to my entrance— has my core weeping with need.

"You want to watch me fuck my hand while I eat that pussy, huh?" He smirks and kneels onto the mattress, his hand on his shaft pumping slowly as my eyes track every move. "Lean back." I follow his orders willingly as he dips down and presses his nose against me. "Spread your legs."

My muscles go taut as his tongue slides through my slit before settling at the top of my thighs where that sensitive nub begs to be touched. He doesn't keep me waiting as he pulls it between his lips, gently sucking and laving against it until my thighs are quaking. My gaze focuses on the muscles of his forearms. The movement of his wrist. The way his fingers stroke up and down his length. I'm fascinated and so turned on that I can't help myself as my core starts pulsating and my hips rock upward, seeking friction. Seeking *him*. My toes curl as he continues to lick and suck, but all I can focus on is the way his fingers tighten over the head of his cock, fucking against that fleshy web between his thumb and forefinger.

Dane sits up suddenly, and before I can be too disappointed, he swipes his length through my wetness, soaking himself from root to tip. I gasp as he continues to lap up my desire. His palm squelches as he thrusts into it. My hips buck harder, and my hands find his temples, grinding against his jaw as my eyes track his hand. Up and down. Slowly then slightly faster. The sheen of my wetness coats his cock as he pumps into his fist harder and harder.

And suddenly, that knot at the base of my spine bursts, and I'm coming, my thighs pulsing as my eyes roll back into my head. My fingers pull at his hair, yanking him into my center as I ride the wave of ecstasy. My pussy pulsates, and just when I think it's over—when my vision returns to Dane's forearm still flexing—a new wave crashes against me, and I roll over the edge again.

"Fuck, fuck!" I gasp as I grind against his tongue. He never lets up, never slows. He continues sucking and licking me until I'm wrung out. Completely spent. My limbs floppy against the bed and my eyes droopy with exhaustion.

But even though my body's slowly returning to Earth, my mind and heart are still eager for more. I grab Dane's cock, pushing his hand out of the way, and gently pull him toward me. He obliges just as I sit up on my elbows. My mouth waters, and I lower to him—my tongue sliding along the velvety skin. I taste myself on him, and it spurs me onward until I'm pushing him back onto the mattress, his cock standing at attention before me. I take him fully into my mouth, sucking him down as far as I can go until he hits the back of my throat.

"I need to be inside you, baby. *Now*," he whispers as his hips thrust up and into my cheek. As much as I'd like to taunt him, tease him, make him wait, my body's ready for round two. I want him inside me just as much, and I'm done denying myself.

I climb over his thick thighs, my breasts hanging at his eye level. Before I can be self-conscious, Dane palms both of them and suckles first one, then the other. "Fuck, I could get off just from your tits, Del. They're magnificent."

I smile and raise to my knees as I position myself over him. "Do I need a condom?" he asks.

I shake my head. "IUD."

He grips himself, sliding through my wetness again as he lines up at my entrance. My eyes meet his, those pupils as round as quarters as I slowly lower myself onto him. Inch by inch, my pussy takes him wholly, and I bottom out with a gasp.

My face breaks into a smile as our eyes still hold, if only because this feels perfect. It's been so long that I can't even remember, but I know I'll remember this moment, this night, with Dane forever.

"Slow, Del. Slow…" he murmurs as I roll my hips and feel the fullness. We're connected. We're one. And as much as I want to ride his cock and come again, we need to get comfortable first. So I lean forward, press myself against him, and grind onto his thick cock while my nipples drag across his chest. Every inch of him is taut, and I love the feeling of being in control. But I also love knowing that, at any second, Dane could toss me over onto my back and fuck me into next week. His breathing is shaky, so I know he's tempering himself.

But a part of me wants to make him snap. Drive him to that unrestrained desire I know is inside. I saw it that night when he ate me out on his kitchen table. And I want to see it again.

I sit up straight and run my fingers through my hair, arching my back. I let out a moan as I grind on his cock. *Hard.* I lower my hands to my chest and roll my nipples through my fingers until the buds are hard. And then I reach back and stroke his balls.

"Fuck. *Fuck,*" he moans. His eyes widen, and I know I've won as he leans forward and grabs me. We roll together, and it's like a dance of limbs until my back presses into the mattress and he rises over me. "I told you to go slow, baby."

I smirk as he takes control, pressing so deep into me that I gasp, and then nearly pulling out, repeating the in and out over and over, but incrementally going slower each time until I can't take it anymore.

My legs wrap around his ass, and I grab his hips, pulling him into me as I beg for more. "I-I'm coming!" Only then does he speed up, slamming into me so hard and fast that my orgasm intensifies, and I feel a gush between my legs as I explode.

"Jesus Christ, Del, come all over my cock—come all over my cock," he begs as he leans down, captures my lips with his, and his body stiffens.

We ride the wave together, our bodies connected from head to toe. And after what seems like eternity, we both exhale, our lips slowly pulling apart, and come back down to Earth.

I'm stunned. Speechless. My arms and legs are like jelly, and my body's been zapped of all energy. I stare at the man who's lying next to me, his chest heaving and his eyes staring into my own, and as I blink and my mind returns to equilibrium, I wonder why it took so long to realize…

I'm in love with Dane fucking Lukes.

As much as I want to curl up in bed and avoid the entire world, the life of a mother allows for none of that. I basically drag Kayce out of bed on Monday morning and shove sugared cereal down his gullet while he zones out on his iPad. I'm attempting to look half-presentable and smearing concealer under my eyes when his angry footsteps interrupt me.

"I forgot to tell you. I need to wear stripes today." There's either a smear of dried milk or toothpaste on his upper lip.

I press my mouth into a firm line and traipse into his room, searching high and low for one of the two striped shirts he owns. I locate the first one crammed in his drawer and extricate it—wrinkles and all. As I yank off his Ninja Turtle tee and replace it with the Waldo-esque red-and-white shirt, I realize too late that this shirt is much too small.

"Shit."

"Shit," he repeats with a mischievous gleam in his eye.

I don't even have the energy to scold him. Instead he gets the "mom eye" before his tiny cheeks turn red and he mutters "Sorry."

"Help me find the blue-and-gray striped shirt that you got from Nana."
I take the closet while he digs through his drawers.

Nothing.

"Oh!" he proclaims. "I know where it is!" I watch, horrified, as he crawls under his bed and pulls the long-sleeved tee from the depths of the darkness. A bright orange Cheeto dust stain coats the front, like it's been tagged with graffiti.

"Absolutely not," I inform him as I grab the shirt and toss it into his dirty clothes basket. "You'll just have to go without stripes today, buddy."

"But *Mooooom!*"—he wails like a dog—"*everyone* will be wearing stripes. I *have* to wear stripes, too!"

I glance at my watch and notice we're running short on time. My makeup's only half done, I'm barely dressed, and my son is shirtless with his arms folded over his baby-smooth chest.

"One striped shirt doesn't fit, and the other is dirty. Put your Ninja Turtle tee back on and go clean up your breakfast or you'll miss the bus." I square my shoulders and match his stance. Two can play this game.

He stomps his foot. "I hate it here. I want to live with my dad!"

The world tilts. It's like I've been slapped, the way his words hit me. I'm not sure if I stumble back or if the power of his anger has literally pushed me away, but my back finds the wall. I blink as the tears cloud my vision. It's the first time my son, my sweet child, has ever told me he hated anything other than broccoli and watching *Frozen* with me.

I knew this day would come, but it doesn't make it any easier.

Before I can calm myself and allow my heart to grieve for this monumental moment, my cavewoman brain reacts and grabs the too small striped top.

"You want to wear a shirt that's too small? Fine!" I pull the toddler-sized top over his mop of curls and yank his arms through the sleeves. His belly is showing, as are the entirety of his wrists. But at this point, I don't care. "There!" I snarl. "Now go clean up your breakfast."

The defiant glare he sends my way has me nearly roaring like Sue the T. Rex, but as I stand in his empty room, breathing deeply through my nose to calm my nerves, I can't help but replay his words.

I want to live with my dad.

CHAPTER TWENTY-SIX

Dane

I add one last phone number to the list of lawyers that I've accrued for Delia. Setting it aside, an alert pops up on my phone.

Tomorrow, December 5

I bite my lip and grab the notebook once more, flipping it back a few pages to the menu. I've been planning and preparing for several weeks. I check the details once more. A salad made with homemade Caesar dressing—complete with anchovies that I'd ordered fresh from Chicago. The city may be a heaping pile of dung, but it's got a hell of a foodie scene, and getting fresh anchovies to the middle of nowhere, Michigan, would've been impossible. The salad will pair perfectly with bacon-wrapped chicken cutlets. The finale: a decadent no-bake panna cotta drizzled with fresh raspberries.

The last few ingredients were delivered while we were out of town, and I'll be spending the rest of the day prepping.

I jog downstairs and flick the restaurant lights on. Surprisingly, Crystal did a great job holding down the fort while we were in Chicago. Everything is stocked and cleaned. She may not have her life together most days, but she's certainly able to prove me wrong when I least suspect it.

I pour a heaping amount of coffee grounds into the machine, expecting that Del will be ready for her caffeine fix momentarily. Last night was amazing. Better than amazing. Words can't describe what it was like, and as I recall the flashes of memory, my cock strains against my zipper. I adjust myself and fetch two mugs.

Ultimately, I didn't want Kayce to see me sneaking out in the morning, so I kissed Del goodnight and slept at my own place. Besides, she needed to rest. To think. And as much as I wanted to be there for her, I knew I had to tread lightly in this situation.

After all, Kayce isn't my son, no matter how much I want him to be. No matter how much anger I, too, feel at this situation, I know Del feels it multiplied by a million. And until I can figure out what to say—how to fix this—it's best that I be patient.

This morning, I've already reached out to several acquaintances and did a little bit of Internet research to find a list of custody lawyers in the greater Michigan area. I plan on sharing my findings with her.

Just then, Kayce trudges down the stairs. His hair's a mess, coat unzipped, and I'm pretty sure he's wearing a shirt I haven't seen in years. He plods up the bus steps, and it's only a few moments later that Delia enters the restaurant.

She, too, looks rough—although I'd never vocalize that. Purple shadows ring under her eyes, which still appear puffy.

As she approaches the counter, I hastily grab a mug and pour the coffee. "Rough morning, huh?" I pass the hot cup across to her as she narrows her eyes.

"Yeah," she mutters quietly as she settles in. She wraps her hands around the mug.

"So, uh, I did some research and made a list of custody lawyers." I reach for the notebook and flip to the appropriate section. I rip the page out and pass it across to her. "I can help you call, if you want. I'll have time between prepping for the Rotary Club event."

She glances at the paper and then folds it in two, shoving it into her purse. "Thanks, Dane. I appreciate it." She reaches for me as she slowly smiles. It doesn't reach her eyes, but I can tell there's effort.

I take her hand in mind. "What else do you need, Del? I'm here. You know I'm here. Tell me what you need, baby."

She inhales slowly and looks up at the ceiling. "Nothing. Honestly. I mean, this was always a possibility. It's just, the longer he stayed out of our lives, the less likely it became." She takes a swig of her coffee. "And I'm just so mad at my parents, too."

"Do you..." I pause, thinking of the best way to word the next sentence. "Do you think we should postpone... everything?"

Her brow wrinkles. "The wedding? No..." she says slowly. "No." More forceful now. "If anything, it will show the judge that Kayce needs to stay here full-time in a two-parent household." She blushes. "Not that we've discussed the logistics of where we'll be..."

I swallow the knot in my throat. I don't have the heart to ask any other questions, because I honestly want the same thing Del does: a home with her and Kayce.

"Besides, it'll show my parents that they were wrong to share my information with Marshall."

I let go of her hand. "Right.. and that's the only reason we're still doing this..."

She shrugs and finishes up her coffee. "Well, yeah. That and now this custody situation."

I suppress the hurt that seizes my gut. *Now's not the time*, I tell myself. She's going through a lot. Besides, I know there's something more there.

We both do. I just need to be patient and be there for her, as I've always done. "Hey," I call out as she's heading out the door. "Don't forget about tomorrow..." I grab her mug and start wiping down the counter.

"Tomorrow?" Her eyebrow cocks as she turns back.

"The Rotary Club event. 6 p.m. You still good to help me out?"

She chuckles a little and shrugs. "Oh, yeah. I remember. December 5th. Right."

And then she's gone.

"Dane! The food is delicious," Marigold Fraser crows from her position at the head of the main table.

Everyone around her nods and gushes with agreement, complimenting everything from the salad to the crispness of the hickory-smoked bacon and juicy chicken. I smile warmly, my cheeks and forehead certainly covered in a sheen of sweat.

And then I glance at the door for the twelfth time.

Where the hell is Del?

She was supposed to be here forty minutes ago to help set up. I'd texted once—only once—because I wasn't going to be that person.

That person that begs to be important. Noticed. Loved.

But as the minutes ticked by and the club members grew restless, I knew I had to begin serving. Alone.

"I'd love some more dressing, Dane." Mr. Jacobson holds his fork aloft, and I nod, forcing a smile onto my face.

I grab the homemade Caesar dressing and hurriedly return to the jeweler's side. Only, as my eyes glance back to the table overloaded with food, I notice I've carelessly knocked over one of the fuel canisters, and now the tablecloth is aglow.

"Shit!" I set the dressing bowl down next to Mr. Jacobson with a loud clatter and rush back to the buffet table. Using one of the chafing dish covers, I smother the flame and release another tirade of curses.

It's only when I turn, the flame long gone but a giant singed hole left in the tablecloth, that I notice the group's eyes on me.

"Well," Marigold Fraser frowns at her table mates, "I suppose we should finish up our meal and begin with new business."

I retreat behind the buffet and begin packing away the remaining entrees. I carefully set out the dessert, the panna cotta still looking delectable even without the garnish yet added. And as I bring around the delicacy, offering each person a drizzle of fresh raspberry syrup, only two members meet my eyes.

My dreams of owning the lot on Miller's Run Avenue are definitely as toasted as the tablecloth.

CHAPTER TWENTY-SEVEN

Delia

Before I can open the message and call, another text appears on the screen.

Despite the mood I've been in, a chuckle bursts from my chest, and I press the *send* button. It doesn't even ring before Savannah's screaming into the device. I lift my phone away from my ear and cringe at the squeal.

"I'm engaged!" The sound of the ocean's waves are in the background.

"Wow, congratulations," I say, careful not to be too loud lest I wake Kayce. I sit up and cross my legs under myself. "Tell me everything!"

I hear the creak of a door and soft footsteps, the sound of the ocean fading to nothing. "I don't know, everything is such a blur! One minute we were taking a walk on the beach after dinner, and the next he was dropping to his knee and asking me to marry him. Can you believe it, Del?"

I giggle. "Well, yeah, I can believe it. You two have been living together for, what, four years?"

"Five, but who's counting?"

"Well I'm glad he finally did it. I'm happy for both of you."

"Listen, I know you've got a lot going on with Marshall, but I need you to be my maid of honor, okay?"

"No matter how deep my depression is, nothing could stop me, Sav. Of course I'll be there for you just like you'll be there for me!" As teenagers we'd always dreamed of being each other's maid of honor, and now that dream is becoming a reality. If nothing else, at least one thing is working out. "Can you believe we're both getting married? We always dreamed of this!" I suffuse joy into my voice.

"Well, right. I mean, my engagement ring actually means something, but yeah..."

My blood runs cold. I chuckle awkwardly into the phone as my body tenses. "What do you mean, your engagement ring actually means something?"

Savannah sucks through her teeth. "Oh, you know. Just that Jack and I... Our engagement is *real*."

I recoil as though I've been hit with a pillow. "M-my engagement is real, Sav. I have the real ring to prove it. Dane got down on one knee. Just like Jack. And I said yes."

"Oh, of course... that's not what I meant."

I swallow over the lump in my throat. "So what did you mean then?"

"Nothing. Just drop it."

"That's a little hard now that I know there's something you want to say. So say it." My voice is harsh. Devoid of emotion.

"Ugh," she growls into the phone. "Listen, I didn't want to get into this with you *tonight*. Not on *my* night, okay?"

I don't say anything. I just sit and wait for the other shoe to drop.

"It's not like your wedding is actually going to happen, Del. I mean, your engagement is all *pretend*. Isn't it? There's no way you're going to have the guts to go through with this whole fake marriage thing. And then you'll just be right back to where you were before."

My vision swims, and the backs of my eyes prick. "You know, having a kid at—"

She growls into the phone again, interrupting me. "And there you go, using Kayce as an excuse for your situation."

"What are you talking about? Where is this coming from?"

"You had Kayce when you were twenty-four, Delia. Not sixteen. You weren't a teenage mother. You have a college degree, for crying out loud. So stop acting like you can't live your life and do what you want. If you want to marry Dane, then marry Dane. If you don't, then don't. But don't do it because your parents pressured you to find a father for your son."

"I can't believe you're—"

"Just stop playing *pretend* if you want me to take you seriously, Del. You may be lying to everyone else, but be honest with *yourself*."

My tears blur everything and then immediately tip over, rolling down my cheeks. My nose stuffs up, and I sniffle loudly over the phone.

"Are you there?" she asks, not unkindly. "I didn't want to get into a fight with you. I love you. You know that."

"Yeah..." I respond quietly as I hold in the sobs that threaten to wrack my body. Not my best friend, too. Everything is going wrong, and I'm flailing in the water. Alone in the dark.

"Anyway, I gotta go. *I love you*," she repeats.

"Yeah..." My brain is short-circuiting. "You too."

And before she can continue, I click *end*.

I frown at the *closed* sign on the door. "Mom?" Kayce tugs on my sleeve, drawing my attention to the bus's open door.

"Oh, right. Sorry, buddy." I press a kiss to the top of his curly head and usher him toward the steps of the bus.

But my mind is on the empty restaurant to my right. Where is Dane? Just then, my phone rings. I glance at the caller ID and see my mother's name flash across the screen.

Great. Except with the mood I'm in, I'm ready for a fight. I refuse to ignore it, so I swipe to accept and go in for the kill.

"*What*?" My growl reverberates off the brick building behind me.

"Is that any way to greet your mother? I assume you meant to say hello or good morning."

"You caught me before I've had coffee," I manage to eke through clenched teeth. I glance both ways and cross the street quickly, avoiding a pothole and oncoming car. There's a biting chill in the air this morning.

Maybe Dane is under the weather. As I reach the other side of the street safely, I glance back at the building. My gut flutters with unease. Should I go check on him?

"Are you even listening to me, Delia?"

"No," I answer honestly. "And why should I, Mother? Don't you have anything to say to me?"

The line goes silent for the briefest of moments. "Oh my God, Delia..."

My fist clenches as my heart pounds. "Here we go," I mutter to myself—

Just as my mother asks, "Are you pregnant *again*?"

I literally snort out a laugh, my breath visible in the chilled air. "Are you serious right now? No, I'm not *pregnant*, Mother."

"Then what do I need to say to you, exactly?"

"An apology would be lovely." My heels dig into the sidewalk as I approach the bank.

"An apology? For what? Setting the date and booking a beautiful church for your wedding? Goodness, what horrible and unlovable parents you have."

I shake my head as the backs of my eyes prick. "Ha, yeah right. And no, that's not it. Although *thanks* for booking a venue that my fiancé and I hadn't even decided upon."

"Then what exactly have I done now to deserve your ire?"

I chuff once more. "You're the one who told Marshall. About me. My *address*. My *marriage*. And now—because of *you*—he's suing for joint custody of Kayce."

The line goes silent. I wait like a sprinter for the pop of a gun. Like a boxer for the bell.

Finally, she says, "What are you talking about, Delia? I, for one, haven't been in communication with that man other than forwarding Kayce's birthday cards he sends to the house. Why on *Earth* would you think I had anything to do with him?"

I lean against the bank building, the limestone scraping against my coat. My throat feels tight and my toes tingle. "Well, if it wasn't you, it was surely my father, then."

An uneasy laugh echoes in my ear. "Like your father wants anything to do with him either. Please, Delia. Be serious."

My brow crinkles as I attempt to make sense of the puzzle. If my parents didn't say anything to Marshall... didn't give out my address or make him aware of my life... then who did?

I close the door to the oven and set the timer on the microwave to thirty-five minutes. I reread the recipe on my phone one last time, a sense of purpose and calm settling over me for the first time in days.

"Kayce!" I holler down the hallway. "I'm going to invite Dane to dinner. You good for a few minutes?"

"Yep!" He continues making smashing noises with his mouth, and the telltale sound of metal clanging against metal hits my ears. I swear, when Dane gave Kayce his old case of Matchbox cars, I never knew the gift would be so important. Kayce loves nothing more than cars. Except maybe his stuffed octopus.

I pocket my phone and bend to check the chicken and rice dish bubbling in the oven. Everything looks good, so after folding the towel and hanging it on the rack, I hurry to the front door and practically skip across the hallway before knocking on Dane's apartment.

Not only had I reached out to a family lawyer on my lunch break today, but I'd also found the perfect wedding dress in a thrift shop two towns over. When I saw the listing online, I knew I had to try it on. Luckily, the small shop owner was willing to hold it through the weekend.

My heart hammers in my chest as I eagerly wait for Dane to open the door.

I knock again, my knuckles stinging at the contact with the cold door. The chill of early winter has set in as the last leaves fall. I bounce on my socked toes to keep myself warm.

When Dane still doesn't answer after the third knock, I pull out my phone and, before I can swipe up and open the text messaging app, I notice the date.

December 6th.

Fuck. I was supposed to help Dane with his event last night.

My blood runs cold—colder than the temperature as the sun dips below the horizon. Disregarding the messaging app, I click into the phone and dial Dane's number. It rings and rings, but there's no answer.

I don't bother leaving a voicemail because what can I actually say?

I'm sorry I was such a piece of shit, and that the one time you needed me, I completely forgot because I was too self-involved to care about anyone but myself.

Fuck! This time I scream it aloud, the curse echoing off the limestone walls of the building.

I glance back at my own apartment door and ensure it's closed before I race downstairs to the restaurant. I fling open the door and find Crystal, her hip cocked against the counter as she slides her thumb over her own device.

She startles when I rush in. "Where's Dane? D-did he say where he was going when he left?"

Crystal's brow furrows and she chomps loudly on her gum. "Um, let me think."

I wait, my heart racing a mile a minute, while she places her hands on her hips and looks up at the ceiling.

I'm just about to tackle her, shake her, do anything to bring about some response, when her face brightens. "Oh, yeah! He said he was going to Miller's Run Avenue."

"What's on Miller's Run Avenue?" The town limits stretch just one block beyond, and there's not much out that way except for a vacant building that used to be a liquor store... or something. It's been abandoned since before I moved to town.

"You're kidding," Crystal says as she narrows her eyes at me. "That's the location Dane's been wanting to move to for, like, *years*."

"New location...?" I can't believe how stupid I've been. How selfish and self-important. Dane's had plans beyond me. Beyond Kayce. Beyond being my safety net. And all this time I've been completely ignoring what he needed.

Freedom away from my issues.

I nod as tears prick the backs of my eyes. I blink rapidly to clear them away and sniffle. "Thanks, Crystal."

"Want me to tell him you stopped by? He should be back anytime now that it's getting dark." Her gaze goes to the windows and the setting sun.

"No. No," I repeat. "Don't tell him I was here."

Chapter Twenty-Eight

Delia

I dump a pile of last night's chicken and rice into a Tupperware container and toss it into my lunch bag along with a brown-spotted banana and a can of Coke from the fridge.

"Mom? I'm going to be late!" Kayce hurries me from the front door where he waits with his shoes and book bag, ready to go.

"I'm coming, bud." I glance at the dusty coffee maker in the corner of the kitchen. I can't remember the last time I used it, but as I consider firing it up for the first time in forever over stopping at Dane's, my chest tightens.

I don't like him avoiding me. Or me avoiding him. Whatever's going on... I don't like it.

"Mom!"

"All right, all right." I hoist my purse over my shoulder and zip the lunch bag before taking the stairs slowly. There's a palpable nip in the air, and I pull Kayce's beanie over his ears. "Make sure you don't lose your gloves or hat at recess, okay?" As we hit the sidewalk, I press a kiss to my fingers and lovingly tap his cheek as he climbs the steps to the bus.

I stand, watching the bus pull away, while I work up the nerve to step inside Dane's. I know he's in there. I can see the light streaming onto the sidewalk. If only—

"Hey..." His presence at my side startles me, and I nearly yelp as my hand covers my chest.

"*Jesu*—" I look him up and down. The rings under his eyes are noticeable, as is the shaggy growth along his jaw. How have I never noticed? Are my problems causing Dane to worry? Am I the reason he looks like he hasn't slept or shaved?

"Sorry," he murmurs as he indicates the bucket of salt-melt he's holding. "Just tossing a little down in case it gets icy."

I step to the side as he sprinkles the crystals onto the slick pavement. My breath puffs into the air between us as his does the same. Mixing together with all the things I want to say. "C-could I get a cup of coffee?" I mentally berate myself. Here I am asking for more from this man who's only ever done everything for me. "I mean, I can get it myself if you're busy out here."

A small smile lifts at his lips. "No, I'm done." He sets down the bucket, and I follow him inside. I take a seat while he slides behind the counter and retrieves a mug and then pours.

"None for you this morning?" I cradle the mug in my palms.

He shakes his head. "I've had two already. Long night..."

"Dane, I-I'm so sorry. I forgot about the Rotary Club dinner." My eyes meet his, and my chest tightens. The one man who has— and would continue— to do anything for me and I've royally fucked it up. "There's no excuse. I am the worst."

He leans back, putting space between us, and crosses his arms over his chest. Then he nods slowly, lips pressed together as he looks down at his shoes. "You're not the worst, Delia," he sighs. Those navy eyes meet mine and I break. My heart shatters into a million pieces. I let him down. Just like I've done to every man I relied on in my life.

The coffee sits untouched between us. I don't even want it. All I want to do is jump over the counter and beg Dane to hold me—to look at me like he did before. Before he realized that I am a complete fuckup.

I want to tell him about Savannah. About the dress I've found. Ask him if he still wants to do this all with me. Be my safety net, my rock, and my best friend.

But instead, I push away my coffee, give him a small smile, and tell him to have a good day as I leave.

I turn left and then right, assessing my silhouette in the mirror. The ivory gown fits me like a glove. The delicate laced bodice clings to my chest just so and, as I run my fingers over the dress, I still can't believe I've messed up the whole situation.

"Mom, can we go yet?" Kayce lays sprawled across the divan behind me, his grimy shoes pressing against the upholstery.

"No. And get your feet off the couch," I hiss at him. I return to looking at myself in the mirror, transfixed by the woman in front of me.

My hair looks flat and thin. When was the last time I actually washed it? There are dark half-circles under my eyes and my face is pale. Lifeless. My eyes dull. Frankly, I've looked better.

But I avoid my facial reflection and, instead, focus on the dress.

My idea of a wedding has changed over the last six years, but the dress and how it would make me feel never wavered.

This is it. This is the dress. I fetch my phone from my purse and snap a few pictures and, after only a moment's hesitation, send one to Savannah.

After all, this may be the dream dress, but I'd hardly call wedding dress shopping with my six year old son my dream.

The response is immediate.

> *Holy shit…*

> *I'm going to cry!*

> *It's perfect.*

I smile at the slew of texts. Even if things haven't quite returned to normal, I know this moment trumps any anger or animosity either of us feels.

I type out a response.

> *I don't even know if he still wants to marry me, but at least I'll have this dress to comfort me.*

> *What do you mean?*

I realize I haven't filled Savannah in on the many ways in which typical Delia has screwed up. So I take a deep breath and hit *send* on my phone. It rings once before my best friend picks up.

"That dress is gorgeous, and if you don't get it right now, I'm calling the shop and buying it for you," she says before I can even get out a hello.

I chuckle. "I'm getting the dress. But…" How do I explain everything that's gone wrong?

"Before you start catastrophizing and thinking you've done something wrong, I need to apologize, Del. I'm so sorry I was such a horrible friend the other night. I just..." She breathes deeply into the phone, and I step off the dais and return to the dressing room. "I just don't want to see you jump into something—a *marriage*—only to make your parents satisfied. I know you've got all this trauma around them and their expectations, and I only want you to be happy."

"Thanks," I respond slowly.

"And if that includes a fake engagement to Dane, then I hope it's enough for you. But you *deserve* love, Del. *Real* love."

There's a gentle knock on the dressing room door. "Ma'am, have you made a decision?" The elderly shopkeeper's voice has me cutting Savannah's conversation short, and I toss my phone back into my bag with a promise to see her soon.

I open the door and spy Kayce on the divan, his feet now firmly planted on the floor. I swallow the uncertainty a I catch my reflection again. Savannah's been right this whole time. I've been using my son, my past, my trauma as a reason to avoid living my life. I've been too scared to take the leap, get the guy, and have it all—not only as a mother, but as a woman with dreams and goals. "I'll take it," I announce as I peek at myself once more in the mirror, my smile finally blooming.

"I cleared out a drawer for you," I say to the man standing in the doorway to my bedroom as I indicate the empty compartment.

He smiles, although the joy doesn't reach his eyes, and nods before traipsing over to the wooden dresser, his hand lingering on the decorative knob. His eyes trail over the empty recess before catching on mine. "Thanks. That means a lot."

I bite my lip and lean back on my bed. He sets his overnight bag on the floor and starts placing his neatly folded clothing into the drawer. "Is it enough?" I ask as the pile gets higher.

He glances at me. Those navy eyes flash in the early evening light from the window. "It's fine." He turns away. "But I'll just take the couch, you know."

My heart sinks into my gut. Of course.

I stand and move toward the doorway, lingering as my hand trails over the fading woodwork. "We have dinner," I murmur.

He sighs heavily and finally looks my way once more with eyes that remind me of the lake. The depths of which I'll never explore because I've screwed everything up.

"Mama!" Kayce's voice echoes down the hallway, and before I know it, he's leaping onto the bed and jumping up and down frantically. Dane chuckles. The mirth finally reaching his eyes for real this time.

I grab my lanky all-knees-and-bony-elbows boy and set him onto the ground. "You hungry, buddy?"

"Yeah!" Dane hoists Kayce high into the air. He squeals and giggles. "I'm gonna get chicken nuggets!"

"You're going to turn into a chicken nugget," Dane responds as he stalks out of the room, Kayce lifted over his shoulder.

And as I follow behind, I only hope I can hold everything together for the next few days and not fuck up too much.

CHAPTER TWENTY-NINE

Dane

The drive to the Boatyard is filled with an awkward silence that even the newest pop song blasting from the radio can't fix. Kayce babbles to himself in the backseat as he rolls his toy cars along the window frame. And yet Delia and I both stare into the sinking sunlight on the horizon ahead of us.

As we pull into the restaurant, Delia points out Jack and Savannah's rental car, and I park close by. The black sedan with tinted windows fits perfectly with the other vehicles in the lot. All sleek and expensive. My beat-up truck is definitely an anomaly, but that doesn't bother me. It's paid off, along with the rest of my debts, and I officially signed the closing paperwork on the Miller's Run Avenue lot this morning.

If only Del had been there to celebrate with me.

Instead, I'd returned to the diner and fixed myself a nice salad and fresh batch of garlic bread for lunch.

As much as I want to forgive her for forgetting the Rotary Club dinner, there's a part of me that's still upset. It hurts to know that she and Kayce are both at the top of my list. I can't even begin to guess where I'm located on hers.

It clearly isn't as high as I'd thought.

We meet Jack and Savannah in the lobby, and our group is quickly ushered to our table. As soon as we're seated, Jim, the restaurant owner, comes out and shakes my hand. He's known me for years. Ever since his son, Reggie, and I played on the same baseball team as youths.

"Trina, make sure this table gets the best bottle of wine. On the house," he tells our server with a fatherly pat on my back.

"Oh, that's not necess—" I begin, but he holds his hand up to stop me before I can continue.

"I just heard the news. Congratulations, you two! When's the wedding?" His eyes dance between mine and Delia's.

Del clears her throat. "Um, this weekend," she murmurs as two pink circles dot her cheeks.

"So soon?" Jim's eyes beam with curiosity. "Ah! A shotgun wedding, no?" He slaps me on the back.

"No, no. Nothing like that," I respond as I take Delia's hand protectively. I don't like the insinuation here. That she's some loose woman forcing me down the aisle. Trapping me into being a father. "We just didn't want to wait to start our lives together." I circle my thumb against her wrist and she turns, smiling at me as her eyes shine brighter in the romantic restaurant lighting.

"Well congratulations either way. And enjoy your dinner." He ruffles Kayce's hair and nods to Jack and Sav before returning to his place behind the host stand.

"That was awkward," Sav mutters under her breath as she opens her menu. Jack snorts, and my hackles rise.

"It's one of the occupational hazards of living in a small town. Everyone knows your business," Delia adds. "But it also means that people truly care about one another. Jim's known Dane since he was a kid, and he's simply looking out for him."

I blink at the woman next to me. How'd she know about Jim? I don't recall ever telling her, but I must've. And she remembered.

"So what do you recommend, Dane?" Jack's friendly smile finds me from across the table.

"What do you like?"

"Anything. Especially if it's fresh. We've been spoiled living in Florida." He glances at Sav, and she offers him a loving gaze in return. They really are a happy couple, if a little boastful of their relationship.

"Honestly the pork chops are great. And so's the salmon." I snap my menu closed and take a hearty swig of the wine. "But with this wine, I'd probably recommend the chops."

Jack nods and glances over the menu one more time before setting it aside. "I don't know too much about wine, although Sav's dad is the wino in the family."

She chuckles and rolls her eyes. "Jack's more of a whiskey drinker." She sends him a wink and points out something from the drink menu. They both blush and chuckle.

"What's so funny?" Del asks as she closes her menu. She doesn't even have to bother looking. A creature of habit, I know she's already going to order the steak salad with parmesan-peppercorn dressing.

"They carry my favorite whiskey," Jack responds.

"It's *my* favorite whiskey," Sav retorts. "You only started drinking it after you figured out it was *my* favorite!"

I glance between the two of them. So clearly in love despite all the obstacles. Not only is there a significant age gap, but Jack used to be Savannah's bodyguard when her father was governor of Michigan.

And yet they've made it work this long.

I notice the ring on Savannah's finger. "W-when did you two get engaged?" My eyes bop between them as a smile blooms on my face. "Did I miss something?"

Savannah's cheeks turn pink. "It just happened a few days ago. I'm surprised Del didn't tell you." She raises a dark brow at her friend.

Delia's cheeks redden, and she glances down at our hands, still connected. The urge to pull her hand closer bubbles through my chest, but instead, I let her go. My fingers tingle with emptiness.

"Well," Savannah says, her eyes clocking the hand release and then meeting my eyes across the table. "I know it didn't come as quickly as your engagement, but sometimes real things take time."

I swallow once. Twice. And then I take yet another moment before I speak. Because I was raised to always count to ten before saying something I might regret. And once I hit fifteen, I know that what I say, I'll never regret. "I don't know about you, but six years is a long time." I turn my gaze back to Delia, who's examining some hidden thread in the tablecloth. "I never entered into a fake engagement with Del. It's always been real, at least to me."

And as I turn my attention back to Savannah and Jack, I hope the congratulations I give them sounds more heartfelt than I feel.

Delia's couch may be my new least favorite thing, aside from Chicago-style pizza and Kayce's biological father. Not only is it some kind of oversized love seat masquerading as a real couch, but the cushions smell of her. In fact, the whole apartment reeks of Delia.

The drive back from dinner had been a silent one. I glanced over at my passenger as she played with the engagement ring on her finger. Twisting it around and around as her teeth sunk into her bottom lip. As much as I wanted to ask her what she was thinking about, I forced myself to keep eyes on the road. Even as we passed Miller's Run Avenue and the vacant lot, the giant Sold sign plastered across the billboard out front, I swallowed the urge to open up to her.

I needed to put the ball in Delia's court.

So, I'd carried Kayce upstairs, helped tuck him in, and read him a bedtime story when he requested. Del stood in the doorway, her eyes watching both of us like a mama bear. And I wouldn't have it any other way. Her love for her son is one of the many things I admire about her.

"Dane?" Kayce whispered as I set the finished book on the floor next to his bed. "Will you be my new dad?"

The back of my neck heated with Delia's gaze. I swallowed and looked down at the mop-headed boy. An octopus stuffed animal from Marshall under one arm and his baseball mitt under the other. *My* baseball mitt. My throat tightened, and I inhaled shakily. "Yeah, bud. You know, I'll always be here for you. I may not be your real dad, but I'll do whatever you need. *Be* whatever you need." My arms ached to lean down and hug him.

"I love you, Dane."

And suddenly, I couldn't help myself. I leaned forward and wrapped his tiny body in a hug, nearly pulling him from under the covers. "I love you too, Kayce."

Delia sniffled from behind us, but when I'd tucked him back in and turned, she'd gone.

And now, as I lie here, struggling to get comfortable on a piece of furniture much too small for my frame, I wonder how this has all fallen apart.

Sure, it *was* a fake engagement, but I had every intention of making it real.

But was that ever going to happen? Was I ever going to pretend my way into a family of my own—a wife and a kid?

I've been alone for so long. Maybe that's all I'll ever be.

I shake my head, and it's only then that I see the willowy figure standing in the hallway. Her reddish-brown tresses glowing in the moonlight.

"I-I know the couch can't be comfortable. Why don't you take the bed?" She lingers, her bare feet toeing at the rug.

I sit up. "Del, you're like two inches shorter than me. You won't fit comfortably either."

"I can bunk with Kayce." She shrugs, which draws my attention to the tank top and flowy pajama pants she's wearing. The way the light from the street hits just so, I glimpse an outline of her pert nipples.

"It's fine," I respond, my eyes transfixed on the ethereal beauty before me. Before I know what I'm doing, I rise and pad toward her. My feet soft along the wood floor.

Has she been thinking of what I said tonight at dinner? *It's always been real, at least to me.* I want to ask if this has all been real for her, too. But, to be honest, I'm afraid of the answer. Was her forgetting the dinner an indication of my importance in her life? Or was it just a fluke?

The way she looks tonight, her eyes sad and her steps unsure, I don't know that I'll get the truth out of her. So instead, I shut off my mind and let my hormones do the talking.

She presses her back against the wall just as I grab her and pull her mouth to mine. Her leg lifts, locking around my hip, and I push into the wall to anchor us. I tuck a tendril of hair behind her ear, if only so I can lick along her jaw. She swallows, her throat muscles pulsing, before releasing a moan that spurns me onward.

I grind against her. Up into her core as her back arches and she gasps. My hands find her tits, loose beneath the thin tank, and I lean forward to pull the soft flesh into my mouth. I work the nipple until it's hard while simultaneously pressing my thickening cock against her.

"T-take me to bed," she begs, her voice barely above a whisper.

And once again, I do exactly as she asks.

CHAPTER THIRTY

Delia

The moment I cross the threshold of my bedroom, Dane turns feral. He shuts and locks the door, his dark eyes hungry with need.

"Get undressed," he commands, his voice low. It's nearly a growl. My core instantly heats, and as I keep my gaze trained on his while I lift up my top, I don't miss how his pupils dilate—or how his gaze zeroes in on my breasts.

"How do you want me?" I ask once there's not a stitch left. His tongue licks along his bottom lip as he eyes me up and down. My skin pebbles. Whether from desire or the December chill, I'm not sure. But my nipples are already taut. Pointing directly at the man in front of me.

"On the bed. Ass in the air." He advances and keeps a secure palm on my glute as I situate myself. Then, just when I think I'm comfortable, he presses his hand against my upper back, shoving my face into the mattress. My hips are hoisted even higher into the air, exposing *all* of me to him.

For the first time, I feel self-conscious. I raise to my elbows, attempting to look behind me, but he presses me down again. "I said, ass in the air,

Delia. And I meant it." His palms run over either side of my cheeks. From glute to thigh he coasts his skin over mine. The feeling is amazing, and I rock my hips backward, searching for a stronger touch.

"Ah, ah, ah. So eager..." The gentle caress turns into a sharp smack as his hand connects with my ass. I hiss between my teeth, but my core is throbbing with desire. "I want to see how you touch yourself when I'm not here."

I hesitate, not because I'm uncomfortable, but because there's a drawer full of vibrators just next to my bed. Am I allowed to get them?

"Go on now, baby. Show me." I glance behind myself and meet his eyes. He nods; his tongue barely sticking out between his thinned lips.

I quickly crawl on all fours to the bedside table and retrieve what I need. I choose my favorites. A bright red bullet finger vibrator and a purple rabbit. "So greedy, aren't you?" he asks as I flick on the rabbit. I pass him the finger vibe, my eyebrow cocked in challenge.

He glides the toy onto his forefinger and examines it. The silence is dulled by the buzzing of my toy, and yet I'm certain the way my heart speeds up — *thump thumping*—can be heard over it all. "Back into position. I want to watch you fuck yourself."

I oblige, leaning down and angling the toy against my already dripping pussy. I slide the elongated tip over my clit, warming myself up to the pulses. It's only then that I realize Dane's eyes are literally at eye level, watching it all from behind through my spread legs. His hand meets mine as he takes the vibrator and guides it to my opening, wetting the end with my desire before sliding it inside.

I groan as the vibrations work their magic from inside me, and Dane pumps the toy in and out. The rabbit ears graze my clit, and I rock backward, seeking friction. Seeking *more*. I'm already so close, but just when I think I'm about to tip over the edge, Dane withdraws the toy completely and sets it on the bed.

"Nuh-uh, Delia." He *tsks* over the buzzing. I moan with disappointment as my wetness drips down my thigh.

His tongue meets the droplet and he laps it up on his way to my pussy. His nose presses against my ass and I spread my legs wider, if only to give him easier access. But just before I can enjoy the pleasure, he pulls away again.

"What're you—" I say as I rise to my elbows, but that pesky palm of his presses in between my shoulder blades and my face meets the soft sheets instead.

"You can come when I say you can come, baby." His face returns to my splayed pussy, and he's lapping away, his tongue slowly edges higher and higher. When it reaches my ass, I groan loudly. "Shh," he murmurs against the puckered skin.

And then the finger vibrator turns on. The soft silicone meets my sensitive hole, edging around the rim as Dane tongue fucks me there. He finally pulls away just as the toy presses gently—then slightly harder—against the entrance. My fingers find my clit, rubbing and swirling the bundle of nerves between my thumb and forefinger.

"Please," I beg as my hips rock up. "Let me come..." I'm so close; the feeling at the base of my spine climbs higher and higher as my body begs for more.

But Dane denies me. Instead, he withdraws the vibrator, and again, I mewl with disappointment. "What did I tell you, Del?"

I groan and rock my hips, my body needing him so much that it can't control itself.

"What did I tell you?" he repeats as his palm smacks my ass cheek.

"I can come when you say so," I respond dutifully.

"That's right, baby."

"I-I need to come. *Now. Please.*"

His hand runs over my smacked skin just as his vibrator-clad finger finds my hole again. A dollop of wetness hits my ass. He spit on me, coating my hole as he glides the pulsating toy over it. Working the wetness inside me. "I already do so much for you. Why should I let you come?" He presses deeper as the vibrator clicks to a faster setting.

"B-b-because," I begin as tears of frustration well in my eyes, but I can't even begin to create a coherent thought. All I can focus on is his palm rubbing against my backside while his vibrating finger glides in and out of my ass.

My clit throbs and my muscles tighten. I'm nearly there, just a few more—

But he pulls away. Leaving me aching and on the edge of tears. I raise to my elbows and glance behind me, meeting his gaze with fury and desperation. "Why—?"

But I don't get the rest of my question out before his rock-hard cock finds my pussy and slams into me. The finger vibrator meets my ass as his cock thrusts in and out. It only takes a few times, the mere press of the vibrator against my hole, before I finally come undone.

I ride the wave as it inexplicably catches up to my body and cry out, louder than I've ever been. I bury my face into the mattress and moan like an animal as Dane meets me thrust for thrust. Then he's coming, too.

My orgasm continues even as he withdraws and spends all over the crack of my ass, the warm liquid sliding between my cheeks.

And only when I come back down to reality and am met with a warm washcloth and Dane's comforting embrace do I realize that there's absolutely no way I can marry this man.

"What do you mean you can't marry him, Del? The wedding is tomorrow." Savannah sips a homemade mimosa from a plastic cup at the kitchen table while I spread orange creme frosting over store-bought cinnamon rolls. The canned rolls were a luxury for me during college, and as we celebrate what was supposed to be my last day of freedom, I lick the frosting from the knife before tossing it into the sink.

I carry the dish over to the table and take a seat, my own glass untouched. "I just can't seem to shake the feeling that I'm doing something wrong. It's not right to begin a marriage this way."

Savannah eyes me as she takes another swig. "What *way*, exactly?"

My eyes travel over the apartment. Kayce's basket of toys take up an entire corner of the living space while the rest of the room contains the oversized love seat. There's not much here, and if I picked up and left, would anyone other than Dane even notice? "I... I'm in love with him, Sav." Saying the words I've known for so long out loud should give me relief. But instead I'm only left with a sinking feeling in my gut.

"So what's the problem? If you're in love with Dane, don't you want to marry him?" She reaches across the table and takes my hand, her thumb rolling along my wrist the same way that Dane does.

I swallow the lump in my throat. "Of course I want that. But to begin a marriage with a lie? Under a fake engagement? It seems like a bad omen." I sit back, withdrawing my hand and crossing my arms over my chest.

"Did you even listen to what he said last night? None of this has been fake to him. I mean, I even put on my bitch face for your sake. Do you think I like being mean on purpose?" She cocks a dark eyebrow at me before lifting a gooey bun to her lips and taking a bite. "As your bestie, I had to be sure that he was serious. And trust me... that man is seriously in love with you. Besides, I've been telling you to shoot your shot for years. And maybe if you'd taken my advice, you wouldn't be in this predicament."

"I don't need your judgment right now."

"No, you don't," she says between bites. "But you're going to get it. You two are perfect for each other, Del."

My mind spins and flashes six years' worth of memories all at once. Dane bouncing a crying newborn while I hurriedly warm up a bottle. Dane pulling a costume-clad Kayce in a wagon on Halloween. The two of them playing catch in the park, Dane practically on his knees to ensure that the ball goes *right* into Kayce's mitt.

"Maybe he's only doing all of this because of Kayce." I shrug and finally take a sip of the orange drink in front of me.

Savannah eyes me. "Maybe he is." She looks down at her plate. "But if you never put yourself out there—if you never tell him that *you're* in love with *him*—you'll never know if he was doing all of it because of *you*, Delia."

My throat burns, and the truth hits me suddenly. Hard. I'm not afraid that Dane doesn't love me. I'm afraid that he does, and I'll just be one big letdown to him.

CHAPTER THIRTY-ONE

Delia

As much as I'd like to rush right out and inform Dane of my feelings, Savannah has us booked solid for the day. After our leisurely breakfast, we head to the next town over and take part in some much-needed girl time. Between an appointment for a mani-pedi followed by a brief stop at the craft store to find the perfect fake flowers for my bridal bouquet, Sav and I make it back to Oselka just in time to meet Kayce as he hops off the bus.

"Hey, buddy!" Sav says as she wraps him up in a hug. As the only child of only children, I never had any fun aunts and uncles, so I'm glad that Savannah treats Kayce like her nephew. "How about you come upstairs and help me arrange these flowers into something that resembles a bouquet?"

Kayce peeks inside the bag and smiles. I know one day he'll scoff at helping, but for now he's simply excited to be included. I start to follow, but Savannah holds up her hand, stopping me in my tracks. "Nope," she enunciates as her head dips toward the restaurant door. "You've got to handle your shit. *Now.*"

My shoulders sag as I glance through the diner's windows. Dane's back is turned, but as he wipes the counter, I don't miss how his hips shake from side to side.

"*Go.*" Savannah gives me a gentle shove.

I pull open the door just as Savannah's footsteps echo up the stairs.

As the bell dings over the door, Dane turns, his smile faltering when he realizes it's me. "Hey." I approach the counter slowly, the bags in my hand weighing a thousand pounds.

"Hey," he responds as he drops the rag. "What've you got there?"

"Just a few decorative pins for my hair," I respond as I set the purchases on the chair next to me. "For tomorrow."

He nods slowly as his jaw works. I let the silence fill the space between us for as long as I can, and then I splay my hands on the counter. "I got my nails done, too." God, I'm the worst. I just need to get it out, but I'd rather derail the conversation by talking about fingernails.

"Nice." He curls his nails toward his wrist and examines them. "Should I have gotten mine done too?"

I chuckle and shake my head. "There was a man getting a pedicure. Maybe next time I go, you'll come too?"

"I'd like that, although my feet are extremely ticklish." He winks and my face heats.

My eyes drop to the ring on my still-splayed hand. Before the silence can grow into something awkward, my brain pushes me over the edge. *Just say it already!* "Dane, I can't marry you."

His brow crinkles as his mouth falls open. "What?"

"I mean, I don't want to marry you. Not like this."

"What do you mean exactly, Delia?" His forearms flex as his jaw ticks.

"You've always been there for me. For Kayce. You do *everything* for us. And I can't even hold up my end of the bargain t-to help you out the one time you need something."

He just stares at me. Waiting. So I continue.

"And not only am I a shit friend, but I talked you into this fake engagement. Well, Nana did... but still. You wouldn't be doing this if I hadn't asked you to. You wouldn't have tied yourself to my sinking ship if you weren't so... so *amazing*."

"So you can't marry me because I'm amazing?" His lip curls.

"No, it's not that. It's everything. It's—"

Just say it, you idiot!

"*I'm in love with you!*" The declaration comes out louder than I intend, and it hangs in the air between us like the first snowflake on a cold winter day. New and exciting. But so tiny and fragile, too.

"I'm in love with you," I repeat.

His eyes narrow. "And you can't marry me because you're in love with me?"

Hearing it out loud is ridiculous, so I work it out in my mind. Trying to clarify the knot in my brain. "It wouldn't be right to go through with this when things have changed."

He leans back, crossing his arms over his chest as he assesses me through those cloudy navy eyes. "And how, exactly, have things changed, Delia?"

I chuff out a breath. "I just told you. I'm in love with you." What doesn't he get?

"And?" There's a smirk on his face. It's so irritating I want to smack it off. Or kiss it away.

"And I've been lying to you—to *myself*—this whole time! I just..." I go silent. My mouth literally snaps shut as my heart drops into my stomach. "You knew?"

He cocks an eyebrow at me. That smirk turns into an all-out smile.

"You knew this whole time..." The realization hits me like a ton of bricks. This whole time I thought I was hiding some secret. Holding some emotion close like it was CIA-worthy information. "How?"

"It's pretty obvious when I feel the same way, Del."

My heart swells as my core heats. "You...?"

He uncrosses his arms and reaches for me. Our fingers entwine as we lean in. "Delia, I've loved you since the day you walked through that door and sat in that exact same seat. I wasn't faking when I asked you to marry me, and you're not backing out now. Tomorrow I'm going to marry you because I love you, too, not because of some fake agreement."

My throat shrinks, and I try to swallow, but fail. Dane notices, because of course he does, and his brow furrows. "What... what if I screw it all up? What if I mess up—let you down?"

His lips curl to the side as though he's pondering the possibility. "I'm not sure I understand the question, Del. How, exactly, could you ever screw up and let me down?" That thumb of his circles along my wrist, soothing my entire soul.

I pull away because I don't deserve to be comforted. "I just..." I pause, searching for the right words. "It's just that I always screw up. I'm a complete mess. I let down all the men that care about me. My father, Marshall...you." Granted there are only three, it's enough that it can't be a coincidence, right?

Dane's brows slam down over his navy eyes. "Forget about my situation for a minute," he says as he flicks his hand through the air. "How on Earth did *you* let *them* down?"

I blink. Isn't it obvious? "I-I got pregnant. I had Kayce. Out of wedlock." Hearing the words out loud, admitting them into the ether for someone else to hear, makes me second-guess myself.

"You think gifting the world with that *amazing* little boy was an accident? Something to be ashamed of?" He reaches forward and pulls my hand into his. Really grabs me, refusing to let go even as I withdraw. "Whoever made you feel that way is the one with the problem. Not you. You created a life and are strong enough to press forward every day, never giving up at being the best mother to that wonderful kid. How can you feel anything but pride at that, Delia?"

I've never had anyone tell me that having a baby as a single mother—working my ass off to provide the best life for him—is something to feel *proud* of. But it's true. And Dane was the one to see it in me, even when I couldn't see it in myself.

"Jesus, Del… I've got my work cut out for me, don't I?" He winks and I melt.

I'm speechless. My heart pounds so hard it can probably be heard in the next town, but as I lean in and capture Dane's mouth with my own, I know that at least maybe part of my life is going right.

"Geez, Del, you look amazing." Savannah tucks a stray curl behind my ear as her eyes skim over me. My face heats, more from joy than embarrassment. "I seriously can't believe you found this dress at a thrift store."

I glance down at the lacy gown. It hugs in all the right places and fits like a glove. Savannah passes me the bouquet that she and Kayce had worked to create, and as I pull it into my chest, something shiny catches my eye. Buried inside is a tiny toy car.

Kayce's favorite toy car. A truck that, ironically enough, resembles Dane's.

My eyes prick, and I blink rapidly to assuage the onslaught of tears I feel coming on.

"Don't you dare cry!" Savannah admonishes as she drags her forefinger under her own eye. "I'm already feeling a little emotional, and if I see you break down, I'm done for."

I giggle slightly and sniff as I nod. Only then does Jack appear. He wears a suit and tie, and I can understand why Savannah's eyes light up as they eye one another. "It's time. You ready?" He holds out his hand to Savannah, but directs his question to me.

"I'm ready," I respond as I follow the two of them into the entryway. There's a slight chill in the air, but the sun outside is shining. While the stained glass inside is beautiful, being in the church feels like a heavy weight pressing down on me. My breathing feels stilted. Like I'm not getting enough air even as I take deeper inhales from deep in my belly.

"You okay?" Sav asks, her hand reaching out to grasp my forearm. Her brow crinkles.

"Y-yeah. I'm fine. I just—"

She smiles slowly. "I know. But look..." She points through the open archway and down the aisle, where Dane stands next to Kayce. They're chatting quietly and both wearing dual smiles.

I turn back to Savannah. "I'm okay. You two go." I shoo them up the aisle as the organ kicks into the wedding march. The deep notes hit me square in the chest, and that familiar tightening is back. My breath hitches again.

As Savannah and Jack creep slowly up the aisle, I peer at the attendants. While there aren't many, the ones we invited showed up. Pete, my assistant, sits alone while in front of him are Crystal and Antonio, chatting animatedly. My parents occupy the front pew, their spines ramrod straight as they glance forward. Nana's next to them, her neck craned toward Sav with a proud smile beaming on her face.

Once Savannah and Jack reach the front, I know it's my turn. Marigold Fraser had been incredibly detailed in her instructions earlier this morning. I step into the center of the archway and inhale, yet my lungs don't seem to fill with air. Instead, it feels like I'm choking. I tell myself to remain calm. To count to ten and take long, luxurious breaths, but nothing helps. So instead I focus on my walk. One foot in front of the other. I try to time myself with the music, but it's impossible, and before I know it I'm halfway up the aisle and nearly panting like a dog.

I can't breathe.

My eyes seek out Dane's, and in an instant, I can tell he knows there's something wrong. Because he knows me. He's there for me.

I stagger to him, my body shaking and my mind a whirlwind of panic. Why can't I breathe? I turn to pass the bouquet to Savannah, but instead it falls heavily to the floor. Kayce's toy car tumbles out and rolls toward my father's foot.

I'm horrified. This isn't how it was supposed to happen.

And just as I turn my eyes back to Dane's, I realize something is terribly wrong.

"We can't do this," he says as his palms cradle my elbows.

And I collapse.

CHAPTER THIRTY-TWO

Dane

I catch Delia just as her knees buckle. One arm snakes around her waist while the other holds the back of her head. Savannah's there, helping me gently place her on the altar. I turn around, my brain slowly absorbing the way Kayce's eyes widen and his mouth gapes.

"Get him out of here," I direct to his grandparents. They snap to attention, rushing up the steps and ushering him away.

From her place in the front row, Nana struggles to stand. "Stay there," I admonish with my hand raised toward her. But she sends me a scowl and hoists herself up nonetheless. I don't have time to argue with her. I turn my attention back to Del, whose eyes flutter open.

"Shit," she whispers, her brows wrinkling together. She tries to sit up, but my palm on her chest stops her. "Where's Kayce?" She looks behind me.

"Your parents took him to the foyer." I nod to Savannah and she scampers away to tell him that his mother is fine. Awake. "What happened?"

She bites her lip as color returns to her pale face. "I didn't exactly eat anything today."

"Jesus Christ, Del. Why not?"

Her eyes widen. "You can't say that in here!"

I roll my eyes toward the ceiling. "Sorry." Then I look back to her. "Why haven't you eaten?"

"I wanted to make sure the dress fit. And I've just been so nervous..."

I blink. "I'm nervous too, baby, but—"

She shakes her head. "No, not nervous about this." Her hand floats between us. "Nervous about all of *this*." Her eyes scan the room. "Being back in a sanctuary after so long. It felt... wrong. And then you said—"

"I said we can't do this." I sit back on my haunches and nod. "Because you're right." It was the exact feeling I'd had. This place does feel wrong. It's not *us*. It's not what we wanted. Never mind the weird start to the engagement, but there's no way either of us would've agreed to get married in a church had we actually taken the time to plan our nuptials.

"We should just call the whole thing off," she says as her eyes turn glassy. Her gaze dips away from mine. To her Nana, who's standing quietly at the foot of the stairs.

I turn and look at the elder Delia. The one who started this whole thing. The one who knew all along. She suspected what we felt for each other. As though she can hear me, her lips press firmly together. *I'm not going anywhere* I'd once told her. And I meant it. I *mean* it. "No." I reach my hand out and pull Delia up to sitting. "We're not calling anything off."

Her hands run through her hair as she meets my eyes. "A-are you sure? We can wait..." She's giving me an out, and while she expects me to take it— like every other man in her life—I refuse. Because I'm not giving up on Delia. I'm not giving up on us.

I stand and extend my hand to help her stand. "I love you, Delia. Nothing changes that. Not the way we first met. Not the way we became engaged. Not the venue. *Nothing* changes that," I repeat.

Her gaze travels around the church. "But..."

I smile. "But we're not getting married *here*, baby." I give her a conspiratorial smile and take the few steps down toward Nana with Delia in my wake. "You two stay right there. I'll be back." I get both of them settled on the pew and then head toward the door.

There's something I need to take care of before I can marry Delia.

"Absolutely not," Delia's father practically roars in my face. We've stepped away from the few guests after I reassured Kayce that his mom was just fine. I even implored him to find a cup of water for both her and Nana, Savannah in his wake to ensure he didn't get lost.

"You know as well as I do that this place isn't right for Delia. Or me," I add. "We'd be much happier getting married in the park just across the street. But we need your help, sir."

Tom Evans crosses his arms over his lean chest. He glares at me under gray bushy eyebrows. There's no way he's going to agree to my terms. "You know how her mother feels about this."

My thumb and forefinger kneed at my forehead. "I do. But I also know that there's no religious reason for us to marry in a church, other than *your* preference."

The reverend doesn't say anything. But he uncrosses his arms and goes to stand near the window, his gaze taking in the small gazebo across the street in the park. "What do you know of religion? According to my daughter, the two of you don't attend church."

I sigh. "That's true. We don't. But I've attended in the past. I was raised in the church. *This* church, actually."

His mouth gapes as he stares at me.

"In fact, I know that *we* are the church, and our covenant—our *union*—is between Delia and myself before God. The location is a moot point." I cross my arms and cock an eyebrow.

His hands bracket his hips. "So why are you even bothering to tell me all this if you're just going to go against my wishes?"

"Because all of *this*"—I indicate the room, the church, *all of it*—"means nothing to Delia. She doesn't know the officiant. She doesn't have a connection to *any* of this. But she has a connection to you, her father."

His throat bobs as he watches me. Waiting for me to continue.

"And I think it would mean a lot to her if you were the one to marry us. Out there." I point to the white gazebo in the distance, the winter sunshine beaming down on the brownish-red shingles.

He snorts and shakes his head. "You really think my daughter wants me officiating her wedding? She didn't even ask me to give her away."

I shrug and back away, giving him some space. "Maybe she was afraid you'd have said no."

He turns to me quickly, eyes wide. "Is that what she thinks? That I'd deny her that one simple request?"

My lip quirks as I tilt my head. "Can you blame her for thinking that?" And then I step toward the door and reach for the knob. "Think about it. We'll be out there if you're interested. But hurry. It's cold."

And I set off to tell everyone the new plans.

"We don't have any speakers out here," Savannah hisses at me as her chin quivers. Yes, it's freezing in the park, but luckily everyone's wrapped up in their winter jackets. Everyone, that is, except for Savannah and Jack.

"I live in Florida. I don't own a heavy coat anymore," she said when I asked if she'd be warm enough in just the sleeveless dress and faux fur wrap. Her fiancé rolled his eyes and handed her his suit jacket. She gave him a grateful peck on the cheek before sliding her arms into the sleeves.

I glance hurriedly at Marigold Fraser, who's still giving me the church-lady glare from just beyond the gazebo. She, too, had been less than eager to assist in the change of scenery. Now, as she awaits my signal to send Delia down the makeshift aisle of freshly fallen leaves and up the steps of the gazebo, I don't want to admit that this seems to be a failed attempt at a wedding where nothing's gone right.

Strike two.

Delia's father has disappeared, along with her mother. Nana's shivering on a picnic bench that Jack and I moved closer to the gazebo, and there's no music for Del to walk down the aisle to.

Just as I'm about to give up, Kayce tucks his tiny hand into mine. I look down at his mop of curls sticking out from his Ninja Turtle beanie. "I know Mom's favorite song," he says as his eyes dart between me and Savannah's phone.

Before I can even ask, Delia's maid of honor swipes open her music app and passes the device to Kayce. I crouch down. "Want me to help you spell it, buddy?"

His brow furrows. "I know how to spell The Fray, Dane." He types it into the search and presses his thumb to proceed.

Suddenly "Look After You" streams loudly from the device, echoing through the open frame.

Kayce continues to hold the phone as I nod to Marigold Fraser. If nothing else goes right today, at least Delia got to walk down the aisle, in a beautiful dress, over a bed of crisp autumn leaves, to her favorite song.

CHAPTER THIRTY-THREE

Delia

The lyrics to my favorite song spill from my lips as I take one hesitant step after another on my way to the rustic gazebo. The orange and red leaves crunch underfoot as my soles sink into the soft soil. It's cold, yes, but I don't feel a thing as my gaze lands first on Kayce, his hand extending the phone up high as he sways back and forth to the gentle guitar strums.

And there, towering over my son, stands Dane. When my eyes land on him, I catch him already staring at me, and I blush. Not because I'm nervous. No, not this time. This time everything is right. Our few guests stand as I pass, their smiles glowing with a warmth that seeps into my cold hands. And before I know it, I'm already taking one step at a time up into the gazebo.

I stop right in front of Dane just as the chorus explodes around us.

I can't help but smile up at him as Kayce slowly lowers the phone and then clicks off the song. Behind him, Jack nods and gently pries the phone from his mittened hand. Only then do I realize that we have no officiant. No one stands before us to consecrate our union, to bind us as one.

My mouth falls open just as Dane speaks. "I know. I asked..." He swallows and his throat bobs as his jaw twitches.

I look out into the faces below us standing in the grass. Nana blinks up at me from under a mountain of blankets. Besides our original guests, a few townsfolk have joined, stopping on the sidewalk beyond the park limits to watch with curiosity.

"W-what are we going to do?" I turn back to Dane.

He inhales slowly, his lower lip tucking under his teeth as he looks away from the crowd and toward the other side of the street. "It doesn't matter, Del," he finally says, meeting my eyes. "None of the conventions matter to me. All I ever wanted was you."

I smile as my heart speeds up. It's all I dreamed of. My favorite song. A good man. And my son beside us.

Pulling Dane toward me, my smile breaks against the chill of the day. I press my lips to his and soak up the moment. Because as hectic as life is, these moments are few and far between. But, with Dane by my side, maybe I'll get lucky and have many more to come.

"Look." Savannah taps my shoulder, and I turn to see her pointing behind Dane. Sure enough, my mother and father stride toward the gazebo with purposeful steps. I gape at what I'm seeing. My father wears white wedding robes, which billow in the chilly breeze.

Dane and I both watch silently as my father takes the gazebo steps two at a time and then approaches us. "I hope I'm not late," he says sheepishly.

"I-I thought you weren't coming."

His gaze snaps to mine as something unreadable flits across his features. "I'd never miss your day, Delia." He looks down at the outfit. "I had to bribe the church reverend to use his robes, though. And he drives a hard bargain."

Lines appear between Dane's brows. "What'd you offer him?"

"A trio of visiting sermons. One for the next three months." He looks between the two of us. "I hope you plan to keep that extra apartment because I'm going to need it."

"You didn't have to do that, dad. You could've married us in your suit. I mean…" My hand swivels out to encompass the park.

His lips flatten. "I'm accepting your decision to marry in a park, Delia. But I'll perform the ceremony in the correct clothing as an ordained officiant."

I smirk and turn my gaze back to Dane's. His eyebrows are raised as he listens to our interchange. I suppose, for now, that's the best I can hope for from my father.

"Dearly beloved," he exclaims loudly to the meager guests. "We are finally gathered here, on this beautiful December day, to unite Dane and Delia in marriage."

As Dane takes my hand, I contemplate how we got here. To this time. To the two of us finally recognizing the love we shared but hid from one another. Had either of us been braver and acknowledged the truth we attempted to ignore, this day would've happened long ago.

But I can't dwell on the past. I can't dwell on the should-haves. I can only focus on the man in front of me. The man who, as he runs the pad of his thumb over my wrist, loves me for everything I am.

"Now Delia and Dane stand before us, ready to take the biggest step of all— into marriage. Delia, if it's in your heart, please repeat after me." My father pauses, and I swallow. He proceeds, going slowly, step-by-step, and I respond accordingly.

"I, Delia, take you, Dane, to be my husband, to have and to hold from this day forward, for better or worse, for richer or poorer, in sickness and in health, to love and to cherish, until we are parted by death. This my solemn vow."

Dane's face blooms into a smile as he repeats his vows. And all the while, all I can think about is how in love I am with this man. The man who has bent over backward, in *my* sickness and health, to be there for me and Kayce.

"This is my solemn vow," he finally repeats.

"As you exchange the rings, look upon them as a symbol of these vows. Tokens of your commitment and promises you've made."

Dane pulls a beautiful diamond-studded gold band from his jacket pocket and slides it on my finger. My mouth gapes at the thought of the cost. We agreed to something simple, yet I can't deny the beauty of the jewelry. It sits atop my engagement ring, but as soon as I'm able, I'll swap the two so the band is closer to my heart.

Savannah passes me the ring for Dane. As I hold it out, eager to slide it onto his finger, the engraving on the inside of the band catches his eye and he blinks once. Twice. "I hope you didn't put anything inappropriate on that ring, baby," he mutters under his breath as I lean in and work the circle over his knuckle.

I purse my lips and look up at him through my lashes. "It's the coordinates to the restaurant, you goof. Where we first met. Where we..."

"And finally, you may kiss the bride," my father announces as our guests clap, their hands muffled with mittens and gloves.

"Where we fell in love?" Dane asks as he leans in, his nose touching mine.

"Exactly," I respond through a beaming smile that pulls at my cheeks. And then our lips meet, Kayce hollers "Gross!" and we seal our union.

"Come sit down, husband," I admonish as Dane bustles around the tables in the diner. He was adamant about cooking for everyone as part of our special day.

"I'll just be one minute. Nana's water looks a little low." I have to smile that he cares so much about me and my family. Even now, he's gone out of his way to ensure that there is more than enough food for everyone. From my perfectly breaded chicken parm to a dish without red sauce for my father, Dane has outdone himself.

"I got it, boss!" Crystal calls from her place behind the counter. She agreed to work the tiny wedding reception in lieu of a gift, not that Dane was expecting anything anyway. We're just grateful she showed up on time and didn't miss the nuptials.

Dane finally takes a seat next to me, and my hand comes to rest on his thigh. I run my freshly manicured nails up and down his slacks, my mind envisioning stripping him out of the fancy duds. It's not every day I get to see him all dressed up, and it likely won't happen again anytime soon. So I need to make sure I take my time enjoying every last bit of it.

His hand captures mine, and he pulls it to his lips, pressing a chaste kiss to my knuckles. My face heats as I catch Savannah eyeing the gesture from across the table. She may have originally had her doubts, but as a slow smile stretches her lips, I know she understands the truth behind our relationship.

It may have started as fake, but it's blossomed into something real. And maybe it always *was* real, and we just needed the little extra push to make it happen, but I couldn't be happier with the man sitting at my side. The man who I'm going to spend the rest of my life with.

From a booth nearby, Pete clinks his fork against his glass. "Kiss!" Everyone cheers as they join in the glass clinking. Kayce, especially, enjoys the game, but before I can tell him to be more gentle, my mother places her hand over his and offers a warm smile.

Dane captures my chin between his fingers and pulls me in for a long kiss. In front of our closest friends, he quickly slides his tongue over the seam of my lips before pulling away. Those dark eyes burn with desire as his lids lower. Whether from the kiss, or the grandmotherly relationship finally forming between my mother and Kayce, I am truly happy.

CHAPTER THIRTY-FOUR

Dane

My fingertips trail over Delia's back as she pulls her frail Nana in for one last hug. "I'm so glad you could make it," she says as she helps lower her grandmother into the backseat of her father's sedan.

"I wouldn't have missed it, my darling. Especially as the matchmaker behind the scenes, I feel partly responsible for this farce wedding." She winks at me, and I chuckle. Before Delia closes the door, my hand connects with the side and I prop it open.

I lean past Delia and pull a tiny bottle of brown liquid from the chest pocket of my suit. "A little wedding favor," I whisper as I pass her the goods. From behind me, Delia gasps as Nana chuckles and tucks the bottle into her purse.

"You really are a good man, Dane Lukes," she says as I retreat behind Delia.

"All this time, all he needed to do was ply you with liquor." Delia shakes her head before gently closing the door.

As we turn toward Del's parents, I'm grateful they are preoccupied with saying their goodbyes to Kayce. I don't want there to be any reason for them to dislike me now that I've finally smoothed things over, and I'm pretty sure slipping grandma alcohol would be pretty frowned upon.

"Thank you for coming," Delia says as she reaches for her mother, "and for bringing Nana."

Her mother tuts loudly and wraps her arms around Del, patting her on the back in a hug that seems never-ending. "We're so glad you included us in your special day." She pulls away and blinks through shining eyes.

While Delia gives her dad a hug, too, I stand awkwardly aside as her mother looks me up and down. "You know, I didn't think much of you when we first met. But I suppose you've grown on me. And I appreciate all you've done for my daughter and grandson." I clear my throat and shuffle on my feet. I suppose this is the best I'll get from her, so I accept it with a flat smile and a nod.

Delia's father, however, reaches out to shake my hand. "Thank you, Dane, for everything." I clasp his hand firmly and wish them both a safe drive home.

Only once their car has pulled away do I exhale. While the day is nowhere near over, I know it will eventually become a mere blur in my memory. I look around at the group before me. Del crouching down to pull Kayce into a hug. Jack's arm draped over Savannah's shoulders as she leans against him. This. This is what it's all about. The family you make for yourself.

"Behave for Sav and Jack, okay buddy?" Delia plants a kiss on Kayce's forehead. His tiny suit long discarded, he stands before us in a too-short pair of joggers and an oversized sweatshirt. I'm beginning to realize that his clothes won't fit until he stops growing, and at the rate he's going, that may never happen.

"I will," he responds as he rolls his eyes at his overbearing mother. My *wife*. Savannah's maid of honor duties aren't quite over, as she was kind enough to offer to take her de facto nephew for pizza and a movie while Del and I are able to celebrate a night alone.

The tyke jumps toward me, wrapping my legs in a bear hug as he squeezes tightly. I bend down and lift him up for a real hug. I may not have been a part of his creation, but I'll be a part of his raising. He'll be a better son, a better friend, a better man because of me.

"There's extra cannolis in the fridge for you," I whisper in his ear as his eyes light up. Then I set him down, take my wife's hand, and lead her upstairs.

My fingers tug gently at the zipper as it travels down Delia's spine. The exposed skin is soft and smells of lilac mixed with something a little heavier. My mouth waters, and I lean in, pressing tender kisses along the nape of her neck and over her shoulder blades. The skin pebbles beneath my touch, and I don't miss the way her back arches and shivers. If I reached around, I imagine I'd find her nipples hard and her pussy wet. As it is, my cock presses painfully against the zipper of my slacks, begging to be released.

The day passed by with such speed, so now is the time to slow it down. To remember every single moment. To *enjoy* it.

And I intend to do just that. My mouth continues its passage along her spine. Licking and nibbling the sensitive skin while my fingers trail down her sides, floating over the white lace. When I reach her hips, I tug the dress farther down until it pools on the floor at her feet. She wears a white silk thong, the fabric tucked between her cheeks. I use my teeth along the band to pull her panties down over her ass and then massage the full glutes with my palms.

As I roll the muscles up and over, then down and around, I get a glimpse of her puckered hole. It's begging to be touched. Played with. But not yet. No, not quite yet. Instead, I turn her around. Her pussy is still covered with the silky underwear, and as I press my mouth against the fabric, she grinds against my jaw. My tongue tickles along the silk, and it's only when Delia reaches down and yanks the panties all the way past her thighs that I'm left eye level with her sopping wet core. She grabs either side of my head, her fingers tangling in my hair, and pulls me into her. I lick and lap at the apex, pressing my fingers into her as she widens her legs slightly.

"Dane," she whispers as she grinds against my face. I smile against her pussy, my jaw now covered in her desire.

I pull away and let my thumb work against the nerve bundle while my fingers pulse in and out. In and out. Before too long her knees buckle and she settles against the side of the bed as she struggles to hold herself up.

I stand up, my face inches from hers. "You like that, wife?" My cock throbs with need. And, as though she can hear my innermost thoughts, Delia reaches between us and unbuttons my slacks. She slides the zipper carefully over the length before diving into my boxer briefs and pulling me out. I suck air through my teeth at her touch.

"I want this. I want you. Now," she demands, lining me up with her entrance.

But I pull away. Not because I don't want it, too, but because I know this would be over in five minutes if I allowed it her way.

"Patience now." My fingers withdraw from inside her, and I press her down onto the mattress. Lay her out like a reclining goddess ready to be sacrificed with sexual torture in the form of multiple orgasms. My mouth finds her pussy once more, my tongue dipping deep into her entrance as my thumb holds steady on her clit.

"I need to taste you, too." I give into her demands and flip over, my thighs bracketing her face. Her palm wraps around my shaft as she lifts her head and flicks her tongue along the tip. I continue tongue-fucking her pussy while she takes me fully down her throat. Her mouth is wet and warm. Her tongue runs along the underside of my cock, and I release a shuddering breath. I don't know how much longer I can prolong this. I want to be deep inside her so badly.

She alternates between using her mouth to wet my length and sliding her palm up and down, jacking me until my thighs quake. And I do the same. Suck and lap at her core and then finger-fuck her until she's gasping against my cock.

"*Please*," she begs once more, and this time I don't have the strength to hold out. I roll over and pull her on top of me, giving her a minute to adjust until she's lined up— her dripping pussy hovering inches above my pulsing cock.

And then I lift my hips and slide home, both of us gasping as she seats herself all the way to the base. My hands hold her hips as she grinds against me, and I breathe through my nose in order to contain myself. But what I really want to do is thrust up into her. Use her like I've done with my hand so many times, imagining it was her.

That feeling starts to build in the base of my spine, wrapping under until it settles in my balls. I flip her over onto her back and hoist her legs over my shoulders. Then I drive into her. Deep. I bottom out and see stars.

"More. *Fuck*—more!" She writhes against the sheets.

"Touch yourself," I command and she obliges, reaching her freshly painted fingers between us and pressing to her clit. "Put 'em in my mouth."

She slides her wet forefinger and middle finger between my lips, and I suck, which spurs me on even more. She pulls away and touches herself again, using my saliva as lubricant.

I'm so close, and I try to slow down and control myself, but when she arches her back and gasps my name— I lose it. I drive into her like an addict chasing his next fix.

"I-I'm coming! I'm coming—don't stop!" She cries as her fingers reach up and grab my hair.

I couldn't even if I tried, so I don't bother. I ride out the wave of ecstasy, spilling so deep into her, and yet she still climbs higher and higher, her legs tense as her body quakes. I stay seated inside until she relaxes, and then I slowly withdraw, my cum mixed with hers.

And as much as I know we should clean up, I can't help but wrap her into my arms and inhale.

It's the smell of lilacs and sex, and on Delia, it smells amazing.

CHAPTER THIRTY-FIVE

Delia

Winter sunlight streams through the apartment window, casting everything in a cool glow. I roll over and discover Dane—my *husband*—missing from the bed. I sit up and pull the sheet to cover myself. It's then that I hear the sound of cutlery coming from the kitchen.

"Dane?" My voice sounds raspy, and I clear it loudly before catching my reflection in the window. My auburn hair looks like a bird made a nest in it while my cheeks are flushed with color. I look thoroughly fucked. And *happy*. I let a small smile bloom across my lips.

"Bon appetit!" Dane enters carrying several plates stacked up his forearm, as though he's delivering a family's order to their restaurant table.

My eyes widen as the delicious smell of bacon and syrup hit me, and in my fervor, I let the sheet drop.

"*Fuck*, I'm not going to be able to focus on breakfast with you on display, wife," he says, eyeing my nakedness.

My face heats with pleasure, and I hoist the thin sheet up once again as he sets down the plates like a picnic. He sits next to me, but while I peruse the delicious options, Dane runs his fingers over my bare shoulder.

"You made all this for us?" I take a piece of bacon and hungrily devour it, hardly even enjoying the crisp saltiness before it's gone and I'm grabbing another.

"Hm, you mostly," he says, leaning forward to press kisses against my skin.

"You're not hungry?" I set down the second piece of bacon and frown at him.

"I'm starving." His lips trail up my shoulder, across my clavicle, and meet the sensitive skin along my throat. "For *you*." He nibbles at my jaw.

His hand yanks the sheet away from my body before his soft palm fondles my breast. I moan against his temple as his thumb and forefinger work my nipple into a point.

"But the food," I mutter without much conviction. Because in all honestly, I'm also ravenous. But not for breakfast, either.

"It'll keep," he says before lifting me into his arms. I squeal as he carries me through the hallway and into the bathroom, where hot steam already rolls over the shower curtain.

Then we're ensconced within the warmth of the shower, our bodies loosening with the heat of the water. Dane sets me on my feet before spinning me to face away from the shower head.

Before I can even wet my hair, he spreads my legs as he lines up from behind. His chest meets my back. One hand glides down my stomach to my clit while the other tightens around my hair, pulling it back until my neck is exposed.

"When I came over to fix the water heater that day... I imagined fucking you like this, baby," he admits as he enters me. *Fills me.* I gasp, not from pain, but from the sheer fact that he glides in so easily.

I manage to glance back at him. The hot water drips from every surface—down his jaw, over his chest, and even in the place where we're connected. I moan as his fingers gently press against the bundle of nerves at the top of my thighs while he fucks me slowly from behind.

He releases my hair and moves both hands to my tits. Fondling them, working the nipples, he presses me up against the cold tile. I gasp at the change in temperature as my senses work on overdrive.

But before I can become too comfortable, I'm flipped around and eye to eye with him. My ass is lifted, one leg hooks over his hip, and he thrusts into me again. We're slippery, struggling to stay connected, and it's not until my back connects with the tile that I gain enough traction for that knot of desire deep in the base of my spine to unspool.

"Harder," I beg, my wet hair hanging down either side of my face. Dane's gaze darkens, his jaw twitches, and we inhale each other's breaths as the water sluices over us. I run my fingers through his hair, yanking at the ends as we work toward the high together.

"I can't believe I get to fuck this amazing pussy for the rest of my life, Del." His breathing is coming harder and faster now, just like mine. "Fuck, I love you baby."

"I love you," I say as the delirium builds and my brain hyper focuses on him. Only him. "I love y-y—"

And then I shatter.

My gasps and moans echo through the bathroom as I squeeze my eyes closed and lean back, my head pressing into the tile. My nails scratch against his scalp, pulling his hair as my very cells implode inside my skin.

And then he's coming too, cresting with a groan as he shudders inside me. We stay connected like that, slumped against the wet wall as the hot water coats our reddened skin.

It's only when I raise my face from his neck and meet his with a matching smile that know I'll never get enough of my new husband.

I stare dreamily at the engagement ring and wedding band combo that now decorates my fourth finger. I haven't taken the set off in days, and I don't think I'll ever be without it. I flutter my fingers and sigh like a princess in a cartoon fairy tale. So this is what real, all-encompassing love feels like.

After a secluded twenty-four hours together—hidden away in my apartment—Dane and I had eventually emerged to collect Kayce and say our goodbyes to Sav and Jack.

"You know, the beach makes a perfect honeymoon spot," Savannah whispered in my ear as we hugged.

I smiled warmly and squeezed her just a little tighter. Dane and I discussed taking some time away, just the three of us, once school let out for summer. But maybe there's something that can be booked in time for the spring vacation in a few months. I click open a tab on my computer, type in "tropical beach family vacations" and then search. The images on the screen portray happy moms and dads with their children frolicking in the sand—dads playing in the pool with the kids while moms kick their feet from the ledge. I find myself all warm inside. This is what Dane and I have created: a true family. I select a location near Savannah's home and scroll down to the amenities.

"Del?" My assistant's voice interrupts my daydreaming. I quickly minimize the screen filled with white sand and bright sun. "Mr. Patrick is here to see you."

"Thanks, Pete! Send him in."

I stand as Phil enters and extend my hand. "How are you doing, Mr. Patrick?"

"Just fine." He avoids my handshake and sets his briefcase on the chair. Standing behind it, he pulls a folded manila envelope from his back pocket and passes it my way.

My brow crinkles as I take the package. Did I ask him to bring in additional forms to update his file?

"You've been served, Ms. Evans. Or is it Mrs. Lukes now?" He smirks slightly.

My blood runs cold, and my eyes widen as he picks up his briefcase and stalks quickly from my office.

And suddenly it all makes sense. It wasn't my parents who told Marshall where I lived. It wasn't my parents who told Marshall about my marriage. It was never them.

It was that fucker Phil Patrick.

Kayce and I are cuddled on the couch when Dane comes home several hours later, a brown bag hanging from one hand. I stand, covering Kayce with the blanket we'd been sharing, and approach my husband.

He smells of the diner—a mix of frying oil and tomato sauce. I reach for him, wrapping my arms around his middle as I rest my head against his shoulder. "Well, damn, baby... Is this how you always greet your husband after a hard day of work?" He presses a kiss against my temple.

But I don't let him go. No, I need his safety. His protective net that catches me each and every time I stumble. And when my arms tighten around him, refusing to let go, his tone changes to one of concern. "What happened?"

I pull away and dip my chin at the stack of paperwork sitting on the kitchen counter. The contents of which are as spelled out, clear as mud, in legalese. He sets down the paper bag and picks up the packet, skimming through the documents with a frown on his face.

I step aside and uncurl the brown bag. Peeking inside, I find not only a takeout container of chicken parm, but a few slices of pepperoni pizza for Kayce, and the signature pink box tucked full of cannolis. Dane continues to peruse the forms as he moves from standing to sitting at the kitchen table.

I set the food out, one box next to another, and grab a stack of plates from the cupboard. "Kayce, you still hungry?" He shakes his head, hardly looking away from the cartoon on the TV. "Hey!" I admonish before his doe-eyed gaze snaps to mine, a blush blooming on his cheeks. "We'll turn it off if you can't answer."

He blinks at me. "Are you still hungry?" I repeat.

"Can I have a cannoli, please?"

My lip curls. He'd eaten a decent helping of macaroni and cheese with hot dogs for dinner, followed by a few cookies for dessert. But as my gaze slides to Dane and the paperwork he's set down in favor of his phone, I can't help but feel that mom guilt coming on. The guilt that wants to give her child anything—*everything*—so that he'll never say "*I want to live with my dad!*" again.

"How about half?" I compromise as I turn back to him and cut the pastry into two. I plate up a portion for him then grab a glass and pour some milk before taking the dessert over to him. As I return to the kitchen and the delicious food waiting for me, I stop behind Dane, my hand coming to rest on the back of his chair.

Between devouring the documents, he's Googling the jargon. Despite the anger I feel whenever I set eyes on the custody paperwork, my heart warms considerably as I watch my husband glance back and forth between the device and the stack.

"Hey," I say as I lean down and brush my lips under his ear. "Put that away and enjoy some takeout with me. I hear the chef's amazing." I saunter over and retrieve the remaining boxes, setting them on the table and taking a seat myself.

Dane only grunts as he continues to peruse everything. "I've suddenly lost my appetite."

I reach across the table and turn over the stack of papers. Then I lean down until he's forced to meet my gaze. "Listen, I know. I feel the same way. But, right now, I just need to have dinner with my husband. And share about our days."

He presses his lips together and nods slightly before sliding his phone into his back pocket. Then his hand reaches for mine, and he rubs his thumb along my wrist in soothing circles.

This. This is all I need, I remind myself. "So, tell me about your day."

CHAPTER THIRTY-SIX

Dane

"Maria can stay an extra hour as long as we send her home with a Maria's Special," Delia says as she rounds the corner from the back stairwell and slides into the booth next to me.

I smirk. Maria's been ordering the same thing since she was a little kid. Her mom and dad would bring her into the diner for her special birthday dinner—a pepperoni pizza drizzled with honey mixed with chili pepper flakes. Eventually, I learned how to infuse the honey with the chili, and named the menu item after the muse herself.

The woman across from me clears her throat with obvious annoyance. Delia blushes and even I find myself feeling chastised. "Sorry, Miranda," Delia exhales as her brows meet.

I'd ask if she has kids, but judging by the bare ring finger and perfectly coiffed ensemble, I'd guess not. Besides, it'd be highly unlikely that a mother could simply jet from Washington DC to the upper Midwest on a whim if she had children.

"So, tell me about the situation, Delia. The Senator relayed Savannah's information, but I'd like to hear it from you." My hand instinctively goes to Del's thigh and gives a gentle squeeze. While I'd given Del a list of high-powered attorneys in the greater Michigan area earlier in the month, I never expected her to already have someone in mind.

A shark, she said with a dangerous glint in her eye. Someone who's worked for Savannah's father for years and understands how to "make people go away." And now, as this self-proclaimed ocean predator sits in front of me, her appearance couldn't be more at odds with her nickname.

Miranda Abbott has worked for Senator Smith, Savannah's father, for years. While she started out as a glorified babysitter through college, she quickly obtained her law degree—as well as a degree in fixing shit no one else can. While her hair is a similar cut to Delia's, the shade is a much brighter red. It's also pin straight. Matched with her elfin features and diminutive frame, she resembles more of a seal pup than a killer.

"My ex—Kayce's father—is suing for custody. Joint custody, but custody nonetheless."

Miranda's eyes betray nothing, but I can't help but feel like she's bored of us already. "So why am I involved? Why not just call up some local bumpkin lawyer? This is an open-and-shut case, Delia."

My wife looks down. Her chin trembles, and she sniffs. "I-I can't do this alone. But"—and now she glances at me—"I can't ask my husband for help either."

My ears burn. "What are you talking about, Del?" I glance between the two women.

"You need the money to buy the building on Miller's Run Avenue. You can't bail me out of this one without losing your dream, and I won't ask you to choose."

My jaw pops open. "Baby, you don't need to ask. I'll give you every dime I have to fight this fucker. Whatever you need, it's yours. I don't need—"

She places her hand on mine and squeezes firmly. "I know *you* don't need, Dane. But *I* need. I need to not be the reason that you can't afford to chase your dream. So please... let me do this my way."

I lean back as defeat settles in my gut. "I want to be a part of this, Del. Don't shut me out." My mind is suddenly filled with a million different scenarios. Cracks in our foundation, rotting away our relationship.

She smiles at me and shakes her head. "I would never shut you out. That's why you're here. With me. I just can't ask you to be financially responsible for me and Kayce this time."

Miranda's icy gaze meets Delia's. "As touching as this whole thing is, how exactly do you suppose you'll pay me? After all, my pro bono days are behind me."

Delia, my beautiful wife, doesn't shrink as she goes toe to toe with the shark. No, she sits straighter, shoulders back, and purses her lips. "Marshall has never paid a single dime in child support, and I presume that's something you could potentially use to recoup your fee?"

"Ah," Miranda says as she leans back and crosses her arms. "There's the girl I remember. You know, I always liked you. More than Savannah, for obvious reasons. You weren't spoiled. No, you had to fight for everything, and it showed, Delia. So you've still got a little fight left, huh?"

Delia's throat bobs, and she nods, her gaze steady and her head high.

"Perfect," Miranda says. And as she gives Delia a slow smile, I suddenly see it. A shark seeking blood in the water.

"Do you really think this is a good idea?" I ask Delia as she glances at her phone once again.

"Miranda said it's fine, and I trust her." She sets the device on the kitchen counter and pads into the other room to retrieve Kayce.

As much as I want to disagree with both Del and Miranda, I've come to realize that it's best to stay silent. And that's been killing me. Keeping quiet as I watch Delia lose sleep, worry herself out of an appetite, and sink into a state of constant unease has been damn near impossible.

"Here's our guy!" Delia hollers as she ushers Kayce out of his room. He's wearing a collared shirt under a holiday sweater, freshly-pressed khakis, and his worn sneakers. His mop of hair has been tamed with styling powder and a bit of gel, and for once, he's missing the signature waves that I've come to love.

"Buddy!" I exclaim as I hold my arms open. "You look so grown up!"

The kindergartener just stares at me.

My face falls. "What's wrong?"

"I feel like a dork! Nobody else is going to be dressed up. Why do I have to wear this?" His fingers slide between his throat and the buttons of his collared shirt as he attempts to stretch it out. "I can't even breathe!"

I indicate the outfit I'm wearing. Dark denim paired with a white collared button down and a dark jacket. "Listen, I feel like a dork too, but at least we'll be dorks together, right?"

A smile cracks across his face. "Yeah, I guess."

I lean down to his level and pretend to whisper, just loud enough for Delia to hear. "Besides, your mom picked out our outfits, and I'm sure it means a lot to her."

Kayce peeks at his mother, who's wearing a flowy skirt and tight white sweater. She gives him a warm smile and then sends me a wink. It steals my breath, and even though we've been married just over a whole week, I still get the chills whenever I'm near her.

"Go get your coat," I order, sending him on his way so I can bury my face in Delia's neck. I inhale her scent as my cock springs to life inside my jeans. "Please tell me I can unwrap you like a present after all this," I beg.

She ruffles my hair. "Let's see how tonight goes with Marshall first."

At the mention of her ex, my desire immediately sinks below sea level. "We don't have to sit near him, do we?"

She wraps a scarf around her neck. "Of course not. But we do have to be cordial. Or so says Miranda."

My molars meet in the back, grinding together until I'm certain there's nothing left. "I believe we were being way more than cordial when we shared information about Kayce's holiday performance."

She cocks a brow at me. "*We* didn't share anything. Miranda shared it with his lawyer."

Right. I withhold the growl I feel bubbling in my throat and help zip Kayce's coat. After all, as Miranda told us just a few days ago, the goal is to let Marshall believe that we aren't preparing for war.

Kayce stands awkwardly on the stage risers, his face clearly not impressed with the songs that he and his classmates are tasked with singing.

"I think baseball is more his speed," I whisper to Delia. She snorts loudly, then looks around bashfully as other parents look in our direction.

"Shush," she admonishes before looking back, feigning diligence and interest in the holiday program.

In all actuality, the Winter Spectacular is just that. Reining in all these students, teaching them the same song and choreography, and getting them all to perform without a hitch takes a lot of effort. So when the curtain closes across the stage, I'm up on my feet clapping wildly and letting out a boisterous whistle.

Delia gives me a playful shove, her eyebrow raised. "Even if our son isn't a fan, we must support the arts." I bring my fingers between my lips and let it rip one last time before the auditorium begins to slowly empty.

We follow the row behind us as we're directed to the hallway to pick up Kayce. I crane my neck in search of him, but with all the parents and grandparents, it's nearly impossible. I keep my hand pressed firmly against Delia's back as she sends video after video to her parents and Nana via text message. "Ugh, the service in here is awful," she says, holding the device up into the air.

"You can send them once we're outside."

She glances around, spotting an exit just down the hallway. "I'm going to go stand by that door and see if they'll send. You grab Kayce, and I'll meet you at the front, okay?"

Before I can stop her, she's shot off against the stream of people like a salmon upstream. I push my lips together and continue winding toward the group of children, but there appears to be a bottleneck effect as parents and grandparents pose with their progeny against a holiday backdrop.

"Oh, hello," a male voice says from my left side. From the side of my vision, I catch Marshall's muddy-brown eyes.

I don't bother saying hello, but simply nod as I keep my face forward in my search for Kayce.

"Figures," he mutters under his breath. Then his elbow connects with the bottom of my rib, and I stumble into an older woman at my right.

"Hey! Watch it!" she says as her husband glares at me.

"Excuse me," I say with a sympathetic smile before turning a glare on Marshall. "What the hell was that?"

"What?" He blinks as we both spot Kayce at the same time. "As Kayce's *real* father, I'm just here to celebrate with him."

I ignore the insult and advance toward Kayce. "Hey, buddy!" I say, just as Marshall mutters loudly enough for me to hear.

"And it's only a matter of time before I'm fucking Dee again, too, you low-life diner owner."

My arms are outstretched, ready to swoop Kayce into a hug, and I swear that weaselly little fucker elbows me a second time—in the same spot just under my rib—and that's when my fist connects with his cheek.

CHAPTER THIRTY-SEVEN

Delia

"Yeah, Nana, the concert was great. I'm sending the videos to you now." As I lean against the door, I pull the phone away from my ear and click *share* on the device. "All right, you should get them in a—"

Suddenly, shouting erupts behind me, and everyone starts pushing and shoving as they attempt to get through the door. My phone flies from my hand as I'm nearly trampled, but I hold onto the door jamb and steady myself. I catch a glimpse of my device and wiggle through the crowd like a worm to retrieve it.

"Watch out!" I admonish a family as they rush past me. I lose my balance and catch myself against a bulky man. Principal Holden turns as I smile apologetically. "What's going on?" Even with my taller-than-most height, I can't catch a glimpse through the fray, although it sounds like a heated argument between two men.

And then it dawns on me.

I push past the principal and maneuver through the parents, their arms protectively wrapped around their children to shield them from the fist fight that rages in front of me.

"Stop it!" But between the ruckus of parents grabbing their kids and the shock of the scene before me, I'm not sure that my voice is even heard over Dane and Marshall squared up against one another. "That's *enough*!"

In that instant, Dane looks at me— regret immediately crossing his features— and Marshall lands a solid blow to his jaw.

"*Shit*, Marshall! *Stop it*!" I enter the foray and stand between the two, my hands held out on either side as I attempt to separate them. "What on Earth happened?" I look at Dane. He rubs the bottom of his rib cage with one hand while the other cradles his jaw. "And where the *hell* is Kayce?"

An off-duty police officer appears at my side, his badge visible as he flicks open his wallet. Kayce stands at his side. His bottom lip quivers as his gaze bounces back and forth between the two men in his life. "Ma'am." The officer nods at me. "This your son?"

I rush to Kayce and kneel, pulling him in for a hug. My palms instantly connect with the back of his head as I console him. "Oh, Kayce, I'm so glad you're safe."

Kayce stiffens and I pull away just in time to watch as the officer directs Dane to turn around and place his hands behind him. "Wait, what are you—"

"Ma'am," the officer interjects, his voice deep and serious, as he holds a hand up to stop me. "I'm going to need you to step back for a minute, and then we'll get your statement."

I press Kayce's face against my stomach, wanting to shield him from this, as I watch my husband get handcuffed. He's led out through the school hallway, horrified parents lined on either side, and out into the night.

As I make to follow, Marshall stops me, his hand extended and nearly pressed against my chest. I eye him up and down, my anger tempered for the time being but now—out of eyesight of the police officer—ready to be unleashed.

"You're not taking my son," he says, his eyes not meeting mine.

My molars grind together. "I suggest you step away from us, Marshall. Or you'll be leaving this building in an ambulance."

He pulls out his phone and holds it up to my face. "Is that a threat?"

I clamp my lips closed and clasp Kayce's hand. Leading him down the hallway, I hold my head held high as I pass the gossiping parents and their wide-eyed stares. "Mom?" Kayce's thin voice cracks my reserve.

"Yeah, buddy?" I swallow the lump that nearly blocks my throat. *Just a few more steps and we're clear of the crowd*, I tell myself.

"Is Dane going to be okay?"

"I don't know. But I hope so." And while I thought I'd breathe easier once I was outside, nothing could be farther from the truth. The officer leads Dane to the back of his car, tucks his head down, and closes the door—locking him in. For the first time in six years, I wonder how I'm going to get us out of this mess.

"It's how much?" I gape at the man in front of me, his neck tattoo crawling out from beneath his crewneck sweatshirt.

"Fifteen hundred, love. But you only have to pay one-fifty today to get your man out." My stomach nearly expels the expired granola bar I shoved down my throat on the way out the door this morning. After attempting to talk to Dane last night and being denied, I took Kayce home and we both tried—and failed—to get some sleep. He tossed and turned in the bed beside me; I couldn't bear to be without him in my sight. Not after Marshall's threatening text I received on the way to the police station.

Marshall: I'll be filing an emergency custody order. I don't feel it's in Kayce's best interest to be living with a violent felon.

I'd like to think the text meant nothing, but this morning I received email communication from Miranda, questioning the events of last night. I haven't responded yet.

"All right, can you put fifty on this card and the other hundred on this one?" I plop two separate credit cards on the counter and slide them over. They're practically pristine, but when he scans the second and it gives an ominous beep, my stomach drops.

"C-can you scan it again?" I ask, my voice breaking on the last word. While it's true that I don't have the funds readily available, I'm certain there's enough to cover the difference.

"No problem. This damn scanner's been acting up all morning." I blink at his reassurance and exhale a sigh of relief as it clears on the second attempt. He passes the plastic cards back to me—along with a stack of paperwork to fill out.

I take a seat in a faded and cracked pleather chair and get to work on the forms. When I've finished, I hand it all back. "Take the bottom two to the jail next door, and they'll release him." The bondsman winks, and I smile, grateful for at least one friendly face during this whole ordeal.

After all, the police receptionist had been surly and disgruntled with my questions last night. "We won't have any updates for you until your husband sees the judge in the morning," the overlarge man behind the desk said as he refused to take his eyes from the computer screen. Based on the reflection from his glasses, he was busy playing Solitaire.

Now, as I traipse in hours later with my necessary paperwork and bail receipt in hand, there's a smiling woman sitting behind the desk who greets me. "How can I help you?"

I breathe yet another sigh of relief as I pass over the documents, and she excuses herself to retrieve "the inmate," as she calls him.

I take a seat, this time in a plastic chair that's bolted to the concrete floor, and swipe my phone awake to give Miranda a call. She answers on the first ring.

"What the hell is going on?" I'm suddenly a lanky thirteen year old again and being scolded by Savannah's babysitter for spilling Kool-Aid on the floor.

"I-I'm honestly not sure yet. I haven't spoken to Dane. They wouldn't let me. But I just posted his bail so I'll know more shortly."

She huffs into the phone. "Then why did you call me, Delia?"

Why did I call her? Because I've got no one else to talk to about this. I can't tell my parents, or even Nana, about Dane getting arrested. They might think less of him and I couldn't handle that. Savannah would fly back up here in a heartbeat and go apeshit on everyone, which would solve absolutely nothing. "I-I don't know. I just thought you'd know what to do. Is my... Am I going to lose custody of Kayce?" My voice breaks.

She sighs again into the phone, only this time it's less severe. Almost resigned. "Until I know more, I can't tell you anything."

I sniff. "Oh, okay."

"But unless Dane attacked you or Kayce, I highly doubt it. And from what I can tell just in meeting him briefly, that man would never hurt either of you."

"Thanks, Miranda. That means a lot." I wipe my nose on my sleeve because, as I sit in the county jail and wait to bail out my husband of less than two weeks, why not?

"Call me back when you have more info." The line goes dead before I can even say goodbye, not that I'd expect any less. She may be a cold and calculating shark, but she knows what she's doing and will always strive for a win.

"Mrs. Lukes?" I snap my head toward the officer behind the window. "We're ready for you now."

"So he elbowed you and you jacked him in the face?" I try my best to keep my eyes on the road, so I grip the steering wheel so hard that my knuckles turn white. It's not from anger at Dane.

At least that's what I tell myself.

"Del, there's no excuse for my actions. It doesn't matter if he elbowed me, shoved me, whatever... I can't believe I fucked up."

My eyes go misty, and I blink away the threat of tears. I hate this entire situation. I hate that I've had to max out my credit cards to bail Dane out of jail. I hate that Dane overreacted and got himself into this situation. But mostly, I hate that Marshall is the reason we're even here to begin with.

"I should've known," I say through gritted teeth. "I should've known he'd come into our lives and fuck everything up. This is all my fault."

Dane reaches across the console and pats my thigh. Normally that simple gesture would send shivers up my spine, but not today. "None of this is your fault."

I nod my head. "The moment he showed up I should've sicced Miranda on him. Demanded child support in exchange for a few brief visits each year."

"But that's not you, Del. You're not purposefully cruel. You don't immediately go on the defensive; you give people a chance."

We approach a red light, and I allow my grip to loosen before dropping my hands to my lap. "And look where it got me. And by default, *you*." The tears well again, and before I can stop them, they rush down my cheeks in rivulets. "H-how is this going to affect the custody hearing?" I gasp and smack the base of my palm against my forehead. "How is this going to affect your new location?"

Dane grabs my hand and brings it to his mouth before pressing a kiss to my curled fingers. "I'm not worried about the restaurant right now. Our focus is Kayce."

The light switches to green, and I swallow, nodding as my hands return to the wheel. "When we get back home, we'll call Miranda and go from there. It's all about Kayce and what's best for him," I say as the car accelerates.

Dane's hand finds my thigh once more. "We're a family now, Del. And I'll do whatever it takes to keep us together."

CHAPTER THIRTY-EIGHT

Dane

"**Y**ou've got to be kidding me!"

"Shhh!" Delia responds as she swats her hand at me. Only—I can't be quiet. I need to know exactly what Marshall was thinking when he assumed he could control mine and Delia's co-habitation as a *married* couple.

"Dane, this isn't about you, remember?" Miranda's voice cuts through the phone line. "Marshall filed for emergency custody because he feels that, with you in the home, it's an unsafe environment for his son. Unless you want Kayce to go live in Chicago for the next several weeks, you'll do as I tell you."

I grind my back teeth together so harshly that I nearly taste blood. "And what exactly do I need to do?"

"Move back into your apartment. It's that simple. You're only across the hall, right?"

Delia's shoulders sag. "Yeah, Miranda. Just in the apartment next door."

"And Delia? You need to make damn sure it looks like Dane's completely moved out and has no interaction with you or your son."

Her mouth gapes. "B-but we're newlyweds, Miranda. How is that—"

Miranda tuts on the phone. "I don't care *how* you make it happen. *Just do it.* For your son's sake."

"All right..." Delia clicks end and sets the phone on the counter.

She looks as though she's witnessed her family dog get hit by a car right in front of her eyes. So I go to her. I take her in my arms and pull her against me. "It's only temporary, baby. It's only temporary..."

She turns her face into my chest. "How are we supposed to appear to be separated when we just realized how perfect we are together?" Her hands slide up my back.

I inhale her scent and enjoy the feeling of her nails along my spine. "We didn't just realize, *you* did." She pulls away and narrows her gaze at me. "I'll stay out of your hair."

"How exactly is that supposed to happen when you *live* across the hall and *work* right downstairs?"

I untangle myself from her grasp and instantly feel like there's an ocean between us. "I was going to wait until the new year, but I'll contact the realtor for the new location and see if I can take possession now. Besides, our business isn't exactly busy over the holiday. Better to close up now and get everything moved over." I take a few tentative steps toward the bedroom, but stop the second she reaches out and grabs my hand.

"I'll help you pack your things."

I reward her with a sad smile and then pull her against me. "How am I going to handle not being with you every night? Waking up to you each morning?"

"It's like I got my most-wanted Christmas present, and then it was taken away." She presses a soft kiss against the corner of my mouth.

"It's only temporary," I remind her as, together, we walk backward toward the bedroom.

By the time we reach the doorway to our—*her*—bedroom, we're already pulling at each other's clothes. "I need a shower," I remind her as I extricate myself once again. Hopefully Delia's creams and lotions can wash away the scent of a night in jail. Although I'm not sure if anything can erase the shame and embarrassment of the whole ordeal.

I walk over to her bedside table and pull out one of her toys. Her lips turn down at the corners as I hand it to her. "Are you suggesting I might as well get used to these old things again... *temporarily?*"

My lips connect with the sensitive skin under her ear. "Get yourself warmed up, baby. I'll be out in a jiff."

As much as I'd like to simply rinse off, making this the quickest shower known to man, I can't help but relish the warm soapy water that runs down my skin. My stint in jail may have been short, but it was cold and uncomfortable, to say the least.

After ensuring that I've washed away all the crud from the limestone cell, I quickly dry myself off, tie the towel around my waist, and head back to the room I'd only just begun to call mine.

"Del?" Despite being the middle of the day, the curtains are drawn. Delia's legs are bent, her knees tenting the comforter.

"Hmm...?" she mumbles over the buzz of her vibrator. I creep forward, and as I fling the covers back, discard my towel on the floor. I'm already hard. My cock points straight toward home.

As I climb onto the bed, the mattress dips and she rolls toward me. Her nipples are pebbled, begging to be sucked. I lean forward and roll the flesh into my mouth, laving it with my tongue as a needy whine escapes between her lips. Her forearm flexes as she works the vibrator against herself.

I release the fleshy mound from my mouth and move to her lips, capturing them with my own. My hand slides down her back, tickling along the soft skin, until it reaches the curve of her ass. I pull and hoist her onto me.

"Ride my cock," I beg as I glide my other hand along the shaft. She attempts to set aside the vibrator, but I still her hand. "No, I want to watch you pleasure yourself—*fuck yourself*—with both."

Her cheeks tint as she bites her lip. She gazes down at my length situated between us, standing tall as it presses against her belly. My hands on her hips, I guide her up and onto it, and as she seats herself slowly—*so slowly*—I can't help but release a moan.

My wife's pussy feels like heaven.

She bounces, her tits bobbing up and down as her thighs work, until I'm already so close. "Slow down, baby. *Please*," I beg, my hands pressing desperately on her thighs.

Delia nods, stilling herself as she lines up her vibrator so that it nestles just inside the apex of her lower lips. Then she rolls forward and back, forward and back. I match the rhythm with small thrusts as she chases her orgasm. Her hands trail up her stomach and cup her breasts, fondling the nipples until they're rock hard once more.

My hands continue to grip her hips, but otherwise, I'm useless as she works herself up. She gasps as she continues to rock and grind on my length, and that delicious feeling starts to build along the base of my spine before it flares quickly to life.

Suddenly Delia's hands clench, her face contorts, and her thrusts become erratic as she crests. I watch as my wife uses me—uses my cock—for her sole pleasure, and then I'm following suit. My orgasm comes on fast, and as I grip her hips and hoist her up and down quickly, I spill into her as she releases a moan of delight.

We both slow, our movements becoming lazy and haphazard, and before long she collapses on top of me and presses a kiss to my lips.

"Promise this will only be temporary," she says. "I need you."

"I promise," I say as I hug her close. Because nothing could keep me away from my wife—my *family*. Not even a court order.

"Boss, you forgot to turn the sign to *open*," Crystal says when she waltzes through the door twenty-five minutes late for her shift. "That honeymoon phase has you going crazy!"

I smirk at her before setting two coffee mugs into the box on the counter. "Good thing you're finally here. You can help me pack."

Her mouth pops open. "Pack? Are we closing?"

"Yep," I say as I continue to nestle the mugs into the box. "The Miller's Run Avenue location is officially a go. I got off the phone with the realtor earlier this morning, and we can start renovating and moving in this week."

Crystal drops her purse on the counter and runs around, wrapping me up in a tight hug. "Oh! I'm so excited for you—for us!"

I pat her gently on the back before untangling myself. "It's going to be a lot of work."

She follows my lead and starts pulling the mugs from beneath the counter. "I'm here for it, Dane."

We continue in silence for a few minutes before an idea pops into my head. "Hey, how old are your kids again?"

"Fifteen and thirteen, why?"

"How would they like to make some extra money over the holiday break?"

Her eyes widen and she smiles. "Oh, they'd love to help."

I bob my head. I may not be able to be around my family for the holiday, but at least I can live vicariously through Crystal's.

Chapter Thirty-Nine

Delia

With the holidays approaching, the bank's been busy. Most are making hefty withdrawals for gift purchasing, while others are trying to make deposits into retirements or college funds before the year's end. The tediousness keeps me busy, at least between the hours of eight and five, and there are several days where I choose to miss my lunch so that a coworker can take a break instead.

After all, the opportunity to ponder my loneliness over a ham and cheese sandwich doesn't exactly make me hungry.

I'm minding the desk as a fill-in teller when my cell phone rings in my pocket. An elderly woman is filling out a form, so I quickly glance at the screen and, seeing it's my father, swipe to answer.

"Hello?" I answer, my voice less than enthusiastic. I'm able to plaster on a fake smile when dealing with customers and clients, but that ability falls quite short when it's my personal life.

"Delia? It's your father calling." At this greeting I smile, if only because he doesn't realize that each cell phone has an embedded caller ID.

"Yes, how are you?" The elderly woman approaches slowly, and I beckon her forward with a gentle smile. It's only when she slides her form across the counter and I use the information to key into her account that I realize it's Marigold Fraser.

Damn, I really need to wear my glasses more often.

"We're fine. I was wondering about your plans for the holiday. Your mother and I would like to make a trip to visit Nana for the Christmas Eve dinner and wanted to invite you, Dane, and Kayce."

I frown slightly—not because I don't want to visit my grandmother, but because the meals at her nursing facility are always bland and soft. "Oh, uh, sure. But it'll just be me and Kayce." I withdraw the amount for Mrs. Fraser and run it through the money counter to ensure that none of the bills are stuck together.

"Is Dane busy working that evening? We'd love to see him."

I sigh heavily, but paste a smile on my face as I pass the money over to Mrs. Fraser. She unzips her purse and digs for her pocketbook. "No, it's not that. It's..." I trail off when I notice Marigold peeping at me through her lashes. My expression pinched, I turn around and whisper into the phone. "Dane and I are just busy right now. He's opening the new location and I'm... working a lot. In fact, I've got a customer now, so I'll meet you at 4:30 on Christmas Eve." I know the dinnertime at Nana's by heart.

I click *end* on the call and pocket the device before turning back to Marigold. Except she's already opening the door and on her way out of the bank.

Left on the counter in her stead is a greeting card, wishing me a happy holiday and inviting me to the Christmas Day service. I roll my eyes and fold the card before pocketing it, too.

Kayce swallows the last chicken nugget and tosses the container into the fast food bag. "Now, if anyone asks, you're not hungry because..."

"Maria made me a big lunch," he repeats the excuse we've been practicing the whole way to Lansing, even as we stopped at his favorite drive-thru to get something to hold us over.

"And when you see a food you don't want, you say..."

"Blech, that looks gross!"

I reach back, playfully swatting his leg that dangles from the booster seat. "No! You say 'no, thank you.'"

He rolls his eyes and tugs at his collared shirt. It's a far cry from his usual T-shirt and sweats, but my boy actually cleans up well. "Quit fussing," I admonish.

I cut the engine, tuck the fast food bag under the front seat, and hoist my purse over my shoulder as I exit the car. By the time I reach Kayce, he's unbuckled and pushing open the door himself.

I hold his hand as he jumps out, and then we make our way into the nursing home. It's been a while since I visited, but with everything that's going on, it's been hard to get away. I've picked up extra bank shifts on Saturdays just for something to do, but also for the extra cash. The older Kayce gets, the more expensive his wish list has become.

"What are you going to tell Santa you want for Christmas?" I ask as we head down the foyer and into the brightly lit cafeteria. Every year, the home gets a Santa for the children, and every year Kayce brings his list to share.

This year, I peeked and noticed that there was an Xbox *and* a PlayStation listed, and it was hard not to mentally curse Marshall even more than I already was.

"I want a PlayStation and an Xbox, and all the games to go with them. And I also want the controllers that light up and the matching headsets for each, too."

I gulp, wondering how on Earth I'm going to deal with the letdown that will surely come when he opens his gifts on Christmas morning and sees neither of those gaming systems under the tree. "Now remember, Santa doesn't usually bring really expensive gifts like that. It's really only what the elves can make in the toy shop." My excuse sounds as lame as my stilted voice.

"So can *you* get them for me?"

My mouth pops open as my brow crinkles. "I don't th—" I begin, just as I spot my parents and Nana waiting for us outside the cafeteria. "Oh look! Go say hi." I give him a gentle shove and breathe a sigh of relief when he's distracted with saying hello to everyone.

Nana takes Kayce's hand and leads us to the table she's selected. Our seats are right next to Santa, and Kayce bounces on his toes as he stares at the empty dais. "You have to eat your dinner first," Nana says as she settles Kayce next to her. He gives a squeamish smile, and I hold back a chuckle.

Just then, a frail woman passes—a family member pushing her wheelchair. Nana leans back into the aisle, blocking the path. "Josephine, you better have my goods today." She glares at the wheelchair-bound grandmother, whose eyes pop open as her gummy mouth gapes.

"Nana!" I grab her hand and pull her from the aisle, appalled by her behavior. I look around, ensuring my parents are focused on asking Kayce about school, and lean in. "What are you doing? You're acting like some kind of mobster!"

"Psh," my sweet Nana swats me away. "She's faking it. The other day I saw her run that wheelchair into another lady on purpose."

I stare incredulously and shake my head. "Don't make me regret bringing your medicine." I pat the large tote hanging on the back of my chair.

Nana narrows her eyes at me and turns to Kayce. As the dinner commences, I'm all but ignored. Waiters and waitresses dressed like Santa's elves bring around cafeteria trays covered in Saran Wrap. Pitchers of water, iced tea, and some kind of red juice are set on the tables, and we attempt to dig in.

Judging by Kayce's face, nothing on the menu looks appetizing. "No, thank you," he says as he slides his tray aside.

I roll my jaw as my mother works to get him to at least take a bite of the mashed potatoes.

"We've got a surprise for you tonight, Delia," my father says from across the table.

I raise my eyebrows as I take a bite of the ham.

When I don't say anything, he leans in and whispers conspiratorially, "Guess who volunteered to be our Santa!" Then his eyes slide behind me, and I turn.

There, in a bright red suit, pillow-stuffed belly, and white beard, stands Dane.

Chapter Forty

Delia

We patiently wait our turn to visit with Santa. Kayce holds my hand, swinging it forward and backward, while my parents and Nana wait at the table behind us.

"Kayce, look this way!" my mother instructs as she holds her phone up. Kayce turns and gives a toothy smile as I kneel down, my arms wrapped around him. "Oh, that's a good one. You'll have to show me how to upload it to the digital picture frame, Delia."

My relationship with my parents has blossomed in the last few weeks. I'm trying to allow them into our lives, little by little. The picture frame was just a small gesture, allowing me to send photos directly to the device.

"Next!" One of the elf waiters, now in charge of the Santa line, beckons to us. I step forward tentatively, my gaze settling on Dane as Kayce charges forward. He leaps into Santa's lap, completely clueless.

Dane's eyes skim over mine as he turns to Kayce. "And what would you like, little boy?" He's done an awful job disguising his voice, but the six year old on his lap still has no idea. I cross my arms, waiting for this whole charade to implode.

Kayce withdraws his list from his pocket and begins reciting all the expensive items, mostly from memory. After the fourth or fifth outrageous gift, Santa interrupts. "Now, Kayce, you do know that Christmas isn't just about opening gifts, right?"

His eyes widen as he folds his list and holds it in his tiny hand. "What else is it about, Santa?"

Dane's hand ruffles Kayce's curls. "It's also about opening your heart, son." My throat tightens and I struggle to swallow as I eavesdrop. "Do you know what that means?"

Kayce shakes his head.

"It means being grateful for your mom and all she does for you every day of the year. It means being excited to spend time with her, watch holiday movies, and eat lots of Christmas cookies. It means saying thank you when you open your gifts from her and being happy that Santa found you the perfect present made by his elves."

Kayce nods and his smile blooms slowly at first. Then he reaches forward and gives Santa a big hug. "I love you, Santa! I'll love whatever you bring me, I promise!"

Then he leaps off of Santa's lap and runs toward his grandparents, the conversation likely forgotten.

Dane's eyes meet mine and I shrug. "At least you tried, Santa." I press my lips together as I take in my husband in his costume.

"Why don't you come sit on Santa's lap, young lady, and tell him what *you* want for Christmas." He pats his knee and waggles his eyebrows under the bobble hat.

I turn to look at my parents and Nana, and all three are enraptured with Kayce's list. Then I tentatively take the steps one at a time until I'm standing before him. I settle myself carefully on his knee and hold my body rigid as the uncomfortableness sets in. Although when I look out at the cafeteria, not a single family is paying attention to us. Everyone's busy with their own kin.

"And what do you want for Christmas, baby?" His voice is low. His beard tickles along my forearm.

Despite the getup, my nipples pebble beneath my sweater. Dane and I have only been apart for a few days, but it's enough that I miss him. The *feel* of him. His *presence*. Being so close to him has all my senses going haywire.

I lean forward and whisper in his ear. "Just you, Dane. That's all I want for Christmas." My knee slowly grazes his inner thigh, and he gasps before I pull away. Now is not the time nor the place.

"It's been hard keeping myself away from you," he says as I stand. I adjust the hem of my top and smooth my hands over it.

My eyebrow cocks. "How hard?" I allow my gaze to dip to his lap.

Even through the fluffy beard, his cheeks tint slightly. And then I step down the dais and rejoin my family. Luckily our group was the last in the line, and as Dane disappears, waving to the families and hollering "Merry Christmas!" I can't help but wonder if I now have a Santa kink.

By the time Kayce and I arrive home, it's late. The street lamps are lit, and pretty holiday wreaths hang along each one. I pull alongside the curb of the building, cut the engine, and sling my purse over my shoulder.

Kayce's passed out in his car seat.

As I trudge around to the backseat, I'm grateful I didn't take any of the leftover food home—my backseat is already filled with gifts from Nana for both myself and Kayce. I'll have to come back down to get them later.

I hoist Kayce into my arms and use my hip to close the door. Only then do I see the outline of Dane in the restaurant. He's stacking chairs and tables. Gone is the Santa suit—it must've been borrowed from the nursing home—and in its place are his signature low-slung jeans and a backward baseball hat. I press my lips together as the desire to go to him surges in my belly, but as a brisk breeze gusts over us, I think better of it and take the stairs carefully one at a time.

Luckily my son is a sound sleeper, and I'm able to get him into his pajamas and tucked in without him waking. Only then do I pad into my room and start my own nightly routine. My eyes trail to Dane's drawers—now empty. To his side of the bed—now untouched.

It's funny how I'd come to feel more whole with him around. Now, it's like each part of my apartment holds a memory of him.

I tie my hair into a bun and slide beneath the covers. Only my brain won't shut off. So I turn to my phone for comfort and doom scroll through social media. I click the heart on a picture of Savannah and Jack at her step-mother's house in Florida. *"Miss you! Merry Christmas, you two!"* I add with a Santa emoji.

And before I know what I'm doing, I close the social media app and open my text messages.

> *I've never been into older men before, but seeing you in that Santa getup made me feel a few things.*

The typing bubble appears and then disappears. My stomach drops, and I reopen my socials just as a response arrives.

What type of things, exactly? I need specifics.

I smirk and wiggle my toes under the covers. Then I bite my lip and start to type, letting it all out.

Well, for starters, I wanted to see what Santa was packing. It seemed like quite a large gift.

Fuck, baby, I'm thinking about the gift I want to give you right now...

Tell me.

I'd watch you unwrap it. Your pretty little mouth would pop open when you saw how big it was. How big you make it. And then I'd slide that gift right between those lips, just for a taste. And while you were gliding that wet tongue all over me, my fingers would be inside you. Pumping in and out, massaging that clit, getting you so wet.

I gulp. My body's on fire, and I kick off the comforter. Jesus, who knew Dane was such a wordsmith?

Are you wet, baby?

Yes. Soaked.

Good. Because my tongue's thirsty for you. I'd lean down and lap at your sweetness until your thighs were shaking and your eyes rolled back.

Keep going...

And just when you were about to come, I'd pull away and slide my cock into you. You'd stretch around me perfectly. Fit me perfectly. And I'd fuck you so hard…until you couldn't even remember your name, but you'd be screaming mine.

Oh, God. My nipples poke out beneath my pajama top, and I squeeze my thighs together. I wish Dane were here. Doing all those things to me. And as I gulp and set my phone down in order to touch myself, in order to relieve some of this tension, there's a soft knock at my door.

I already know who it is. I nearly skip with anticipation as I throw open the door. Dane stands before me, his arm overhead as he leans against the frame. I step over the threshold and throw myself against him. He catches me, hands under my ass, and shoves me backward against the door.

Our lips meet in a race of tongues and teeth, nipping and sucking like we're starved for one another. It's hardly believable that we were just in the same room a few hours ago, and as I drag his shirt up and over his head, he backs us into the apartment.

I'm set on the counter that separates the kitchen from the living area, my pajama pants verily ripped from my bottom half. "No underwear?" His eyes gleam as he gazes at my wet core.

My hands connect with his hair as his face dives forward. He throws my legs over his shoulders and I lean backward against the kitchen faucet. It's not comfortable, but the pain turns to pleasure as the cold metal connects with my spine.

"Fuck, *fuck, fuck,*" I murmur as he laves me, his tongue flat against my skin. Then, as promised, those fingers enter me. Hard and fast, as though he can't restrain himself, he finger-fucks me until my toes are curling and I'm hissing his name.

But I want more. I want the whole package. The gift I was promised.

I lean forward and grapple with the button of his jeans, my fingers demanding as they withdraw him from his briefs. I hop to the floor and drop to my knees, pulling him into my mouth as my tongue salivates with need.

His palms come to rest at the base of my skull, and as he sucks air through his teeth, I know we're both about to tip over the edge. But before he gets too close, he pulls out of my mouth, pushes me backward until I'm flat on my back in the foyer of the apartment, and enters me fast and hard.

I gasp out his name as he covers me with his body, pumping into me like it's our last time together. I pull at his hair, my nails drag across his biceps, and the pressure builds so quickly that I'm coming within moments. He leans down, captures my lips with his, and tips over the edge as his cock pulses inside me. Only after our movements slow and we catch our breaths do I realize it's past midnight.

Merry Christmas, indeed.

CHAPTER FORTY-ONE

Dane

"**M**ommy! Santa came!" Kayce's excitement pulls me from the depths of a deep sleep at the ripe hour of five in the morning. As I come to, I realize that both Delia and I are curled next to the Christmas tree with a blanket wrapped around our nakedness.

"Shit," Del mutters under her breath as Kayce rushes to his presents. Her wide eyes are filled with terror as she shuffles under the blanket for her pajamas.

I pass over her pajama top and keep the cover wrapped around us both. "Hey, buddy, why don't you go brush your teeth before presents?"

Kayce frowns at me, his eyebrows lowering in disagreement. "But I want to open my presents first!"

I wink at him. "I know, but your breath is stinky! Phew!" I flap my hand over my nose in jest, and am rewarded with a crack of a smile.

Then he turns and ambles down the hallway, closing the bathroom door with a slam. Only then do Delia and I scramble apart, pulling our clothing over our nakedness with the speed of Rudolph on his last stop of the night.

I button my jeans just as Kayce reenters the room, his pearly whites flashing. "All done! Now can I open them?" He looks between the two of us, and I'm not sure if he's asking permission from Del or me, so I defer.

"Sure, bud. But you need to say goodbye to Dane first." She takes a seat on the couch and tucks her foot under her leg.

"Why can't he stay and watch me open presents?" Kayce whines.

"Well, I've got to go wrap your presents because I totally forgot!" I smack my palm against my forehead.

He nods solemnly, willing to risk missing me in exchange for more gifts, and then throws himself into my arms. "When will I see you so I can open them?"

I glance over his head at Delia, her lips thinned as she watches us. I clear my throat. "Well, uh, I'm helping out at the church later this morning. Serving biscuits, gravy, and bacon."

Kayce turns to his mom. "Can we go? I love bacon!"

Delia swallows, her throat bobbing as her cheeks flush. "Uh, sure. W-we can go to church."

Then he releases me from my hug and dives headfirst into the wrapped boxes. As he stacks his gifts into a tower, he sets one gift aside for Delia before passing another to me. "I made this for you," he says as his eyes brighten. "You can open it later."

My throat tightens as I look at the rectangular gift. It's wrapped in brown paper and decorated with baseballs. "Thanks, buddy," I manage as the back of my eyes prick.

I place a peck on Delia's forehead, my hand lingering at the base of her neck for far too long.

As I head toward the door, my chest aches. Not spending Christmas morning with my family is gut-wrenching, and I despise Marshall for trying to break us apart.

Although I shouldn't be, I'm surprised by the number of people attending church on Christmas Day. As a child, I was raised in this church. Attending Sunday morning services every week, as well as holidays, was a big reason my mother and father were such staples in the community.

"Dane! I'm so glad you're here. What time do you need to start preparing?" Marigold Fraser's felt hat is decked with sprigs of holly and tinsel, and I try to keep my eyes on hers as I answer despite the bobbing of the accoutrements.

"I got everything set up in the church's kitchen. I was able to source a few extra Crock-Pots, and the bacon only needs about twenty minutes in the oven." I clasp my hands together and nod encouragingly.

"My, my. You've got it all handled. Will you be listening to the service, then?" Without waiting for my answer, she guides me up the aisle toward her designated pew.

The same pew where my mother and father sat each week next to Marigold's family. Her husband passed away quite a long time ago, as did my parents, so it's just the two of us that occupy the empty bench.

It's been ages since I've attended an actual church service, but as I glance around at the sanctuary, nothing's changed. "Did Delia tell you I was in the bank the other day?"

"No, she didn't," I answer as I turn my gaze toward my seat mate.

"Well, I had quite the withdrawal, and Delia was working the desk. I swear, I don't even think that woman takes a lunch break anymore. I've been in there several times the last few weeks, and each time she's been busier than a bee."

I press my lips together in a flat smile. If only Marigold really knew the real reason Delia was running herself ragged, and that I'd been doing the same with the new restaurant location. "They rely on her a lot, and it certainly keeps her busy."

Marigold tuts and puts her wrinkled hand on my forearm. "Dane. We both know something's going on between the two of you." She leans in closer and whispers. "And we know about the incident at the school play, too." She settles back against the wooden pew and raises a single eyebrow at me.

I swallow. It's been a long time since I felt like I was being chastised by my mother again. But that's exactly what's happening here. "Kayce's father has filed paperwork for emergency custody, and our lawyer thinks it's best I keep my distance for a bit." I glance up at the enormous wooden cross over the pulpit. It feels wrong to ask for help from The Big Guy when I so rarely seek Him out these days. So I keep my lips closed and look down at my hands.

"Psh!" Marigold chuckles under her breath. "And you thought that was the best thing to do? Keep your distance from your family during the holidays?"

I shrug. If I'm being honest, I hadn't wanted to follow Miranda's instructions, but it wasn't—still isn't—my choice. "What else can I do? I don't want to hurt Delia's chances of primary custody."

Just then the organ starts up, and everyone stands. As I help her to her feet, Marigold says, just loud enough to be heard over the organ, "You let me take care of this."

And before I can question her on what exactly she intends to do, the congregation begins to sing.

"Hey Dane, the new location is really coming along, isn't it?" I smile and nod kindly at the woman whose name I don't know before passing over a plate of biscuits and gravy. "This looks delicious! Will you be serving breakfast once you reopen?"

"I doubt it. Keeping my focus on the Italian recipes." I hand her son a plate, and he beams at me. Suddenly, I realize it's one of the baseball parents. "You been practicing? I expect to see your name on the spring ball sign-up list, you hear?"

"Oh, he would love to be on your team again, Coach! He even got a new bat for Christmas, didn't you Harrison?" The kid bobs his head before scooting off to find a seat. "Merry Christmas!" the mother adds with a small wave as she follows her son.

I scoop another helping of gravy onto a plate of biscuits before I realize that we're nearly at the end of the serving pan. I've got another warming on the stove in the back, and I pass the ladle to the youth group assistant as I retreat.

By the time I return, the line's dwindled down to just a few stragglers and those vying for seconds. I dump the last of the gravy into the warming pan, and this time, I allow the assistant to take it back to the kitchen.

My eyes scan over the crowd. The families that chose to stay are crammed together on foldable card tables, the chairs scraping loudly against the linoleum floor as they scoot closer together to accommodate just one more. The spirit of Christmas is alive and well as people in their Sunday best share their hopes for the new year and thanks for their blessings.

My gaze lands on Delia and Kayce, seated next to Marigold Fraser. The moment she'd spotted my family, she scooped them under her wing and led them to her table. Now, as Kayce finishes his plate and takes it to the trash, Marigold's head bends toward Delia's, and they murmur together. Their eyes occasionally dart my way, and my throat goes dry.

"Can I get another helping?" A lanky teenage boy holds his plate out.

"Sure, man," I respond as I scoop a ladleful of gravy onto his biscuits. But my eyes don't leave the scene at the table. It's only when Kayce runs over and tugs on his mom's shirtsleeve that her attention diverts from Marigold's. She notices me watching and blushes.

"Oh, that's plenty." Startled, I turn my focus back to the teen and realize I've overloaded his plate with way too much gravy. The Styrofoam practically bends in half in my hand.

"Uh, sorry. You want some more biscuits?" I awkwardly pass him the tray.

"No, that's all right..." He uses both hands to steady the plate as his brows squish together. Luckily there's no one else waiting, so I decide to abandon my post and make my way through the crowded room toward Del and Marigold.

An older woman grabs my arm as I pass. "This was amazing, Dane. When can you come back?"

I press my lips firmly together and give a curt nod as her table mates echo the sentiment. "Excuse me," I respond as I continue onward. Only when

I reach my destination do I notice the scrap of paper between my wife and Marigold.

On it is a date and time. January 3rd. 10:15 a.m.

"What's that?" I blink at the paper as I take a seat. Kayce immediately climbs onto my lap and I squeeze his shoulders.

"Oh." Delia blushes again as her gaze flits from the note to Marigold. "I-it's the custody date. Marigold—she offered to watch Kayce." Delia's hand darts out and she pushes the scrap toward the elderly woman.

"Right." Her eyes dip as she folds the paper and tucks it into her bag. "Well, you two enjoy the rest of the day. Lovely meal, Dane." She stands abruptly and hoists her purse over her shoulder. Then she shuffles away to a table of church officials.

I turn my head back to Delia. My gaze narrows. "Okay, something's up. What's going on? You're letting Marigold Fraser watch Kayce?"

She blinks. "Why not?"

"What about Maria?"

"She's busy," she says, a little too quickly.

"Hm." I pat Kayce on the back. "Want to help me clean up, buddy?"

"Sure!" He jumps from my lap and pulls me to stand. "Can I use the faucet sprayer, too?"

"Of course, but you have to promise to keep the water in the sink this time."

"I promise." He lops off to the food table. I start to follow—just as Delia's hand reaches out and grabs my forearm.

"Hey," she says, her eyes crinkling in the corner.

"Yeah?" My stomach clenches. I know she's fibbing about something. Now that Kayce's gone, is she going to reveal what's actually going on?

"The biscuits and gravy were great."

My smile falters. Apparently not. "Thanks." I bend to plant a kiss on her forehead, but I don't miss how her eyes lower or her fist clenches until her knuckles are white.

What is my wife up to?

CHAPTER FORTY-TWO

Delia

Dane knows I'm withholding something from him, but luckily, Kayce and I head up to Nana's after the church breakfast. The weather is mild for December in Michigan, and we make good time, arriving just before lunch.

We meet my parents there and exchange gifts under a small tree with ornaments made by my father, myself, and Kayce. Not a single decoration is store-bought. There's a badly-sewn stuffed bird that I made in second grade art class, innumerable laminated class photos that were once coated in glitter, and a few salt dough handprints from when my dad was a child. Kayce loves putting his own hand in the print and figuring out who has the bigger hand based on age.

"Mom! My hand is bigger than grandpa's at eight years old," he states excitedly. "And I'm only six!"

"Wow!" I chomp on a cheese-covered cracker.

"You know, your grandfather had the funniest looking teacher when he was eight. She smiled like a rat."

I roll my eyes and let out a snort. "My teacher smiles like an angel," Kayce replies as he returns to his new toys. My parents had given him a new set of "church clothes" which were quickly discarded in favor of Nana's color-changing matchbox cars. "Nana, can I play with these in your sink?"

"Of course, sweetheart. Just make sure you put down a hand towel so you don't get everything wet." She winks, and Kayce beams and rushes to the bathroom, where he dumps all his cars into the porcelain sink before cranking the faucet on full blast.

I stand, but my grandmother puts out her hand. "Let the boy have fun and make a mess. It won't hurt anything." I press my lips together and retake my seat on the floor. With my Nana occupying the recliner and my parents seated side-by-side on the couch, I start to tidy up the torn wrapping paper.

"Why didn't Dane come along?" my father asks, his hands clasped together as he watches me clean.

Before I can answer, my Nana interrupts. "Working on the restaurant again?" I narrow my eyes at her. "What's actually going on, Delia?" I flick my gaze back and forth between the three adults before me and cave.

"He punched Marshall at Kayce's holiday program." My shoulders slump as I wait for the biblically-inspired lecture from my father about violence.

Proverbs 3:31 Do not envy a man of violence and do not choose any of his ways.

Ephesians 4:32 Be kind to one another, tenderhearted, forgiving one another, as God in Christ forgave you.

I could go on, reciting nearly every verse my father hopes to throw at me, but instead he lets out a deep chuckle. My eyebrows shoot up into my hairline.

"Can't say I blame him."

"Are you kidding me?" I squawk.

"I have a feeling Marshall likely deserved it. And how does this pertain to Dane not attending family Christmas?"

"Marshall filed an emergency custody order demanding Kayce not reside with a 'violent offender.'" I roll my eyes as I mime the air quotes. "So, for the time being, Dane is keeping his distance." I shrug and clench the ball of wrapping paper tightly as my knuckles turn white.

"And how do you plan to fight this, Delia?" Nana leans forward, her eyes hard as she stares at me.

"What do you mean?"

"I know my granddaughter. She's tougher than any other, so what do you plan to do?"

"I've got a lawyer. Miranda. But she's working out of DC and doing the best she can…"

Nana clears her throat and gives me a withering look. "So what are *you* going to do, Delia, for the man you love and who's raised your son with you?"

I sit up straighter. "W-well, the local town gossip—you remember Marigold Fraser—she's going to get character witness letters for Dane. Prove he's not a violent person and all…" I tuck my lower lip under my teeth. My brain surges as I think of solutions to this problem.

And then it hits me.

"Video cameras!"

My Nana's shoulders relax, and she smiles slowly.

"It happened in a school. There has to be video cameras set up all over that place." I nod slowly as the idea takes shape. "First thing tomorrow morning, I'm emailing the principal and asking for footage."

Nana opens her arms wide and I lean in for a hug. "Thank you for reminding me to fight," I whisper against her Christmas cardigan.

"Anytime, sweetheart."

While I may not have the principal's personal cell phone number, I do know his address. In fact, everyone in town does. One of the perks of living in such a close-knit community. So, while Kayce plays on his iPad in the backseat of the car, I navigate the frosty road in front of us. It takes more time warming up the car than to drive over, but as I tell Kayce to sit tight and I traipse up the sidewalk, I can see a light on in the kitchen and a family sitting around the table enjoying breakfast.

My gut churns as I knock on the door. Am I embarrassing myself by interrupting their family time? But then Nana's question from last night sparks alight in my brain. *"So what are you going to do, Delia, for the man you love and who's raised your son with you?"*

And this time, I knock just a little louder, my gloved fist causing a dog in the back of the house to bark. The side window shade pulls open, and I spy Principal Holden's face pop through the fabric. I smile widely and give a little wave.

The door unlocks and opens slowly. "Ms. Evans? Can I help you?" I swallow at his use of my maiden name.

I bite my lip and glance behind me at Kayce, embroiled in his iPad with not a care in the world. The car is locked and the heater is on. "C-could I come in for just a moment? I won't take much of your time."

With a curious expression, he backs away from the door and allows me to pass. I stand awkwardly in the entryway, wavering from sole to sole, as he closes the door behind me. "Is everything all right, ma'am?"

I clasp my hands in front of me and meet his eye. His family watches me from the kitchen. "Sir, as you know there was an... incident at the school just prior to winter break. I'd like to request footage of the hallway location. For my lawyer, you see."

His lips thin and he crosses his arms. "Are you speaking of the incident involving Mr. Lukes and the father of your son, Ms. Evans?"

My inclination is to lower my eyes as my chest flutters. But I refuse. I meet the principal's gaze straight on. I hold my head high. "Yes. And, actually, Principal Holden, my last name is Mrs. Lukes. Dane and I were married earlier in the month."

His eyebrow cocks as his head tilts. "Ah, I see. So this is a domestic issue, then."

The lump in my throat grows exponentially, but I don't back down. "It is. You see—"

"I'm going to stop you right there, Ms. Ev—Mrs. Lukes. The school doesn't get involved in these matters. You'll need to have your lawyer subpoena the district, our lawyers will review the paperwork, and we will consider sharing the footage if everything is in order."

"That sounds like it could take weeks."

"You're right," he responds crisply. "It could."

My heart plummets into my gut and my shoulders sag. "I see." I turn and lift my hand to grab the door knob, but stop short. "Actually," I say, turning back to the principal, "I've brought a formal written request, and I'd like to leave that with you." I pull the document from my bag and pass it over. "And, as the incident occurred after hours with people from all over the community and not simply students, I believe the Family Educational Rights and Privacy Act wouldn't quite pertain to this situation. Therefore,

I would greatly appreciate if you would consider sending the footage to my email address. I've listed it clearly at the bottom of the document here." I indicate the location and roll my shoulders back, standing taller.

Principal Holden scans the document before setting it behind him on a table. "I'll see what I can do, Mrs. Lukes."

My lips lift in a thin smile. "I appreciate your assistance." Before I leave, though, I hold my finger up. "Oh, and one more thing." I withdraw a decorative Christmas tin from my bag. "I know how much you love Dane's eclairs. I was able to replicate the recipe and made them just this morning. Perhaps you and your family can enjoy them with your breakfast." I nod graciously before passing over the tin.

Principal Holden's mouth pops open as he opens the container. Inside are as many eclairs as I could fit. "Th-this wasn't necessary, Mrs. Lukes, but I do appreciate it. We've been missing these since the restaurant's been closed for the move."

"I hope you'll visit the new location once it opens in the new year. Well," I say as I hoist my now-empty bag over my shoulder, "please apologize to your family for my intrusion. I hope to hear from you soon." I hold out my hand and shake his before turning and opening the door.

The cold slaps me in the face as I step out of the warmth of the house, but as I see Kayce's face in the foggy window of the car, I'm no longer chilly. My body heats with pride.

I'd do anything for my family. And while at one point that only included Kayce, it now includes Dane as well.

CHAPTER FORTY-THREE

Delia

I scroll through my email address one last time and then click off the screen of my phone and set it on the table in front of me.

"Nothing?" Miranda's voice startles me. It's almost like I'd forgotten she was here. In a courtroom just outside of Oselka Harbor.

I shake my head and shrug. "I'm sorry."

She rolls her eyes. "Don't apologize, Delia. Never apologize for caring for your family. It's not something that comes naturally for every family." She clicks her pen and scribbles something on the yellow legal pad in front of her. "Besides, I'm sure it wouldn't matter."

I swallow because I'm not so sure. I *know* Dane, and I *know* he didn't initiate the tussle with Marshall. And if there's anything that would help show this, it's a video from the incident.

My gaze strays to the left and lands on Kayce's father who sits at an identical table. His crisp black suit fits a little too perfectly, and his sleek lawyer matches his nonchalant posture.

My stomach churns as I wait for the judge to enter the chambers. Not only has the last week passed at a glacial pace, but I heard nothing from either Marigold Fraser or Principal Holden, despite my continued outreach.

And, to make matters worse, Dane has been nonexistent. There's been some kind of mistake with the new oven delivery, and he's needed to make adjustments to the infrastructure of the building in order to accommodate the machine. He's also stayed clear of today's proceedings, per Miranda's stern instructions, despite wanting more than anything to be here.

The doors behind us open loudly, and I turn in my seat to find my parents stalking up the aisle. I swallow the lump in my throat as the backs of my eyes prick. Of course I let them know of the court date, although I never expected they'd show up. But ever since the wedding, they've been making a concerted effort to be in our lives more and more.

As they slide into seats in the first row, my father squeezes my shoulder. I offer him a small smile and stand to give my mother a hug.

Only when I'm seated does the bailiff announce that the courtroom needs to rise, and I stand once more. My heart pounds fiercely within my chest, and I'm certain that the entire room can hear its frantic beating.

Neither Miranda nor I have any intel on Judge Lafferty. Even Marigold Fraser, who knows everyone, has been silent on information about this illusive man. The lanky balding man—who wears wire-rimmed glasses over chocolate eyes—enters from a door behind the bench. His gaze, though, is harsh as he takes my measure before turning to Marshall and repeating the same up-and-down assessment.

"You may be seated," the bailiff announces before turning to the judge and sharing pleasantries. We're too far away to hear, but the judge lets out a deep chortle before shaking his head and settling into his chair.

My heart is in my throat, and try as I might, my foot taps mercilessly under the table. Only when Miranda sends me a stern glare do I still.

By then, the judge has read through the papers in front of him, and he addresses both lawyers for the opening statements.

As Marshall filed the petition for custody, his lawyer is allowed to go first. Despite my best efforts, I am unable to focus on anything the dark-headed lawyer spews as he cockily saunters forward. As I take in his slick-backed hair, my ears are filled to the brim with a loud-pitched ringing. It gives off sleazy vibes, and I can't help but be reminded of a lion as his eyes land on me. My heart nearly stops when he narrows his gaze. "At the end of today's proceedings, your Honor, it will be clear why Marshall Hampton deserves custody of his son." He flashes me a dazzling smile, his canines bared like a wild animal.

The ringing in my ears subsides just as Miranda stands and saunters to the front of the room. I can't help but be awed by her confidence. She's wearing a navy blue pantsuit that fits her impeccable figure. Her ginger hair is pulled back in a tight chignon, and her makeup is subtle, highlighting her sharp cheekbones and wide-set eyes. While most redheads couldn't pull off a bright red lip, Miranda wears it like a badge of honor. Blood on her mouth. The shark.

"Your Honor, today I am going to prove to the Court that it is in Kayce Evans's best interest to remain in custody of his mother. I will tell you about this wonderful six year old and his living conditions, his relationship with his custodial parent since birth, and why the only solution is to remain with his mother. I have gathered innumerable pieces of evidence to present to the Court—from medical records to teacher testimony verifying why the child should continue to live with his mother as the primary custodial parent. By the end of the hearing, I believe you'll decide that Delia Lukes should have sole custody of her son. Thank you, Your Honor."

"These financial statements, as well as the location of a world-renowned elementary school within walking distance to my client's penthouse, shows that the child would be best-served in an affluent environment where his every need is provided for. Not only will the child receive a first-class education, he will also have access to tutors, coaches, and every other amenity he would require."

I fight the urge to roll my eyes as Marshall's lawyer presents a folio with the aforementioned documents tucked neatly inside. The judge takes the leather-bound book from the lawyer and flips through the paperwork, his lip quirked to the side. I look at Miranda, my eyes attempting to convey the fear and uncertainty I feel.

How am I going to compete with the money that Marshall's able to throw at all of his problems? I'll never make his salary, and the lump in my throat grows by at least two sizes as I start to doubt myself.

Would it be better for Kayce to live a life of luxury where he wants for nothing? What kind of mother wouldn't wish the best for her child? Private schools and luxury trips. Things I never had could be given to my son.

But just then Miranda places her hand over mine and squeezes. As I meet her gaze, I see the fight within. She's not backing down. There's prey in the water, and she's caught the scent.

Her folio is filled with attendance records from his first year of school, as well as records from his pre-school years. There is a testimony from Kayce's kindergarten teacher, the aide who works in the classroom, and the bus driver.

The final document is from Kayce's doctor. It details the health and wellness of my child, with little to no issues. Beyond a visit for a sore throat or a fever, there have been no major medical interventions of note.

"Your Honor, you'll find that Mrs. Lukes has provided sole custody of her child for the past six years. Within this document are teacher and school staff statements, as well as medical records. My client is able to provide all of this— information related directly to her child— as the boy has lived only with her since birth. She has primary custody and conducts a perfect job mothering her child as a single parent. And that's something money can't buy." Miranda passes the clear folio to the judge, who accepts it with a curt nod. He flips through the papers within, his brows raised.

My heart soars slightly and when Miranda sits down I shoot her a smile. Except her face is flat. "Don't get too excited just yet. The witness testimonies are next. It could all go sideways if Marshall decides to take the stand."

I sit back, my stomach roiling so bad that I feel as though I may puke right here in front of the bailiff and judge. I swallow the bile that burns up my throat and clasp my hands together under the table until my knuckles crack.

"My client would like to take the stand, Your Honor," Marshall's lawyer announces with a smirk. Marshall scoots his chair back from the table, and it loudly echoes through the nearly-empty room. He stands, buttons his suit jacket with one hand, and waltzes toward the bench. The bailiff holds out the Bible and Marshall places one hand on it while the other is held aloft. He promises to tell the whole truth, and my gut bubbles once more.

"You may take the stand, sir."

"And what exactly happened on the evening of December 17th at Oselka Elementary's holiday program?" The lawyer crosses his arms over his chest and leans against the witness box.

Marshall sits forward and speaks into the microphone. Not that it's needed. "Mrs. Lukes's husband assaulted me. He punched me in front of Kayce and the other parents while filing out of the gymnasium after the program."

My foot shakes uncontrollably under the table while my heart beats frantically within my chest. I try to keep focused on the questions and answers occurring right in front of me, but my mind and body are refusing to comply.

You're going to lose your son.

You'll need to have supervised visits.

You'll *be the one paying child support to Marshall.*

"He was arrested and, according to what I know, spent the night in jail."

You're going to lose your son.

You'll need to have supervised visits.

You'll *be the one paying child support to Marshall.*

"I don't believe it's in my son's best interest to share a home with a violent offender. I don't want him taught that using his fists is the answer to the problem, Your Honor."

"Objection!" Miranda's sharp cry pulls me from the depths of despair and back to the nightmare that I'm living.

"Sustained," the judge responds as Marshall's lawyer rolls his eyes.

I breathe a shaky sigh of relief and try as hard as possible to hold myself upright as the questioning ends. Marshall retakes his seat and, before I get ready to be called for the stand, Miranda approaches the bench.

I sit at the ready, my back ramrod straight as I lean forward in an attempt to listen. Finally, the judge nods at Miranda and addresses the meager court. "We'll be taking a fifteen minute recess." The judge beckons the bailiff forward while Miranda retreats to the table.

"What's going on?" The whole court system is a foreign language to me, but I know that a break isn't warranted on a hearing this early in the day.

She smiles slowly. "I think you'll be pleasantly surprised by who just arrived." She nods to the doors, just as they're thrown open and Marigold Fraser saunters through.

She takes a seat next to my parents and passes a small flash drive to Miranda. I watch dumbly as my lawyer takes the slim metallic device and walks it to the bailiff. He nods at her and disappears behind the judge's bench.

Only then do I turn back to my lawyer, my eyebrows dancing in my hairline. "What was that?"

"Footage from the school's cameras," Miranda responds with a slow smile. "You have your friend Marigold to thank."

CHAPTER FORTY-FOUR

Dane

"You're kidding!" I exclaim as I press one more kiss to Delia's soft lips.

"Nuh-uh," she mutters as she pulls away. "Not only did Marigold manage to get the footage, the judge is currently watching it in his chambers, and I'm due back in about fifteen minutes," she says as she glances at her watch.

I tuck an errant piece of auburn hair behind her ear as happiness surges through my gut. Despite what Miranda had instructed about me staying as far as possible from the hearing, when I hadn't heard anything by lunch time, I'd driven over to bring Delia a sandwich.

And possibly find out what was taking so long.

Now, the sandwich long discarded in the backseat of the truck in favor of Delia's story, I unlock the door and pass my wife her mittens. "Better not be late."

She hesitates, her fingers dancing over the door handle. "Why don't you come?"

I blink at her. "I-I don't think that'd be a good idea. Miranda said—"

"Fuck what Miranda said."

My eyebrows nearly touch my hairline. "She's your lawyer. It's best you listen to her…"

Delia pulls at the handle and slams the door behind herself. Then she stalks around the front of the truck and yanks open the driver side door. "No. I'm done being afraid of Marshall and what might happen. I *need* you in there. With me."

Her posture stiffens as she waits my answer. But how can I refuse her? With a pleading smile on her face and lips slightly parted, I step out of the truck just as she wraps her arms around me.

Do I want to screw up Marshall's chance at custody? Yes.

Do I want to see the look on his face when he catches me by Delia's side? Also yes.

Seems like a win-win situation from my end.

My hands turn clammy the moment we step foot through the courtroom doors. Even as Delia's parents smile and wave from the front row, and Marigold Fraser sits beside them with a mischievous grin, I can't help but glance over at Marshall. His face is made of stone as he watches Delia and I approach.

I press a chaste kiss to her lips and slide in next to Marigold as Delia continues onward. Miranda, her eyes nearly piercing my soul, flicks her gaze toward her client as she sits down.

"What's he doing here?" The angry whisper echoes through the courtroom.

Delia simply shrugs and settles into her seat.

"I told you—" Miranda's interrupted by the bailiff returning and indicating that the court needs to rise.

The judge appears from behind the bench and takes his seat. He stares out into the room from his throne, and my mouth goes dry. "Marshall Hampton, please rise," the judge finally orders. Marshall stands. His palms run over his bespoke suit. "Sir, can you indicate the amount you pay in child support each month to Mrs. Lukes? It appears to be missing from the documentation."

Marshall clears his throat as his eyes drop to his lawyer's. "Uh, Your Honor, th-that's something I was hoping to work out with Mrs. Ev— Mrs. Lukes— once custody was decided."

"Hm." The judge thins his lips and flips open a folder in front of him. "And how many times have you seen the child— *your* child— since filing for custody?"

"Twice. Wait, no. *Three* times, your Honor."

The judge makes a noise with his throat. It's a cross between a chuckle and a sniffle. "And how many times were these visits monitored by the boy's mother, Mrs. Lukes?"

Marshall's quiet for a moment. His lips thin slightly before his mouth pops back open. "Nearly all three. Although I took him to the arcade without supervision."

"Hm," the judge says again. I attempt to withhold the smile that's threatening to break across my face just as Marigold grips my forearm, her nails digging into the skin. She knows I'm about to crack, and as I glance at her, there's mirth dancing in her eyes. "After further review of the documents, and the case itself, I am awarding full primary custody to Mrs. Lukes. Mr. Hampton, you may reach out to Mrs. Lukes to create a visitation schedule, per Mrs. Lukes's guidelines, once you begin making child support payments. Your lawyer will need to submit the appropriate financial paperwork to the Department of Child Services, and a child support order will be issued today."

Marshall's face turns an angry shade of red as he glares down at his lawyer. The judge turns to Delia. "Mrs. Lukes?" Delia stands. "You'll also need to complete a financial form so that the court is aware of your responsibilities as it relates to establishing the order guidelines."

"Yes, your Honor," Delia responds shakily.

"Mr. Hampton will work with his attorney to provide a schedule of dates to visit and, should you agree, for the child to stay overnight in his place of residence in Illinois. It is at your discretion, ma'am, on the number of visits, dates, and overnight stays."

Delia nods as the judge addresses both lawyers. "If the parties cannot come to an appropriate visitation contract that works with Mrs. Lukes's schedule within twelve months, we will reconvene and discuss Mrs. Lukes's wishes going forward."

Just before both parties sit, the judge turns toward Marshall one last time. "And, Mr. Hampton, I would advise that you retain a new lawyer—one who deals with criminal cases—as Mr. Lukes may seek out assault charges against *you* based on the camera footage I witnessed."

The judge bangs his gavel and dismisses the group, just as Marshall rounds on his attorney. They exchange heated words, but I'm immediately pulled into a hug by Marigold Fraser. "Congratulations, Dane!"

"For what?"

"I'm sure once you discuss the footage with Delia's ex, he'll drop the charges against you."

I harrumph. Just then, I feel a tap on my shoulder and turn, expecting Delia but instead finding Marshall. His face is grim. "My lawyer advises I drop the assault charge in exchange for the video footage." He nods at the thin plastic stick that Marigold passes to me.

I hold it up, my head cocked to the side. "I think I'll hold onto my copy for now. After all, I haven't even viewed it yet."

Marshall's mouth pops open. And for once, he's silent.

"Let's see how you do making those child support payments and sticking to a Delia-approved visitation schedule. Then we'll chat." I reach around and smack him on the back, feigning friendliness that I certainly don't feel.

And only then does he remove himself from my sight so I can focus on my wife. I pull her into an embrace, my nose coming to rest against the skin under her jaw. I've missed this. Missed her.

"When can you come back home?" she asks, her voice muffled in the fabric of my jacket.

"Now, baby," I promise as I release her. "I never even unpacked."

"That should do it," I say as I close the drawer to the bureau. I look around the room as confusion knits my brow. "Kayce?"

He was just here.

I feign looking under the bed. In the closet. Behind the door.

A giggle erupts from the overturned empty box.

"I wonder where he went?" I drag my thumb and forefinger along my jaw as I glance into the ether.

A squeal of laughter splits the air.

I tiptoe toward the box and lift it high into the air. Kayce is tucked tightly into a ball, the bumps along his spine protruding from beneath his soft cotton tee. "There you are!" I toss the box to the side and hoist him into the air. He lets out another peal of laughter.

I toss him onto the bed as my fingers dance under his armpits. He squirms and kicks wildly. "I'm ticklish!"

"Dinner!" Delia's voice echoes down the hallway and we both still for a brief moment before I restart, this time my fingers moving up along his collarbone.

"Gaaaah!" He squeals as his shoulders flood his ears. I don't relent as Kayce continues to wriggle around on the bed. Only moments later, when Delia clears her throat from the bedroom doorway, do we both look up from our play.

"Hey, it's time to eat," she says with a smile pulling at her cheeks.

"But Mooooom!" Kayce whines, "Dane and I are playing!"

I pull him forward and into a bear hug. "Your mom worked hard to cook for us, and we don't want it to get cold. Or burned," I whisper in his ear. He giggles and gives me a hug.

"Okay, but only if you promise to play with me some more after dinner." The warm stickiness of his breath along my ear has my chest pounding unnaturally fast. Because nothing else in this world would make me happier than playing with Kayce after dinner.

And, for the rest of my life, each and every night, I plan to do just that.

"Go wash up." I set him down and gently nudge him toward the bathroom as I follow Delia through the hall and into the kitchen. Set on the table are three place settings, each loaded with baked chicken, mashed potatoes with brown gravy, and a side salad. "This looks delicious, baby." I pull her in for a kiss.

She settles into the chair across from the one I take, which allows Kayce to sit in between us. He tumbles from the hallway and climbs onto his seat before eagerly diving into his mashed potatoes.

Delia's bites are slower, but as I look at her—my *wife*—and then flick my gaze to Kayce—my *son*—I can't help but finally feel like I've done it.

And it's been a long time coming—six *long* years— but I finally got everything I ever wanted. And more.

Epilogue

CHAPTER FORTY-FIVE

Delia

The test sits untouched on the counter top. It's a test I haven't worried about for eight years, yet I'm just as nervous as I was back in Chicago. From my place seated on the toilet lid, I can easily see the giant plus sign that's formed on the white background.

Pregnant.

My throat tightens as the implications fly through my mind. Another bedroom in our already cramped apartment. A maternity leave that will throw a wrench in my business plans.

And yet I can't stop the smile that spreads across my lips.

Pregnant!

A beautiful baby— the perfect combination of mine and Dane's genetics.

My fingers dance down to my torso as I imagine the bundle of cells already forming into a tiny heart and eyes.

"Mom! I gotta go— bad!" Kayce's knock on the door pulls me from the daydream and I quickly scoop up the white plastic stick and shove it in the back pocket of my jeans.

"Sorry, buddy!" I blink away the emotional tears that have welled in my eyes and open the door to allow my lanky seven year old to pass. I linger, staring at how tall he's grown in the last year, until he sends me a frown. "What?"

"Moooom! Get out!" He points to the door, and I chuckle.

"Make sure you hit the bowl this time or you'll be cleaning up the mess, mister!" I close the door behind me and make my way beyond the hallway and into the kitchen.

Pregnant.

The apartment is in no way set up for an infant. The kitchen table hardly fits three chairs comfortably, let alone a high chair. The new couch, bought because the old one was no bigger than an oversized love seat, takes up most of the space in front of the television, leaving only enough room for a single basket of Kayce's toys.

"What are we going to do?" I wonder aloud as I glance at the meager space. Unless this baby plans to spend the next eighteen years sharing a bedroom with their big brother, we're going to need a bigger home.

"I'm ready!" Kayce announces as he tumbles from the bathroom. His pants are askew and his hair is a mess, but as he grabs his book bag and shoves his feet into his Crocs, I can't help but feel the nostalgia roll over me. I remember, not so long ago, when he was a tiny tot with a gummy smile. And, no matter how ill-prepared we are for this new adventure, I can't wait to welcome it with open arms.

"Delia Lukes, financial advisor and accounting services." Pete's phone greeting is short and sweet, just the way I like it. "She's not in at the moment." He pauses and waits. "Of course I can take a message." He bends forward and begins writing something on the pink pad while I lean against the desk. After a few moments, he thanks the caller and hangs up.

"Who was that?" I pass him the hot cup of coffee. Steam rolls off the lid and curls against the chilled air.

"Savannah. *Again.*" He tears the note from the pad and passes it to me along with two others. *Urgent* is scribbled across the top.

I frown and set down my own coffee before pulling my cell from my bag. I've got two missed calls— both from my best friend. I swipe away the notifications and grab my drink before heading into my office at the back of the building.

Lukes Financial Advising and Accounting Services has been open just under a year. Dane assisted in converting his old restaurant into an office complete with enough space for a conference room. While I'm currently the only full-time employee, I hope to clear enough revenue by the end of the fiscal year to bring Pete on permanently. In the meantime, he's been picking up shifts at the bank across the street.

My office sits at the front corner of the building, and with the blinds open, enough fall light trickles through to forego the fluorescent bulbs that have been giving me a headache recently. I sit down at the desk and wiggle my mouse to wake my computer. I log in and, while the system loads, I pull my phone out once more and click *send* on Savannah's number.

It rings once before she answers, practically screaming into the device. "*Where have you been?*"

"I had to get Kayce ready for school and then I stopped at the new coffee shop in town. What's with the code red?"

"I left, like, eight messages with Pete!"

"I know," I concede as I crumple the pink memos and toss them into the can at the side of the desk. "What's so important that you had to harass my assistant?"

"Del, prepare yourself."

I swallow and lean back against the plush office chair. I swivel around, my gaze trailing out to the street. "I'm prepared," I deadpan as I take another slow swig of my coffee.

"Are you sitting down?"

"Yep, but I have an appointment in an hour. Should I reschedule or are you going to—?"

"I'm pregnant, Del!"

I let out a squeal and stand from the chair, whooping with excitement. "Oh my gosh!" Savannah and Jack have quietly been trying to conceive for months. "I'm so excited for you!"

"I'm about ten weeks," she admits quietly. "I hope you aren't mad for not telling you sooner. I just didn't want to get my hopes up again, especially after—"

"You don't need to say anymore or apologize for anything. I understand." I inhale and take another sip of the coffee. "And I guess I need to tell you something, too..."

"Oh my god," she responds. "Oh my god, oh my god, you're not— *are you?*"

I nod as my smile stretches across my face. "Yes. I just found out this morning. It's incredibly early days yet, but you're the first to know."

"Holy shit, Del. We always talked about this and now it's finally happening!" She sniffles into the phone.

"Are you crying?"

"No!"

I laugh because only my best friend would immediately start crying over sharing a pregnancy together.

"Wait, so you haven't told Dane yet?"

"Nope, he was already at the restaurant when I got up this morning. Had an early delivery."

"Oh shit... When are you going to tell him?"

"I figured I'd stop by at lunch."

She whistles into the phone. "You think he'll be excited?"

I bite my lip and smile once again. Because while we may not have the room for another person in our cramped apartment, there's one thing I do know...

Dane is going to be ecstatic.

I'm not sure how I manage to survive the next three hours, but eventually, Pete stalks through the open office door and announces that he's taking his lunch break.

"I suppose I'll run by Dane's and get something to eat too," I say awkwardly.

He narrows his eyes at me and shrugs. "Okay. I don't know why you're telling me, but enjoy. I'll be back later." He stalks from the room, and I hear the telltale bell ding over the door indicating he's left.

Once I lock up and put the *Back in Thirty Minutes* sign on the door, I saunter over to my car. I finally upgraded the dilapidated sedan and was able to afford a sleek black coup that sits out front. "It raises the legitimacy of the business," Dane had said when I'd stalled signing the lease.

I swallow as I slide into the driver's seat, once again realizing that another part of my life won't fit the changes that are coming. I wonder if upgrading to something with a sliding door is in my future.

The drive to Dane's New Italiano is short, taking no more than five minutes which includes a stop at the only red light in town. I pull into the only available spot and am surprised at how stacked the parking lot is. Normally lunch is fairly slow, but with the tourists in town for the fall foliage, I should've expected more visitors to the nearby establishments.

I enter and take a seat at the counter. The restaurant maintains some of the original stools from the old location, but the booths and tables are all new, sleek, and modernized. The menu, too, has been refreshed. Dane's able to source more local produce from the farmers just outside of town and even has a slew of new servers helping now that Crystal's been promoted to manager.

"What can I get for you, ma'am?" the youth behind the counter asks as I drop my bag on the seat beside me.

I withhold the upper lip curl at his use of ma'am and smile politely. "A Diet Coke and chicken parmesan. Pounded extra thin, please."

He looks confused. "Uh, I don't know if the chef will do that, but I can ask."

I blink at him. "Please do. I'm not in a hurry." My next appointment isn't until later in the afternoon, and the paperwork I'd planned on finishing can wait.

The gangly teenager disappears in the back and reappears with Dane just behind him. "I wasn't expecting you today!" He says as he leans over the counter and presses a kiss to my cheek.

He introduces me to the server and then dismisses him. The boy blushes a shade of red that matches my lipstick and attempts to find something else to do while eavesdropping from the corner near the till.

"I would've had your specialty whipped up ahead of time had I known you were stopping by," Dane says as he fetches my drink from the fountain.

"I'm not in a rush. Not today." He sets down the glass and goes to leave, but I grab his hand and stop him. "Th-there's something I wanted to talk about with you."

Dane stills, even as his eyes scan the restaurant. I can tell he doesn't have too much time, as he's calculating the orders that are surely backing up, so I make it quick. "Do you remember when we discussed moving? We thought something bigger might be needed?"

His eyes widen. "Y-yeah, I remember. But we thought it'd be best to wait until after the holidays."

I allow a slow smile to pull at my lips. "Unfortunately, I think we're going to need to adjust that timeline."

Dane's hands move to his hips as he looks at me closely, his eyes narrowing. "By how much? Once the tourist season is over it's—"

"By nine months, Dane." I allow my hand to fall to my stomach. His eyes track my movement before going round as his mouth pops open.

"Del? Are...Are you sure, baby?" Then, before I can nod my head, he's stalked from behind the counter and wrapped me up in his arms, twirling me away from the stool. "Are you telling me..."

I nod my head as my hands come to rest on his shoulders. "Pretty sure, if this is any indication!" I pull the test from my bag and pass it over to him. He stares at it like a foreign object, turning it this way and that in his hand.

"Shit, baby, I can't believe this." His hands come to rest on my hips as his eyes dip to my belly. And then they flick up to meet mine. "The apartment! Oh no, the car!"

I press my lips to his and take just a single moment to enjoy the excitement that's bubbling through my gut. "S-so you're excited then? This isn't too soon?"

He pulls me in for a tight hug, and my feet lift from the ground. "I couldn't be more excited, Del. And it's definitely not too soon. We've waited long enough for our happily ever after."

Acknowledgements

From the bottom of my heart, thank you for taking a chance on an unknown indie author's story.

If you enjoyed reading *Only Six Years*, please consider leaving a review or recommending it to a friend. Your support, through reviews, word of mouth, and social media shares, helps readers find my story.

Follow and interact with Jenn Lynn Adams on social media:

Instagram @jennlynnadams

TikTok @authorjennlynnadams

On the web www.jennlynnadams.com